# IN TRANSIT

# IN TRANSIT

## KATHLEEN GERARD

**FIVE STAR**
*A part of Gale, Cengage Learning*

GALE
CENGAGE Learning

Detroit • New York • San Francisco • New Haven, Conn • Waterville, Maine • London

**LIBRARY OF CONGRESS CATALOGING-IN-PUBLICATION DATA**

Gerard, Kathleen.
  In transit / Kathleen Gerard. — 1st ed.
    p. cm.
  ISBN-13: 978-1-59414-966-5 (hardcover)
  ISBN-10: 1-59414-966-6 (hardcover)
  1. Young women—Fiction. 2. Policewomen—New York (State)—New York—Fiction. 3. Manhattan (New York, N.Y.)—Fiction. I. Title.
  PS3607.E728I5 2011
  813'.6—dc22                                              2010051989

First Edition. First Printing: April 2011.
Published in 2011 in conjunction with Tekno Books.

Printed in the United States of America
1 2 3 4 5 6 7 15 14 13 12 11

for
D.M.D.

*If you don't know where you are going,*
*you might wind up someplace else.*

—Yogi Berra

# ONE

"Let's go Del Vecchio. I want to go home already!"

The windows lining the perimeter of the police academy gymnasium that had once burst with blinding sunlight were now dark panes of glass that glistened with the reflection of distant streetlights. Rita Del Vecchio struggled harder and harder to make her way over the obstacle course wall. It was her seventh try. The muscles in her arms burned tired and sore, but she kept her fingers firm around the thick, bristly rope even though the flesh on her hands felt stripped bare to the bone.

"This is your last chance. If you don't get over this time, you can kiss graduation goodbye. You hear what I'm saying?"

She heard him, all right. How could she *not* hear him? He screamed at her all day, and the badgering sound of his voice echoed in her mind, haunting her all night. There was no escaping him.

Sergeant Gary Hill.

Rita could see him pacing on the floor mat below. He was watching her, his head craned upon his thick neck and his Popeye-like arms folded, bursting across his muscular chest.

"It's a god-awful shame," Hill said, his words rising up to meet her. "You go through six weeks of hell, for what? Face it, Del Vecchio. You're too damned weak. It just goes to show you— the NYPD is no place for a woman."

Rita glared down at him. From her perspective more than halfway up the twenty-foot-high wall, Hill now appeared the size of a midget despite his bulky six-foot four-inch frame.

Using every ounce of strength she had left, Rita pulled herself up. She groaned, reaching higher. Her hands seared around the thick, splintered knots, while the soles of her sneakers searched for traction, squeaking against the seams and joints in the paint-chipped plywood wall.

"Should've made a trip to the gym instead of going to your ballet class last night. Right, Twinkle Toes?" Hill's laugh bounced off the walls of the now empty gymnasium that stank of manly sweat and body odor. "What kind of cop likes ballet anyway? Are you gonna do pirouettes while you read some poor bastard his rights?"

Beads of sweat trickled down from Rita's forehead and reached her lips. They tasted salty like tears. From day one at the police academy, Hill seemed determined to defeat Rita. But she refused to give in—or give up. She looked past the pus oozing from the blisters on her white hot hands. There were only two more rope knots to go before she would reach the top. She inched up, heaving the last painful weight of her body. But with her fingers too anxious to stretch toward that final notch, she lost her grip and was sent into free-fall.

Down

Down

Down.

Her rump crashed first and knocked the wind out of her until she found herself flat on her back. Her size seven, five-foot four-inch frame was sprawled atop the spongy, rubber mat. *It's over,* she thought, her hands and spine stinging with pain.

When the stars before her eyes finally cleared, she was looking up Sergeant Gary Hill's nostrils. They loomed like the dark tubes of the Lincoln Tunnel.

"Why'd you want to be a cop anyway, Del Vecchio?"

A lump had grown in Rita's throat. She tried to swallow it,

hoping it might alleviate the pressure building behind her eyes.

"What are you trying to prove? And to whom, huh?"

Rita could see how Sergeant Hill's closely cropped, flaxen hair was highlighted with tiny strands of gray. And this late in the day, he had a stubbly look of a five o'clock shadow.

"Well, what do you have to say for yourself?"

What could Rita say? What should she say? She lumbered her body from the mat until she was seated upright. Then she tucked some wayward strands of hair back into her ponytail and straightened her shoulders. She hated his condescension, but she pulled in her chin and braced for more of his verbal gale.

"You women recruits are all alike. A bunch of prima donna idealists who are out to change the world," Sergeant Hill said. "Well, forget about it, Twinkle Toes. Do me and this city a favor. Stick with changing your frilly little underwear . . . or better yet, go stir a pot with meatballs and macaroni. I mean, what's the worst that can happen? You get a tomato sauce stain? You break a nail?" He sighed a mix of annoyance and contempt in an effort to illicit a response from her. But he wasn't going to get one. "Ah, hell," he said, turning from her and tossing up his hands. "I don't know why the city makes me waste my time. What's the use? You were just one of the few token women in this graduating class anyway."

Rita's body tensed into a violent quiver. "To meet guys!" she finally blurted, her fists clenched.

Gary Hill squinted his eyes. He looked at her suspect. "I beg your pardon?"

"You asked me before why I want to be a cop." Rita met Sergeant Hill's gaze dead on. She spoke her piece in one long stream, without even taking a breath. "Well, I joined the force to meet guys—to meet guys just like you. I'm a masochist at heart. How's that? Does that make you feel better? Is that the response you've been waiting for?"

Hill's eyebrows lifted in an arc. He appeared stunned and slightly amused by Rita's comeback. "I hate to burst your bubble, but there are easier ways to meet men."

Rita held up the palms of her hands in surrender. She rose to her feet and marched past him, straight for the locker room.

"So you're a quitter? Is that it, Del Vecchio?" Hill's words chased after Rita and slammed into the back of her head. "Atta girl. Go on. Take yourself and your bad attitude back to your old waitressing job at that grease pit in Jersey."

Rita stopped in her tracks. A sick, empty feeling roiled inside of her. *This is it, isn't it? Everything I've worked for, it's all been in vain? For nothing?* The hum of the fluorescent lights droned beneath the sound of her heavy, pounding heart. When she heard Sergeant Hill's footsteps drum like a slow, solemn cadence and the wooden floorboards pop and creak in response to his approach, Rita tightened herself.

"You surprise me, Del Vecchio," he said, his hand grasping her arm like a vise. "You've put up with more abuse in this academy than any of the other candidates. Why call it quits now?"

Rita turned and bore her gaze through him. She knew this was probably the last confrontation she'd ever have with her sergeant—or any officer from the NYPD for that matter. Why not make her final exit a grand farewell? "Is it all women you don't like," she said, "or is it just *me?*"

Gary Hill's staunch grin curled slowly into a smile. He shook his head and laughed. "You pegged me all wrong, Twinkle Toes. If I didn't like you, I wouldn't have worked you so hard." Hill resumed his leathery facade. "Some folks in this city are a lot tougher and meaner than the likes of me, many are even savages out for blood. If you don't thicken that suburban skin of yours, you're gonna be easy prey."

The words Sergeant Hill spoke aimed straight at the heart of the matter.

"I don't make a habit of giving presents unless it's Christmas," he told her, "but deep down, I like your grit and determination." A glimmer of a smile emerged on his face. He leaned closer to Rita until his warm breath whispered, "How about we let this be *our* little secret."

She repeated his words inside her head. *Our little secret?*

"Better press your uniform and shine your shoes," he told her, releasing his steely grip and letting her go. "You wanna look spit and polished for graduation, don't you?"

*Am I hearing things? Or is he saying what I think he's saying?*

"I'm recommending they assign you to the Transit Department. Good luck, Officer Del Vecchio. You're gonna need it."

Rita opened her mouth to say something, anything, but no words spewed forth. Instead, she just stood there with her mouth unhinged, astounded, staring at Sergeant Hill's broad shoulders as he walked away from her and headed for the men's locker room.

There was an urgency in her voice when she finally managed to spit out the words, "Thank you, Sergeant. Thank you."

Hill made an about-face. "Don't thank me. Just do me a favor and next time you get to the end of your rope, tie a knot in it and hang on."

In Rita's eyes, the image of Sergeant Hill as he disappeared through the locker room door became blurry and soggy-looking. And it was through her tears that she heard him say, "I bet you're one hell of a dancer."

# Two

Having spent eight hours a day with those whom he considered to be the dregs of the earth—at least the dregs of East New York—Sergeant Billy Quinn was now a product of the environments he had policed for nearly twelve years. This drug-infested, lawless zone in Brooklyn had become more of a home to him than his apartment in the white, middle-class, Morris Park section of the Bronx. But today was his last day on this tour of duty. The newly elected mayor and his brand new police commissioner meant only one thing for the NYPD—change. Change for the sake of change. *Show and Glow* is what Billy Quinn and the *Mean Nineteen,* the nickname he and eighteen other police sergeants assigned to the city's Special Gun and Drug Task Force, called it when politicians initiated change solely to benefit their own political agendas.

But Billy Quinn knew that change wasn't always such a bad thing. The Mean Nineteen might soon be scattered about all five boroughs of the city, but they would always share a common bond of lasting brotherhood that would remain unchanged.

Behind the wheel of the patrol car, Billy cruised along New Bridge Avenue while he and his partner listened to Howard Stern on the portable satellite radio. Billy eyed the neighborhood for what would be his last time. The familiar streets seemed more like an underdeveloped, third-world country than a ghetto amid the outskirts of the cosmopolitan city. In the early days, Billy once squirmed at the sight of drunks as they squat-

14

ted on the litter-strewn and excrement-filled pavement, and he felt repulsed by the hollow-cheeked crack-heads as they stumbled, half-conscious, half-dead, into dilapidated tenements. It was amazing how, after all the years, the view beyond the police car window hadn't really changed.

"Pitiful sight for sore eyes," Billy sighed, glaring at the poverty that infested this neighborhood and had only continued to get worse. "If there's one thing I've learned prowling about this hellhole, it's that these niggers and spics make their own damn problems. Look over there." Billy pointed outside the car. He motioned for his partner, Sergeant Tony Sanducci, riding shotgun, to look at an empty lot studded with junked appliances, ransacked automobiles, picked-through trash and burned mattresses. "We're not the ones dumping crap all over. Look at all this junk. Just because these folks are piss-poor doesn't mean they have to live in a sewer. They take pride in nothing."

Tony kept chomping on a wad of bubblegum, a new habit since he'd quit smoking. He didn't say a word. But then again, he didn't have to. Sergeant Billy Quinn was famous for having some of his best conversations with himself. He had a reputation for being grossly opinionated. But why shouldn't he be? After all, he'd more than paid his dues, devoting the past twelve years of his life to policing some of the worst areas in and around the city. Billy had seen more than most. It was more than anyone should have to see, really. Tony Sanducci had been assigned to Billy's jurisdiction of the task force for only the past year. The two became fast friends and allies. It was too bad that budget cuts, division mergers, and the new police commissioner's big ideas were about to break up a good thing.

Sergeant Sanducci was to stay on in this Brooklyn neighborhood, but he was reassigned to a new post within the Housing Authority. Billy was looking forward to his two weeks of paid vacation and then being transferred to a rotating position throughout several districts within the five boroughs. This was billed as only temporary until the Gun and Drug Task Force could be restructured by the new administration.

"Hey, I've been meaning to ask you, how's that kid brother of yours?" asked Sanducci, quickly having a word with Billy when Howard Stern's radio show cut to a news bulletin.

"Kevin?" Billy asked. "Oh, he's a lucky bastard. They'll fit him up with a prosthetic leg and give him some medal of honor or badge of courage. Then he'll probably retire down in Florida someplace."

"But that sucks, man." Tony gave a sympathetic shake of his head. "I mean, he was a really good distance runner, wasn't he?"

"Yeah, that's him. My kid bro. Mr. All-American, Jock-Cop. Finished top twenty in the city marathon last year. But a lot of good it did him. No one can outrun a bullet."

"A bullet is one thing. But a blood clot and then losing your leg? Aw, that just sucks." Tony loudly popped a bubble from his gum.

"Sucks? If you ask me, Kevin was too soft to be a cop in the first place. He hid behind the shield. Tried to be all idealistic."

"But he was a lieutenant, wasn't he?"

"Yeah, but all that label really means is politics. My brother had to kiss up to a lot of people. That's how he rose through the ranks. And there's no respect or honor in that."

Tony just shrugged his shoulders.

"As far as I'm concerned, my brother getting his leg blown off was a gift," Billy said. "Here I put my life on the line every day for the past twelve years and what do I get? Reassigned to another dump, that's what I get. While Kevin gets full pension and an early retirement, all because some pistol-whipped crackhead blew off his leg."

Billy continued his tirade, now drowning out Howard Stern's

16

monologue.

"What kind of faggot cop goes out for his morning jog and fights crime, off-duty and without his gun? Give me a break. And now the city is trying to make him out to be some kind of hero? He was stupid, and as far as I'm concerned, he probably deserved to get shot."

Tony, wide-eyed, looked over at Billy, whose face flushed hot. "Yo, take a chill," Sanducci said. "You know what they say, *'What goes around, comes around.'*"

"Oh, I don't go for that superstitious crap. I figure that if I've lived this long, then I'm untouchable—"

Tony interrupted. "Hey look, over there. There's our Big Mama."

Billy pulled the patrol car over to the curb toward a young black woman. He rolled down the window. "Hey, you got our lunch money or what?" Billy eyed a brown paper bag the woman carried over to the car. She was well-endowed, wearing a low-cut tank-top and a bandanna around her head.

"We cool now, ain't we?" the woman asked, before handing over the bag. "My man wants me to make sure there ain't no more trouble once you fellas are gone."

The woman leaned into the car. She turned a suspicious gaze past Billy, over to Tony Sanducci, who sat on the passenger's side. "I said, we all cool now, right?" she asked again.

"Yeah, yeah, *we cool*," Billy said. "You can tell your man that we're all square, for this week at least. Tony'll be keeping an eye on things, so don't you worry. And I'll come back and visit every now and again." Billy took the bag from the woman and crinkled it open to inspect the contents. He pulled out a handful of green dollars. "Just remember, keep business as usual and everything will stay nice and quiet in the 'hood. Hear?"

The woman nodded in agreement.

As she prepared to leave, Billy asked, "Hey, wait a second.

You didn't forget my going away present, did you?"

The woman reached into the cleavage of her tank-top. She pulled out a tiny bag of white powder, palmed it over to Billy then waddled her hips away from the patrol car. She furtively flipped him the bird and said, "Filthy pigs!" under her breath. "Soon, we'll all be supporting every damn cop habit in this city."

"Why, ain't she a sweetheart," Billy said, pulling out one of the green bills from the paper bag and rolling it up like a straw. He cut two thin lines of the white, sifted-looking powder on top of the blue vinyl dashboard of the patrol car. His face got lost in the shadow created by the brim of his eight-pointed patrolman's hat as he leaned over and snorted one line off the dash. He motioned for Tony Sanducci to do the other, and his partner eagerly accepted the invitation.

"You know, it's times like these that I'm really gonna miss this friggin' place," Billy said, wiping his nose clean.

# THREE

Rita Del Vecchio could never resist a man in uniform. Standing among the boys in blue made her feel like a kid in a toy store authorized to use her parents' MasterCard. A sea of navy blue hats extended as far as the eye could see. Madison Square Garden was more jam-packed than it would have been for a Billy Joel concert.

This was Rita's day. The twenty-two-year-old was only one of twelve women in her graduating class from the police academy and standing there, she had never felt so damned proud and sure—of herself and her decision.

But what was even more mind-boggling was all of these men in uniform. All shapes, sizes, colors and forms. She would have her pick of nine hundred and eighty-seven male rookies, give or take a handful already married. And, added to that, were the thousands of seasoned male veterans already in the field. What more could a young, single girl possibly ask for?

A smile tickled her face. *This is where I belong. This is where I'm meant to be. I've done it. I've finally found my destiny. Me! I've become a New York City Transit Cop. Can you believe it?*

It was a psychic at the Center Hills Mall in Paramus, New Jersey, who'd initially planted the seed that would change Rita's life. Rita would never forget the day she pulled up a chair at the clairvoyant's card table. There, amid a sea of mall-walkers, some pushing strollers and hauling shopping bags, Rita took a chance. Gazing at a plastic crystal ball and battery-operated faux candles flickering on a table in front of The Gap and Bed Bath and Beyond, Rita shuffled the tarot cards and cut the deck in thirds. By the time a series of colorful, medieval-looking pictures were set out on the table in front of her, Rita was convinced she'd been given a lot more than twenty minutes and forty dollars worth of advice.

"You're destined for greatness. And I'm getting a sense that your spiritual guides are urging you to make a major life change," the psychic told her. "They are sending you signals. You need to really listen to your inner voice and have the courage to follow your dreams." She also told Rita, "I see you marrying a man in uniform."

With so little direction for her life, Rita felt obliged to take this woman's metaphysical pearls of wisdom under careful consideration.

But it wasn't just the tarot card reading that set Rita's life in motion. A few weeks later, Rita's beloved Uncle Mike also altered the course of her fate. At the family's annual Fourth of July barbeque, her uncle, a veteran New York City Police Lieutenant, a decorated officer who'd lived and worked through 9/11 and was now nearing retirement, mentioned that the NYPD was looking to hire new recruits. Due to affirmative action, they needed to enlist more minorities, meaning African-Americans, Latinos—and especially women.

When Rita heard this, gooseflesh broke out on her body. She pictured the uniformed 9/11 police heroes, those on the force who'd made a difference and risked their lives by staring into the face of evil. When she envisioned herself wearing NYPD blue, she had a sense that her uncle's passing remark was further confirmation of what that psychic had told her. Maybe Uncle Mike was a spiritual guide, an earthly messenger, who had come to deliver the inspiration that Rita was looking for? Maybe Rita wasn't really floundering in her ambitions, after all? Maybe she had simply been biding her time until the fates could align her life with her one true destiny?

That was all it took to light a fire under Rita.

It was settled. Rita believed that she was, indeed, being called to greatness, convinced that joining the NYPD was the reason why she'd come to the planet. She was so inspired that she finally slipped off her apron and quit her waitressing job at the Darcy's Restaurant on Route 17. How was she really contributing anything to the world by waiting tables? She'd spent every day taking orders and dealing with complaints and dissatisfaction. All she seemed to do was try to please people by slopping plates of greasy, artery-clogging food before them. And no one was ever really satisfied. Oh, the dull, boring, dispiriting drudgery. The biggest thrill she'd had were tips more than fifteen percent, and those were often few and far between. And, if the psychic was right, that Rita would marry a man in uniform, could a man worthy of her affections really be found in a Darcy's restaurant? The only uniformed men she'd met so far were men and boys wearing gray shirts and maroon slacks, the hallmark uniforms associated with the restaurant chain. These potential prospects bused tables, slapped burgers and eggs on the griddle, and verified ages as under-twelve for the children's menu. For Rita, waitressing suddenly felt like a dead-end job.

Now it was almost a year later. Rita had taken and passed the police exam. She'd gone through the academy and had done all the training. And here she was in uniform, sitting in a full-capacity crowd at Madison Square Garden. She had taken charge of her life and had made an important life-changing decision. She didn't care what people thought or the judgments they passed. *With the way the world is, with all the violence and threats of terrorism, why would you want to take your life in your hands?* But no matter what people said, Rita's mind was made

21

up. She went from being an unappreciated and under-tipped waitress to one of New York's finest. How many women have ever made such a dramatic transformation in their lives?

Staring down the aisle where she sat in the middle of Madison Square Garden, Rita was awed at the conformity in the whole graduation ceremony. Finely waxed shoes lined the floors like limitless rows of strategically placed dominoes, ready to roll. Each pair of navy blue pants was creased so sharply that you'd think there were metal rods keeping them in place. White-gloved hands rested alertly on each lap, and the shiny brims of every hat were raised high. She scanned the faces across the aisle. She saw reflected images of accomplishment, success, and those of idealism, all masking the underlying fear that she believed was present in every new rookie cop.

But Rita was confident. *The career part of my life is underway,* she thought. *Now, I'll just have to find my Mr. Right. Maybe we're breathing the same air at this very moment.* Rita oscillated her sights. *Who might be wearing that lucky uniform, possessing it like an undisclosed, winning lottery ticket?*

Rita glanced down the aisle again. At the opposite end sat Sergeant Gary Hill. His chiseled profile was aimed attentively upon the stage. *If it wasn't for him, I wouldn't even be here now.* At the moment she had this thought, he turned and looked at her. There was no smile, no warmth, on his face, just a harsh seriousness that shot through her like the impact of a bullet. As they exchanged glances, someone seated beside Gary Hill leaned forward into Rita's line of vision. It was him again. She remembered seeing him down at the district office over the past few weeks. And during the graduation ceremony, he and other members of the Special Gun and Drug Task Force were awarded departmental citations from the Police Commissioner. Rita and this stranger kept crossing paths. Now they were locking stares, flirting, as if their meetings were somehow predestined.

Sergeant Hill's face blurred out of view, and Rita's gaze remained fixed on the stranger's. She was drawn to his blue eyes. They seemed as transparent as the water of the Caribbean. She tried to determine what was stirring below, but he was too far away to explore their depths. He looked slightly older than Rita, but the dimple in his left cheek and his almond-blond hair gave him a somewhat boyish appearance. He smiled at Rita and tipped his hat, and Rita felt her cheeks flush and her heart jump at his gesture. When Sergeant Hill caught sight of this exchange, he turned to glance at the person seated next to him. Rita felt suddenly embarrassed that both he and her admirer had caught her gawking. Modestly, she ripped her gaze away.

*Pitter-patter.*

*Pitter-patter.*

*Thump.*

*Thump.*

Who was this stranger? She didn't know his name or his precinct, and she had been too shy and, in her own way, too old-fashioned to approach him those few times when she'd spotted him down at the district office. But she knew she could fall for him—hook, line and sinker.

Before her family moved to New Jersey, Rita had spent the first ten years of her life growing up in the Morris Park section of the Bronx. She could have earned a master's degree in outwardly tough street smarts, and she could surely hold her own. But in spite of that fact, the woman of steel turned instantly to mashed potatoes at the sight of this handsome stranger. This twenty-two-year-old was a preschooler in affairs of the heart.

All she knew was that this good-looking guy, a man in uniform, had been keeping an eye on her.

She liked the attention.

She liked what she saw of him.

# FOUR

There was nothing worse than working the midnight-to-eight shift alone in the subways, but this would be the last night for Patrolman Francis "Franko" O'Malley. It was his third consecutive rotation in the past week. In an effort to cut costs, the city began a policy of Transit Cops working underground in solo shifts. However, in the six months since this procedure was adopted, the NYPD budget was overspent because whenever a rookie cop was out sick, the department had to pay a seven-year veteran like Franko the wages of two rookie cops.

But on the day after tomorrow, all that would change. Transit Cops would return to partner shift rotations, and Franko actually looked forward to it. He would be getting a new partner—a woman, he was told—and he would be back to a steady eight A.M. to four P.M. rotation.

That still left him one more night to practice his lonely, whistled version of "Oh, Danny Boy," as he shuffled his growing beer belly and his thick, fleshy hips on and off the Number Five train running from Delancey up to 125<sup>th</sup> Street. So far, it had been a long, quiet night on the Lexington Avenue Line and after a week of double shifts in the subway, Franko welcomed the tranquility of the quiet underground. But by five-thirty in the morning, after his sixth round trip riding the Lex Line, he could sense a heaviness weighing down his tired eyes.

He was long overdue for a cup of coffee, but a break for him was further postponed when a static-filled call came in on his radio requesting that he check out the subway near Central Park and 23<sup>rd</sup> Street. There was a report of "skels"—also known as "skeletons" or "homeless"—blocking the entrance to an apartment building in the vicinity.

Franko rolled his eyes and nonchalantly made his way out of the terminal. *No big deal. No need to rush. Probably just some b.s. call.* Franko knew better than anyone that skels were merely harmless annoyances scattered about the city. The crimes they committed were mostly those of being a nuisance.

When Franko finally arrived at the apartment building in question, he found the doorman standing above a creature scrunched up into the fetal position on a battered piece of cardboard.

"Officer," the doorman said, summoning Franko. "I guess I'm partially to blame for this. I told a couple of homeless folks they could sleep over there, near the alleyway, just as long as they were gone by daybreak. I got rid of a few of them, but—"

"Let me guess. Not that one?" Franko said, finishing the doorman's sentence. He glanced over at the skel, who appeared neither man nor woman, but more like a bestial-looking creature wearing layers of heavy, decrepit rags as clothing. A crumpled felt hat with three soiled white feathers covered the person's face.

"You've gotta do something," the doorman pleaded with Franko. "This is only my first week on the job, and I don't want to get fired because of this."

"You from outta town?" asked Franko.

"Yeah. How could you tell? My southern accent that noticeable?"

Franko smiled and nodded. Although the southern twang in the doorman's voice was obvious, it was the man's actions that spoke much louder than his words. They were the dead giveaway that he wasn't a native New Yorker.

"You want a Welcome Wagon piece of advice?" Franko asked. The doorman shrugged.

"In the future, if you want to do charity work, volunteer at a soup kitchen. And if you want to keep your job, don't *ever* give the homeless refuge near your place of work. That's what shelters are for."

"I hear ya," the doorman said.

Franko wandered off toward the skel, who reeked of urine and unwashed skin even from a few feet away.

"Rise and shine. C'mon, up and at 'em." Franko reached down and prodded the figure sleeping on the concrete slab. When the creature lifted its head, he caught a glimpse of a face embedded with dirt and grime. Franko could make out womanly features.

"C'mon, Dorothy. Let's go. We're back in Kansas."

The woman stirred. Her eyes fluttered open. But it obviously took too much effort for her to focus on Franko. She moaned as if in pain and sank her head back into her folded arms.

"Let's go, lady. Time to get up." Franko nudged the near-comatose body with the toe of his police boot as one would to see if an animal lying on the street were dead or alive.

The woman opened her eyes again and gave him a sneer. Franko gestured his hand to the night stick dangling from his police belt. This time, the woman took the hint. She quickly gathered her things and stuffed them into a shopping bag. As she scurried away, she mumbled something indecipherable in a disgruntled tone. The putrid stench of her lingered as Franko and the doorman watched her silhouetted figure walk down the street, into the rising sun. With the three feathers protruding above her hat, her head resembled that of a rooster.

"Welcome to New York, buddy," Franko told the doorman, shaking his hand. "You'll meet all kinds, that's for sure."

The doorman thanked Franko, and Franko, in turn, was

relieved that he could finally go in search of that coffee. But before long, another call came in on his radio. Another skel was reported to be harassing an M.T.A. clerk in Franko's jurisdiction on the Lex Line.

When Franko got there, he met a familiar face.

"Hey, long time, no see," Franko said. It was the woman with the feathered cap again. She had set up a slumber party, this time close to a turnstile accommodating the first batch of early morning commuters.

"C'mon, you're gonna have to move, Pocahontas," Franko told her, nearing the gate and heading for the woman. "You'll need to get a job or find somewhere else to get some shut-eye, preferably out of my district."

Franko grabbed the woman's arm and tried to drag her out of the way. But the woman refused to budge. When Franko turned to face her, he noticed that within the grime on her face sat two eyes the color of blue topaz. The sparkling sight of them stunned Franko. He'd never seen such vibrancy in another human being, especially not a skel.

"Get your hands off of me, dammit. Let me go," the woman hollered, trying to shake her arm free from Franko's grasp. "All I want is to sleep."

"Yeah, you and me both," Franko told her. "Now, c'mon, lady. Give me a break. I'm only doing my job."

"Do your job with someone else. I need to sleep. Is that a crime?"

"Well, you can't sleep here. And if you do, then it *will* be a crime." Franko pulled and tugged at the woman's body in an effort to move her. The more stubborn she was in her refusal, the more Franko was forced to literally drag the woman's stiffened body, her legs like two-by-fours, down along the platform.

"Why won't you leave an old, poor woman alone?" she

shrieked, her body still contracting in resistance. "Let go of me."

"The only way I'm leaving you alone, Pocahontas, is if you move it."

"All right. All right," the woman finally said, freeing herself from his grasp. She heeded his request and shuffled away, shooting a dragon-like stare at Franko from over her shoulder. "You'll pay for this." Her words lingered like a dark cloud on the platform even after she was swallowed up by the growing droves of early morning commuters.

Franko rolled his eyes. "Crazy skel," he mumbled, convinced his efforts were only temporary. The woman would, no doubt, hop the next train and find sleep there.

Franko wasn't more than two steps out of the terminal when he heard a plaintive squeal of brakes from one of the subway cars and then a chorus of screams. He turned and hurried back down the platform, pushing himself through a crowd that had clustered together and folks peering onto the tracks. Chins were dropped and eyes were wide. Someone had been hit by the passing train. When Franko followed the path of their gazes, he saw a body, mangled and bloody.

"What the hell happened here?" Franko asked a young girl who looked like a college student. She'd cupped a hand over her mouth and was looking, in horror, over the edge of the platform.

"A beggar. I think she jumped," she said.

Franko felt a heaviness cleave to his throat and then shimmy down to his heart. He turned from the body on the tracks and looked at the train, which had since been halted. There, stuck to the cold iron monster, were two bloody white feathers.

Surging with adrenaline, Franko eased back the crowds while he radioed the station house and requested assistance. It wasn't long before a back-up team arrived.

"Well, at least there's one less pain in the ass in this city to worry about," remarked the first officer to arrive on the scene.

"Yeah, but now we're gonna have to stick around all morning filling out paperwork," another cop said, joining the assemblage of officers huddled on the platform.

The first officer replied, "Hey, I don't know about you, but I can sure use the overtime."

A detective wearing a long trench coat made his way past the group. He kicked a pebble over the edge of the platform and disdainfully eyed the sight. "Those damn skels are all better off dead."

The officers went on with their banter, but Franko stood silent in their midst. It took all his strength to conceal his heavy heart. As he turned from the group and glanced down at the victim again, a sinking feeling dropped like an anchor inside of him. The woman's grime-covered face. Those piercing blue topaz eyes. A chill of unshakable guilt crept up and down Franko's prickly spine.

# FIVE

Rita's first day riding the rails gave her a bad case of nerves. Maybe it was all the crowds at rush hour? The close proximity of so many people all breathing the same air underground? The sight of rats foraging and splashing through puddles along the tracks? The damp, acrid scents of urine coupled with body odors, aftershave and strong aromas of perfume? The self-assuredness of her partner, Francis O'Malley? Or maybe it was just a fear of the unknown exacerbated by the bulky, heavy belt fixed around her waist, where a radio, a night stick, handcuffs and her gun combined to hold her captive like a ball and chain. It all came down to culture shock, and Rita was quick to learn that life as a full-fledged police officer in the Big Apple was a far cry from slipping a pencil behind your ear and carrying trays with artery-clogging food to hungry, paying customers.

Rita was so keyed up that first day she had trouble concealing her edginess. After only the first few hours, she scrambled off the swaying train at one of the stops. She quickly found a spot behind the stairs leading up to the street and caved in to a wave of nausea. Wiping her face and mopping sweat from her brow, she reordered her hair beneath her patrolman's hat. What had she gotten herself into? How could she possibly be expected to protect all these people when she, herself, felt so vulnerable? But while she lost her breakfast and feared for her dignity, she was relieved when her partner, Franko, patiently looked the other way and chose not to make matters worse with wisecracks.

30

"First day on the job is like trying to get a bad virus out of your system," he told her. "You only become immune once you become infected. So, trust me. By next week, you'll feel like you've been a part of this dungeon since birth."

He was right. Before long, Rita settled into the hectic morning pace of the city, and she even made friends with some of the regulars she protected and served day in and day out. There were the street vendors down on Canal Street, those whose merchandise Rita could often not resist. Rita loved to browse and negotiate with the merchants, some of whom she got to know by name. They cut her deals and worked up special prices just for her on shoes, handbags and even knock-off brand-name watches.

There were also the restaurateurs in Little Italy where she and Franko often stopped to have lunch. She teased the folks at the four-star Sabini's Trattoria that their food was *almost as good* as her mother's. The maître d' took such a shine to her that she and Franko were always seated at the best table in the house and offered free dessert.

There were also others like Aladdin, the term of endearment she and Franko had given to a taxicab driver of Indian descent. Every Wednesday—his payday, they'd discovered—he illegally parked his yellow cab and blocked the same subway entrance in the Bowery. His initial claim was that he couldn't read English very well—in particular, No Parking signs. But that didn't carry weight for long, as Rita and Franko caught him one Wednesday, parked in his usual place. He and a buddy were scanning the racing form outside the OTB office in the Bowery and spouting off a list of sure bets for the Trifecta over at Belmont Park. When Rita and Franko questioned Aladdin about how he could read the form, he denied his literacy skills.

"I use paper to swat away flies," he told them.

"What? From your eyeballs?" said Franko.

Aladdin became a regular call on the radio frequency. He wasn't what they'd call a troublemaker. He was merely a nuisance, like so many people whom the officers crossed paths with in the city of New York.

Most of the action that Rita and Franko tended to in the subways consisted of people who asked directions or tried to jump the turnstiles. When it came to not paying fares, most cops, Rita discovered, looked the other way—unless they had a quota to fill. But for Rita and Franko, listening to excuses and sob stories became a form of daily entertainment. They used their own discretions and were usually broad-minded when filtering fact from fiction. After all, writing up summonses meant more paperwork, but paperwork was part of the job.

As a team, Rita and Franko seemed the best-matched duo at the Lower Manhattan Precinct, even though they manned one of the most challenging subway lines heading into crack-infested Harlem. They weren't out to break records, and, though thrown together at random, somehow the two of them clicked as if they had chosen each other. Their team efforts on subway sweeps and keeping the line safe from eight in the morning until four in the afternoon, four days on, two days off, proved more than successful for over three months.

Patrolman Francis O'Malley was the more experienced of the two, and the NYPD had hardened him on some level. With his thick-skinned attitude and sardonic city humor, he appeared as tough as a bull. But as Franko got to know Rita better and became more candid and open, Rita learned that hidden beneath Franko's mask was the soul of a sentimental teddy bear.

Rita softened his jadedness, and he tempered her idealism. From their first day on the job, Franko treated Rita with respect and patience, which effectively settled her down. And he gave her three invaluable pieces of advice: 1) Always look like you know what you're doing; 2) Never take yourself too seriously; and 3) Don't ever think you're going to change the world.

"Don't let anyone fool you," he told Rita. "The best part of this job is that you get a paycheck every second week, good medical, dental and eye insurance, and if you can go the distance for twenty years, you can retire with a decent pension."

Franko's philosophy was keenly street-smart and insightful, and also amusing. He was one of the major reasons why Rita liked her job. They laughed a lot, spending eight hours a day together—sometimes more, depending on overtime. The New York Yankees were a hot topic of discussion and debate, as both Rita and Franko were die-hard fans of the Bronx Bombers. To hear their often opinionated banter, you'd think they could better manage the team and the personalities of so many high-priced, high-profile players and their egos than those actually hired to do the job. After only a few months of working so closely, Rita and Franko started to become extensions of each other, and they settled into a comfortable routine.

"There are days in Transit that can be as thrilling as reading graffiti on the trains as they pass," Franko told her early on. "Believe me, after 9/11, be very grateful for shifts like those. But if you want to make the time go faster, you need to have a sense of humor and you'd better like to chat."

This wasn't a problem for Rita, as talking was her forte. It always had been, even from her elementary school days in the Bronx when Sister Leo chronically reamed her out for being a chatterbox at Our Lady of Perpetual Help.

Each morning at six o'clock, Rita would begin her drive to the precinct. She'd step out the front door of her one-bedroom, one-bath basement apartment in the Bronx with a warm cup of tea. By the time she merged onto the Cross Bronx Expressway, the tea became iced. When your funds are limited for so long, you grow accustomed to making do, and one gets used to driving a car without any heat, even in the fall when temperatures prematurely dipped below freezing.

Eventually Rita would dump the tea outside her car door and toss the empty cup on the floor along with the rest of the rubbish collected during the week: junk mail, balled-up clothes, CDs and half-read romance novels always seemed to clutter her car. Her freshly pressed uniform was hung by the back window. And a duffel bag bulging with ballet slippers, tap and toe shoes, tights and bodysuits was tossed on the back seat. After her shift each day, she would faithfully head for the dance studio a few blocks from her apartment. A dancer's workout had been her ritual for years, and she felt she needed it now more than ever, especially while experiencing the hard edge of the NYPD. After working in the trenches of the subway every day, with the abrasive language of city kids and some cops, she welcomed the chance to restore her gracefulness and femininity. She'd never be a prima ballerina, but continuing to study dance as an art form offered her a necessary outlet.

There in her car each morning, Rita pulled back her thick, curly hair and tied it into a ponytail. Her neck felt suddenly cold with the elimination of her natural scarf. She breathed some hot air onto her rearview mirror to clean it off and began to apply her make-up. Why waste a moment of time that stood still at six-thirty in the morning on the Cross Bronx? With one hand on the wheel, she dabbed out a little base make-up and chased that up with a couple of brush strokes of rouge. Never too much. When she was on duty, she wanted to look her best, but there was no need to look like a cover girl.

Every day, there had been traffic. Rain, snow, sleet or hail; sunny or cloudy skies didn't make a difference. By her third month on the force, Rita had become immune to the inconvenience and the various ways that other drivers passed time during the commute. Some read the newspaper or talked, hands-free, on the phone, while others brought along coffee and Danish. Some even had portable computer devices affixed to their dashboards where they watched prerecorded television shows and news. It took Rita a little over an hour to wind her way from the Bronx into lower Manhattan with traffic. She preferred to brave the early morning commute with the rest of the city and work a day shift with rush-hour crowds rather than a night shift with the eerie emptiness and homeless skels loitering about the dark, dreary underworld.

Rita was in the midst of applying her eye make-up when she heard a horn honking. The worst thing about putting on your face in traffic was the complete lack of privacy and being on display. And while the whiney sound of the horn was persistent, it certainly wasn't anything new. A young female traveling alone anywhere in the city gets used to it. Such attention didn't really phase Rita anymore; it simply annoyed her. The men who usually took an interest in her from behind the wheel were gawking low-life types who inched along the fast lane with monotonous rap music playing too loud. And she gathered that her admirers were usually the passersby who found nothing better or constructive to do with their time but stare at her while jammed up in traffic.

Aside from her friendship with Franko and some of the guys in her district, life in the city was much less eventful than she'd thought it would be. The on-again, off-again of her rotation kept her out of synch with the social routines of many of her girlfriends. For Rita, a few days off meant sending out for Chinese food, renting a couple of movies or paging through the latest Jackie Collins or some other steamy romance novel while looking forward to seeing Franko again back at work.

As Rita continued doing her make-up, the horn kept blaring. She tried to drown it out by turning up the radio, but the volume was becoming deafening. She wasn't about to acknowledge some bored lunatic who was probably using her image for one of his male fantasies. And she had a hunch that the fogged windows of her car would've kept her from gaining a clear glimpse of the obnoxious motorist who was now sounding the horn from the lane next to hers.

With mascara applied to only one set of lashes, Rita nearly poked out her eye with the mascara wand and jumped through the roof when she heard a knock on the passenger-side window.

Her heart cascaded down to her tummy. She cautiously wiped the thin film of condensation from the window and uncovered the face of stranger. *Wait!* He was someone she had seen before. The beaming blue eyes and the dimple in his left cheek were unmistakable. *It's the cute guy from graduation. That decorated officer.* When she placed the face, her emotions changed from horror to gleeful surprise. Her fingers fumbled for the button to roll down the window, but she accidentally pressed unlock instead.

"I hope I didn't scare you," he told her, letting himself into the car and jumping into the passenger's seat. "When I realized it was you, I didn't want to let another opportunity pass."

Rita's heart was thrashing in her chest. She was speechless, startled by his presence, and completely shocked by his forwardness.

"I've seen you several times at the precinct house, but I've never been able to catch you alone," he said.

He put forth his hand. "Sergeant William Morrison Quinn, the Third."

Rita studied his fingers as if his gesture were completely foreign to her.

He extended his reach. "My friends call me Billy."

"Thank God," she told him. Rita's iced fingertips melted as they slid inside his warm, firm grasp. "Rita Del Vecchio. The first. The only."

"I've seen you driving this route every morning for the past couple of weeks now. Today was the first time my car actually wound up in the lane next to yours. It seemed like this was as good a time as any to finally introduce myself and say hello."

Rita was caught completely off guard. She didn't know if she was feeling fear or delight.

"Are you stationed in Midtown or in one of the boroughs?" she asked him.

"Right now, I'm sort of between assignments. Being shuffled around. They're trying to coordinate a new task force, so I'm waiting things out. I'm probably going back on special detail in a few days."

The traffic suddenly started to unclog and impatient car horns provided the soundtrack that began to underscore this conversation.

"I better get back, but how about going for a drink some-time?"

At first, Rita didn't answer. She studied his face, wanting to be sure she'd remember this moment if it somehow turned out to be a dream.

"Yeah, sure. Why not?" she told him. Her words seemed to float out of her mouth in a slow, sedated motion. "The easiest way to reach me is probably at the Lower Manhattan Precinct."

"Great, I'll call you," Billy said, hurrying back to his car.

Rita shoved all the make-up scattered about the console of her car back inside her purse. With her hands set at twelve and two on the steering wheel, she moved her foot from the brake pedal over to the gas. She tried to piece together what had just happened. When she turned and saw a red Mustang in the lane next to hers, Billy tooted the horn. He smiled and waved to her. Her heart swelled. She was sure that her warm cheeks must've been glowing. She put up her hand to acknowledge him and before she knew it, his face was like a mirage that floated past her. The traffic in her lane started to advance, and she lost sight of him.

The sun was on the rise. Beyond the potholes that riddled the expressway, glass skyscrapers from downtown hemmed the sky and took on an orange radiance. Rita's confusion began to lift as she drove toward the morning light. It grew bright and sharp, glinting off the hood of her car. A new day had dawned, and all Rita could see was her own glittering future. The whole chance meeting seemed surreal, like a scene straight out of one of those romance novels she loved to read. Only this time it was even better because she'd be the protagonist, the heroine, of her very own story. Maybe Billy Quinn was destined to be her knight in shining armor, the one who would carry her off into the sunset.

# Six

Johnny "the Jinx" Delgado thought he had finally turned his life around. That was before two plainclothes police officers removed a bag containing ninety grams of cocaine and several vials of crack from the twice-convicted drug dealer's jacket earlier in the day.

"You've got the wrong brother. I've turned my life around, and I belong to Jesus," Johnny pleaded with the officers who put him in a head lock and threw him against the wall of a bodega in Spanish Harlem.

"I thought Jesus was big on bread and wine?" one cop remarked, palming vials of drugs as he continued frisking the Jinx. "I never knew the Son of the Almighty was a big crack-head."

"I belong to Jesus. I belong to Jesus," the Jinx chanted, while he burst into tears. "Jesus. Help me. Help me, Lord. Forgive them for they know not what they doin' to me."

As the cops dragged the Jinx out of the building, closer to their squad car, he shook his head. "I's telling you. I don't do the drugs no more. These ain't mine—"

"Ah, shut up, Johnny. We all got problems," the cop said, opening the door to the squad car and pushing the Jinx inside.

"You have the right to remain silent, scumbag. You have the right to an attorney . . ." While the cop read him his rights, Johnny tugged on the handcuffs set securely around his wrists. The Jinx had rotten luck, maybe the worst of anyone in the whole city, and it looked as though things had just gone from bad to worse. Much worse.

Internal Affairs agents greeted the Jinx at the precinct house in Harlem, and the hand-cuffed Johnny was now more than eager to cooperate.

"You cops get payoffs all the time from the local dealers in return for not busting hot spots," the Jinx told investigators. "Hell, before Jesus saved me and I was deep into things, I'd seen uniformed cops pistol whip dealers in plain sight. There's a whole network of you guys out there."

"Oh, yeah? Well, then, tell us, Johnny Boy. Who's running the dirt? We want names. And where, exactly, *are* the hot spots?"

"If I talk, you don't bust me?" the Jinx asked. "You don't bother me no more if I do your dirty work?"

"If you'll be our eyes and ears for a while, then we'll pull a couple of strings and see to it that you'll be *born again* with the law. But that's only if you keep quiet and do as we tell you," a suited investigator told him.

The twice-convicted drug dealer needed less than a second to consider the offer.

"Deal." The Jinx gave a sharp nod toward the Internal Affairs team. "I'll help you combat the snares of Satan because I belong to Jesus now."

"We don't really give a damn who you think you belong to," one of the Internal Affairs suits mumbled under his breath, while rolling his eyes in response to the Jinx's sermon. "The only thing that matters now is that you belong to us."

# SEVEN

*I'll call you . . .*

Famous last words.

Guys had fed Rita that line a million times, but somehow Rita hoped that William Morrison Quinn, the Third, would be different. So far, he was turning out to be like all the rest.

Three weeks had passed, and he still hadn't called. Just as she was about to write him off, floral delivery men began paying her regular visits at the Lower Manhattan Precinct, always presenting her with a dozen long-stemmed roses. No matter who the florist or what color the roses, the card attached always read the same: I HAVEN'T FORGOTTEN YOU. YOUR SECRET ADMIRER

*Secret admirer?* Who was he kidding? It was no secret. With no other prospects in sight, Rita knew the roses could only be coming from Billy Quinn. She liked the flowers. The whole idea of them arriving was storybook romantic, but she would have preferred a telephone call, as promised. She had no other choice but to wait and water the flowers until they wilted.

In the interim, the guys around the precinct began teasing her, calling her "Rose," and of course, Rita ate up the attention. For the first two weeks, she played up the aura surrounding the mystery of the flowers. But by the third week, she was beginning to wonder if this was someone's idea of a cruel, terrible joke.

"You should know that a slew of rumors are flying around,"

41

Franko told her. It was ten o'clock in the morning, and she and Franko were among the last batch of standing freight crowding a subway car.

At first, Rita didn't respond to Franko's innuendo. He had been very cautious about asking her questions. But Rita could tell that Franko's patience, much like her own, was nearing its limit. He wanted details.

"Did you hear what I said, Ree?"

"About the rumors, you mean?" Rita tried to act unaffected. She knew about as much as Franko, and the answers he was seeking even *she* didn't have.

"Who's the flower man?"

Rita played coy. She tucked some stray hairs beneath her police hat and poked them under the brim.

"C'mon, Ree. The precinct house has been receiving more floral arrangements than McCleary's Funeral Home. I'm your partner. I'm entitled. You have to tell me. District policy."

"I can't," she told him. At the next stop, she walked out over the gap between the platform and the train. Franko trailed behind her like a shadow.

Rita smiled at a Transfer Annie, an old lady beggar shuffling down the platform. She dragged a heavy bag filled to the brim with what looked like all her worldly belongings. Rita passed the woman and meandered along the platform, away from Franko. She clenched her hands behind her back and slid the soles of her boots along the concrete platform as though she were skating on ice. *Thin ice,* as far as she was concerned.

Franko chased after Rita, pressing, "Why can't you tell me? What's with all the mystery? Have you landed yourself some rich guy? Is that what this is all about?" As Franko passed the bag lady, he pulled some bills from his pocket and handed them to the woman.

When Rita turned, she saw Franko slip the money to the

woman. "Look at that. You did it again."

"Did what?"

"Why do you throw so much of your money away to the skels like that?"

"Don't try to change the subject," he told her.

"How much money do you give to street people on an average day?"

"I don't know. A couple of dollars here and there. It's not a big deal."

"But I don't get it."

"Why, do you need some money?" Franko pulled a wad of money from his pocket. He thumbed a few bills off the roll and playfully offered a few to Rita.

"C'mon, Franko. Don't be evasive."

"Oh, look at who's talking? The Queen of Evasive herself."

"But is there some special reason why you feel compelled to tithe your salary with these people?"

"Look, it's no big deal. It's one or two less beers a day that I can surely do without," he told her, running his hand along the rounded curve of his flabby belly.

"So you'd rather give your income to skels than to Anheuser-Busch?"

He laughed. "Yeah, what's the harm? You know you might even try being charitable yourself, even just for a day. It feels good. Good for the soul."

Rita shrugged. "I don't understand it, but if it's fulfilling some need in you, then more power to you, I guess."

"Okay, are we done psychoanalyzing me? Can we get back to you now?"

Rita played coy. "Me? *Moi?*"

"Yes, you. Your secret admirer, remember?"

The two of them were playfully dragging this out. And with Franko keeping the tone light, Rita was once again eating up the attention.

"To be honest with you, Franko, your guess is as good as mine," Rita began. "He's a mystery man. I met him about a month ago. On the Cross Bronx, of all places."

"The Cross Bronx? What, were you broken down?"

"No. We were stuck in a traffic jam, each in our own cars, a lane apart. The only contact I've had with him since we met has been through FTD. And don't get me wrong. I love the flowers. They're beautiful. But I don't get it. He could save himself a bundle of money and a lot of trouble if he'd just pick up the phone and call."

This tidbit of information seemed to capture Franko's complete attention. Rapt, he leaned his elbows atop a tall garbage can and rested his chin inside the palms of his hands. His deep-set brown eyes hung anxiously onto her every word.

"Does this mystery man have a name?" Franko waited for more, eager for Rita to tell him the next chapter that had yet to be written.

Rita didn't step out of Esposito's Dance Expressions in the Bronx until nearly ten-thirty that night. It was later than usual, but a guest teacher, a retiree from the New York City Ballet was a visiting instructor, and Rita couldn't pass up the opportunity to study with her. Surely the extra hours were well-spent, although Rita was exhausted. It had been a long day, and she looked forward to getting home and taking a hot shower. As the soles of her shoes clicked along the pavement toward her apartment building, she heard footsteps behind her. The streets of the Bronx were desolate by this time of night, and a woman walking alone could become an easy target. Or, even worse, easy prey.

She rounded the corner, cautiously quickening her own pace, trying not to appear alarmed or nervous. But the footfalls behind her doubled their cadence. Someone was on her trail. Rita's heartbeats quickened to match the rhythm of her own footsteps. Reaching for the gun tucked inside her purse, she suddenly remembered that she'd left it in her locker at the precinct. The stranger was moving closer.

"Rita? Is that you?" a voice called from behind her. "Rita? Wait."

Her heart was pounding as she quickly turned. Her sights were set on a hand holding a dozen red roses, complete with baby's breath. Then a familiar face emerged from beneath the yellowish glow of a nearby streetlight. It was Sergeant William Morrison Quinn, the Third.

"I tried to call out to you as you were leaving the dance place, but I guess you didn't hear me."

Rita put a flat hand over her beating heart. She worked hard to catch her breath.

"I'm sorry," Billy said. "I didn't mean to frighten you. Not again!"

"What are you doing here?" she asked. Steam from her breath rose into the crisp autumn air.

"I felt so bad not getting in touch with you sooner. They switched me to an undercover narc assignment. I wasn't able to call anyone directly. That's why I wired you the flowers. I didn't want you to forget me."

"But how did you find me here?"

"When I finished my assignment, I knew I had to get in touch with you as soon as possible. A buddy of mine works in Central Records. I hope you don't mind, but he pulled your file and found out that you dance a few nights a week at Esposito's. When I called the studio, they told me you were expected tonight. I thought I'd come over and surprise you."

"And surprised, I am," Rita said. She wasn't sure how she should feel—mad, flattered, angry, scared? Should she still feel insulted that he hadn't called sooner? And what about his buddy taking the liberty of pulling her confidential records?

"There was a guest dance instructor tonight. We danced later than usual," she told him, filtering his story through her mind. His absence seemed plausible and he'd gone to great lengths to find her, like a real Sherlock.

"I really wish you had told me that you'd be out this way. I look awful. I'm still all sweaty from class."

"You look fine to me," he said, handing her the bouquet of roses and smiling boyishly.

"They're beautiful. Stock in FTD must be going through the roof these days."

"You're worth the investment," he told her.

Beneath the street lights, she searched his face, trying to gauge if he was genuine.

"I hope you can understand why I didn't call you all those weeks. No one outside the squad could know my whereabouts. I felt awful, but there was really nothing I could do."

She decided to accept his apology. His efforts—and his explanation—sounded sincere.

"I know this quiet little place on the other side of town," Billy said. "Why don't we go for a nightcap?"

Although he'd courted her with flowers for all those weeks, the only thing Rita really knew about Billy Quinn was that he was a handsome stranger who was without a precinct and currently working undercover. He also liked to send roses, had been checking up on her and so far, he'd made his appearances unpredictable. While her attraction to him was strong and she wanted to instantly accept his invitation, the old-fashioned pragmatist in her warned that she exercise caution. He must've sensed her reservations.

"C'mon, what do you say? You up for it?"

"I appreciate your offer, but it's kind of late. And I'm tired," she said, resisting her urge to be impulsive. "I've been dancing for hours, and you just got off a big assignment. Maybe it would be better if we shoot for another night."

"One drink? C'mon, we won't stay out long. I promise." He raised his right hand, pleading his case.

"No, thanks. But I'll take a rain-check."

"Okay, then how about tomorrow? And not just a drink. How about dinner, too?"

Trying not to appear too overanxious, she paused before answering. "All right. That sounds good to me."

"Great. C'mon, I'll walk you home."

"No, that's okay. I live only a few blocks from here."

"I know," he said.

"Central Records?"

He nodded.

"Aha," she said.

"You're not mad, are you?"

She shrugged. "Just surprised, I guess."

In all her life, no man had ever gone to such lengths to find Rita. And woo her. Since she'd already turned down his bid to go for a drink, and it was clear that Billy Quinn wasn't the type to take "no" for an answer, she let him lead the way as they headed off in the direction of her apartment. A few steps in, Billy reached for Rita's duffel bag stuffed with her dancing garb, and she let him take it from her like a boy might walk a girl home from school and carry her books. A perfect gentleman. Rita had thought they didn't exist anymore, at least not outside romance novels.

The short walk beneath the streetlights to her apartment allowed them to become better acquainted. And Rita was glad that she'd postponed his proposition because knowing a little bit more about Billy and his manner had eased her mind and settled her doubts. By the time they'd reached the front stoop to the apartment building, Rita almost wished they could keep on walking a while longer.

"So I'll pick you up at seven tomorrow?" asked Billy, watching as she entered the building.

As she slipped through the door to her apartment, Rita suddenly felt exhilarated, as if she'd been given a second wind. She could easily get used to all the attention he was showering on her. Perhaps William "Billy" Morrison Quinn, the Third, would finally give her social calendar a lift.

# EIGHT

The headlights cut parallel swaths down along the ramp from the West Side Highway that curved onto 125th Street. There it was all lit up—The Cotton Club. The long, white building looked silvery tucked amid the shadows from the highway overpass. Spotlights shined upon the pristine-looking facade that was capped by a tidy black awning and a circular sign that sported the name of the club in stark black-and-white lettering in art deco style. A slew of polished old cars and limousines were angled in front of the place, and patrons, dressed to the nines in ball gowns and tuxedos, cluttered the street.

"Well, what do we have here?" Trapped in a blaze of floating brake lights, Sergeant Dirty Roy McSweeney inched the unmarked car in front of the club. The nickname *Dirty Roy* was first bestowed upon McSweeney years before, back when he walked a beat through the city and had a penchant for flipping through porn magazines at newsstands.

"What we've got is a sea of Bentleys and Rolls Royces," chimed Sergeant Tony Sanducci, his eyes wide through the back-seat window. "Look at how everybody's all dressed up. Like a throwback to the heyday of this place in the thirties—"

"—Well, it's the twenty-first century, bro. To me, it looks like big doings at the gateway to hell." Sergeant Billy Quinn's tone made it clear that he was unimpressed by all the fanfare as he rode shotgun alongside Dirty Roy. "And The Cotton Club isn't the only place in Harlem putting on a big show tonight. Right, fellas?"

The three cops shared a laugh as the car idled at the traffic light beneath the elevated subway tracks at 125th and Broadway. As the roar of the train approached overhead, the ground beneath the steel-belted radials began to quiver. Sparks from the rails scattered down like fireflies, dipping toward the shops and bodegas lining the darkened street below.

When the traffic signal changed from red to green, Dirty Roy hung a left onto Amsterdam Avenue and turned the car north in the direction of Hamilton Heights.

It was easy for these three officers to fall back in step with their old banter. Under the new mayoral administration, it took the city three months to recreate and reform the Special Gun and Drug Task Force that had finally reunited this decorated trio of police sergeants: Dirty Roy McSweeney, Tony Sanducci and Billy Quinn.

"How long has it been since we patrolled this hellhole together?" Billy asked.

"Too long. I'm broke," sighed Dirty Roy.

"For all the talk of revitalization, this place still looks like a dump to me." Billy gazed through the passenger-side window at neighborhoods that seemed to change from bad to worse, block by city block. The deeper they drove into Harlem, the more the place seemed hemmed in on all sides by public housing, the projects, and tumbledown tenements. Gangs were huddled on street corners. Kids wore baggy pants, and thick gold chains and medallions glistened around their necks. They chugged forty-ounce bottles of King Cobra beer. Frenetic baselines from rap music served as a soundtrack while they hurled verbal insults like rocks toward the unmarked car.

Sanducci leaned toward the front seat. "Hey, don't forget," he said, giving Dirty Roy a poke in the arm, "we've gotta get over near Jackie Robinson Park."

"Yeah, yeah. I know," Dirty Roy told him. "Quit being a backseat GPS!"

Dirty Roy veered the car right, then took a couple of quick lefts. Down a dark and narrow one-way, a coned beam of light from a streetlamp widened upon a shiny car parked below. The three officers *oohed* and *aahed* when they were close enough to spot Nick "the Spic" Zapato's souped up, black Monte Carlo. It was vintage 1986, parked right where they were told it would be—outside a boarded-up social club and tenement house.

"I don't know about you guys, but I'd take Nicky's car any day over those Bentleys and Royces over at The Cotton Club," said Billy.

Dirty Roy slowed the car and glanced up at a square of light blazing from a window on the third floor. "Looks like Nicky's already upstairs, counting and cutting his loot."

Billy pummeled his fist into his palm. He craned his neck and followed the trail where Dirty Roy was looking. "Tonight's the night that poor bastard's gonna regret he didn't cut a deal with us before he got back into town."

"You sure we've got the right time?" Dirty Roy asked.

"Yeah, I heard Nicky's girl say that he opens the safe and starts to cut the new stuff around seven o'clock." Sanducci unwrapped two long pieces of chewing gum. He folded them in half and in half again, then shoved them into his mouth. "Looks like we're right on schedule."

Dirty Roy pulled the car as close as he could to Nicky's totally refurbished Monte Carlo. Those who knew Nick "the Spic" Zapato knew his car was his pride and joy. His baby.

With a grimace, Dirty Roy said, "Nicky boy's gonna have a coronary when he gets a load of what we've got planned."

Sanducci cackled as he pushed open the car door and slipped out from the backseat. He grabbed a dented metal lid off a nearby trash can. Then he turned back and asked, "Okay, *Queey.*

You going up?"

Billy stepped gallantly from the car. "Pleasure's all mine."

"We'll meet you upstairs," Dirty Roy said to Billy.

Billy drew his weapon as he neared the dilapidated tenement house. Before he entered, he turned to his cohorts and mouthed in a whisper, "Have fun. And don't you guys miss me too much while I'm gone."

It was a cinch for Billy to jimmy the door lock. Once he had it open, he tiptoed up the creaky front stairway. The walls were so thin that when he hit the third floor landing, Billy heard Nicky counting out loud.

"Four thousand . . . Five thousand . . . Six thousand . . ."

Billy mumbled under his breath, "I'm surprised that bastard can spout off numbers that high." He looked at his watch—6:56. With his body tucked into the shadows filling a nearby alcove in the hallway, Billy pictured Dirty Roy and Sanducci on the front sidewalk, also eyeing their watches and giving a go-ahead nod to each other. Billy firmed his fingers around his gun. He braced himself, waiting for Sanducci to pull his nightstick off his belt and whack it as hard as he could against the metal garbage lid.

*CRASH!*

The impact of the sound clamored right on schedule. It was loud enough to hear even inside the building. Then Dirty Roy screamed, his voice lighting up the quiet with, "Jesus Christmas, dawg! What the hell's wrong with you? Look at what you did to that car! Why don't you friggin' watch where you're going?"

It didn't take long for Dirty Roy and Sanducci to start their noisy pseudo-brawl before Billy, from inside the alcove, saw Nick rush into the hallway and dart down the stairs. With Nicky gone, Billy slipped into the vacant apartment. In his haste, Nick had left his weapon behind and the safe wide open. Billy wasn't surprised to find drugs and stacks of crumpled green bills crowding the kitchen table. In the safe, hidden behind a makeshift cupboard, was a gym bag bulging with money. The zipper was undone, revealing bricks of cash inside along with an oozing stash of loose dollars. Billy yanked the bag from the safe. As he headed back toward the door, he lifted a few baggies filled with Quaaludes and cocaine, along with some piles of C-notes, from the kitchen table. He stuffed his pockets.

Nick was breathless by the time he flung open the door of the building and burst onto the front stoop. Leaning against his Monte Carlo were two familiar faces.

"Hey there, Nick," Sanducci greeted.

"What's up, bro?" asked McSweeney.

At the sight of the two smiling officers, Nick did an immediate about-face. He turned on his heels and charged back into the building. Taking two steps at a time, he flew up the three long flights.

Nicky, a middle-aged convicted drug runner who had recently been released from prison and had just returned to his old neighborhood, bolted through the door to his apartment. In a fury, he swept the drugs and money off the table and tried to cram everything into the safe. But Nick didn't get very far. When he heard a creaking sound, as if from hinges in need of oil, he turned and froze. Emerging from the shadow behind the opened door inside the apartment was Sergeant Billy Quinn. With his revolver already aimed, the officer took a step toward Nicky and put a bullet into the Spic's ankle with one perfectly placed shot.

"Nothing like falling for the oldest trick in the book," Billy said as Nick dropped to the floor. "It's a damn shame you didn't cut a deal with us while you had the chance. It's hell living without police protection, isn't it?" Billy slipped the gun into his holster while Dirty Roy and Sanducci rushed into the apartment, weapons drawn.

"What've we here?" Dirty Roy asked, first eyeing the Spic curled into the fetal position, then making a visual sweep of the remaining drugs and money piled atop the kitchen table.

"This suspect was trying to flee the scene. He left me no other choice," Billy announced, looking on as Nick moaned, a growing pool of blood encircling his leg. When the three cops nodded in agreement to the facts of the story, Billy tossed the overstuffed gym bag he'd lifted from the safe Sanducci's way. "Critical piece of evidence for the Gun and Drug Task Force. Get this down to the car, *ASAP*."

"Will do." Sanducci cradled the bag like a precious newborn. On his way out of the room, he chomped on his wad of gum and said, "I'll give you guys a few minutes to finish up here, then I'll radio for an ambulance and some back up."

"Someday, I'm gonna do all you dirty mothers in," Nick the Spic shouted, blood oozing through his fingertips while he clung in desperation to his ankle. "Especially you, Quinn."

"Do that, and I'll come back and take target practice on your other foot." Billy kicked the steel toe of his police boot into the Spic's stomach. From down on the floor, Nicky let out a gut-wrenching groan.

"What do you think the bag's worth?" Dirty Roy asked Billy.

"I'd say at least ten grand apiece."

"I'll take it. Perfect start for my kid's college fund."

"Yeah, not bad for five minutes of work." Billy put up a hand in Dirty Roy's direction. They clapped their palms together in a high-five gesture over Nick the Spic who was twisting himself up as tight as a pretzel on the floor.

Dirty Roy asked Billy, "So do you want to do the honors or should I?"

Together, the two officers started to recite the memorized

litany as if in harmony. "You've got the right to remain silent. You have the right to an attorney . . ."

# NINE

"We can talk about anything you'd like, but I'm not at liberty to discuss what goes on in the Gun and Drug Task Force. Got it?"

Rita was somewhat taken back by Billy's curtness, but she respected his privacy.

They stayed at Finnegan's Pub in the heart of the Bronx, talking until nearly one o'clock in the morning. The dimly lit bar, with its wooden floors and tables, brass fixtures and emerald-green accented décor was conducive to conversation. Plaques engraved with old Irish proverbs, along with pictures of Ireland and photographs of Irish and Irish-American writers like Samuel Beckett, James Joyce, and Flannery O'Connor were hung crookedly on the walls. A television over the bar was tuned in to a college football game, and the men crowded on stools all seemed to know each other. Rita could tell that Billy, too, was a regular here at Finnegan's. The place felt lived-in and comfortable. It probably offered the comforts of a home away from home to most of the patrons.

During their date that night, Rita admired Billy's complexion as it glowed from the flickering candle at the back of their table. He told her the story of how he had descended from a long line of Quinns who had worked their way through the ranks of the NYPD. Billy was the third direct generation, and he was proud to join the "family business," especially that he was a part of the police force during the terror attack of 9/11.

Rita had a sense that he took his job very seriously. He was a dedicated cop, loyal to the bonds of police brotherhood and stories about the force. He even shared a little about being stationed at Ground Zero and the horrors he'd witnessed. He'd lost a few buddies in the attack, and Rita could tell that was hard for him, emotionally.

But beer after beer, Billy talked more freely, moving from topic to topic, and Rita soon learned that she'd met her match. He loved to talk almost as much as she did. But the way she let him ramble on was a real switch for Rita Del Vecchio, the girl who was voted *most talkative* by her senior class in high school. When she was with her partner, Franko, sometimes they'd cut each other off mid-sentence. But in the case of Billy Quinn, Rita—nervous, shy and overwhelmed by such a good-looking potential admirer, a decorated police officer and an older man to boot—became a willing listener.

It was rare for Rita to discuss work when she was wearing civilian clothes. Most of her girlfriends, when they'd meet for dinner or happy hour, pressed her for details about life in the NYPD. One friend in particular was a wanna-be writer whose over-active imagination tended to glorify Rita's job.

"You mean to tell me that you're a part of the hotbed in the greatest city in all the world, and you don't see any action? I don't believe it," she'd said.

Rita would laugh and tell her, "I think you watch too much *Law & Order*."

"But you must have some dirt. A perp who got away? An arrest gone awry? Give me something. Anything!"

"Trust me, outside of overtime, there's a whole lot of downtime. And a ton of paperwork."

Most people had similar misconceptions about cops, and Rita had a hard time convincing them otherwise. Because of that, she could just as easily tell people she was a veterinary assistant (she was petrified of animals—even fish), an administrative assistant (she had absolutely no computer literacy), or even a nurse (she became queasy at the sight of blood) if the circumstance called for it. In Rita's mind, many of those jobs were probably far more interesting than hers.

When it came to answering the question of "What do you do for a living?" Rita had found that most civilian men felt threatened by women cops and turned off the whole idea of romance quicker than a light switch. But sitting across the table from Billy and listening to his thick New York accent put Rita in a hypnotic-like trance. She remembered the psychic from the mall and her prophecy. A man in uniform, it appeared, would truly understand and accept Rita. And she wanted to have it all. A career, marriage, kids, and to finally settle down. Billy, it seemed, wanted those same things, too.

"Just between you and me, my birth certificate says I was born on September 21$^{st}$, but I was actually born May 21$^{st}$. My mother had the certificate changed because I was conceived before she and my father were married," Billy told her. "It would have been a sacrilege if their marriage certificate read December 1$^{st}$ and I was born five months later."

"But couldn't they have claimed you were premature? I mean, it sounds like they went to an awful lot of trouble for the sake of appearances."

"Oh, you don't know the half of it," Billy said. "Upstanding, church-going Irish Catholics will go to great lengths to avoid black truths. Trust me."

The whole rationale seemed odd and ironic, especially when Rita later learned that Billy's parents had been separated for years—as far back as Billy could remember. But they lived separately under the same roof. This made their lives and the lives of their offspring miserable, at times, until they'd finally divorced when Billy was in his twenties.

The story of Billy's parents was so sad when she compared it to that of her own. Rita's mom and dad had a long and enduring marriage, and she admired how tight they still were after more than twenty-five years. The longest relationship Rita had ever experienced was probably shy of twenty-five days. More than anything, though, she longed to have the type of union her parents shared. Sitting there, listening to Billy's story, it was obvious that his childhood hadn't been as happy as hers. And swept up in the details, she suddenly felt sorry for him, so she tried to lighten things up and change the subject.

"On to other important things," she told him. "What's your sign?"

"You're into signs?" he asked.

"Of course. I'm a superstitious Italian. What else do we Guineas do for fun and recreation?"

Billy chuckled, obviously amused by her. "Well, I tell everyone I'm a Virgo, but with the whole birth certificate thing, I'm actually a Gemini."

"Aha, the twins," Rita said, conjuring what she remembered about the May-June birth sign. "Creative. A tendency for a dual personality. A real ladies' man."

"None of the above." Billy grinned as he raised his beer bottle to his lips. "I'm just a cop's cop, dedicated to the job and old fashioned. What about you? What's your sign?"

"A Leo. But I'm sort of surprised you don't already know."

Billy didn't say a word. When she saw confusion reflected in his face, Rita spun around her sweaty, white wine spritzer glass and fished out the cherry from the bottom with her straw.

"It's just that I figured with all that checking up you did at Central Records, you'd know *everything* there was to know about me. I guess you missed the birth sign angle."

"Not quite," Billy said, blushing. "They only list birth dates, not signs, down at Central Records. I guess astrology doesn't make it into personnel profiles."

59

"Oh, I see," Rita said playfully.

"Besides, my contact at Central Records didn't give me carte blanche with your file. He only told me baseline, preliminary stuff."

"What kind of preliminary stuff?"

"Name, address, phone. Where you might be located after hours. Even with connections, no officer can know everything about a person. However, there *are* many more things I want to know about you."

"Like what?"

"Like everything, including why you drink white wine spritzers with a cherry at the bottom."

Rita grinned. She was enjoying this banter. "Well, wine spritzers are the perfect drink if you're not a big drinker. And the cherry jazzes things up so the drink looks exotic. Plus the fact I'd rather splurge my calories on pizza."

"And why did you become a cop? What possessed you?"

The gap between the question of wine and why-did-you-want-to-become-a-cop was like a canyon. Rita's path was certainly not mapped out as Billy's had been, and she wasn't about to tell him the whole mall psychic story. At least not on a first date. It seemed much too flighty. Therefore, she took a more circuitous route and told him how she grew up in the Bronx and how, when she was nine, her parents decided to move to *the country*—a.k.a. the suburbs of New Jersey.

When she admitted to Billy that she'd kicked and screamed and cried like a baby for weeks after they'd relocated, he reached for her. His thick fingertips interlaced with hers and the meshing of their hands gave Rita a sense of a perfect fit.

"For the next twelve years," Rita said, "I lived like a fish out of water, trying to find some reason to move back to the city."

Rita's passion for New York and being a New Yorker only intensified once she had been taken from it. Her speech, dialect and sense of humor made her stand out among her peers amid the refined quiet of New Jersey. During high school, she spent many weekends back in the Bronx with friends she'd stayed in touch with until they, too, eventually took off to other places and carved out lives of their own elsewhere.

"When I heard the NYPD was in search of new blood, I figured with no strings or commitments in my life, I had nothing to lose. So I gave it a whirl. I figured I'd go as far as I could. And voila! Here I am."

Billy nodded. "Wow. That's pretty free-spirited thinking."

"I think the planets aligned for me at just the right time. Of course, it helped that I've never been the academic-type. I'd had enough of college after my associate degree. And while waitressing was fun, it didn't seem like a career. Yet, I couldn't bear the thought of spending the rest of my life sitting in an office cubicle somewhere."

"But being a cop can be a rough life, especially for a woman."

"Maybe. But being in Transit, at least so far, hasn't really been any more difficult than waitressing. And you get great benefits," Rita said. "Plus the fact, between my police badge and being legally armed, I'm probably safer than most people in this city, male or female."

Billy chuckled.

"What's so funny?" Rita asked.

"You. The way you put things."

"Well, I think the NYPD is the best thing that's ever happened to me, especially my coming back to New York. I've returned to the city I've loved and missed. I'm doing something worthwhile, and I've made a lot of new friends. My partner, Franko, is great, too."

"O'Malley? Really?" Billy sounded surprised. "I don't know him well, but I've heard that he can be a real hard-nose prig, except with the homeless. With them, he's got a reputation for being a soft touch."

Rita played dumb, hoping he might enlighten her. "Is that right?"

"Yeah, something about a lady skel making a swan dive off the subway platform and going splat on the tracks just as he was trying to apprehend her. It wasn't too long ago, I think."

"That's terrible," Rita said, piecing together Billy's comments with what she herself had witnessed of Franko's charity kick with the homeless.

"Yeah," Billy went on. "Word around has it that since the skel incident, your partner has been seeing Dr. Preston, the department head-shrinker."

"That's news to me," she told him, feeling suddenly uncomfortable with the information and not wanting to say anything negative about her partner. "Franko might appear to be a 'hard-nose,' as you say, but from my perspective he's a good guy and a good cop. Loyal as they come, at least with me. And I think he'd go the extra mile for anybody."

"Wow, listen to all that," Billy said. "Franko's one lucky s.o.b., having you as his partner *and* singing his praises. We should all be so lucky."

Rita blushed. Billy was certainly saying all the right things. She picked up her wine spritzer and took a sip as if it were a love potion.

"I'm glad we finally hooked up and got to hang out like this tonight," Billy told her, not taking his sights from hers. "I feel like I've known you a lot longer than just a few hours."

"Me, too," she said. "I hope I haven't been talking too much."

"I could listen to you go on forever, Rita Del Vecchio."

Rita was captivated by Billy Quinn. He was charming and dreamy, everything Rita hoped for and then some. She could tell he was smart, and she liked the way he looked at her when she was talking. He asked questions and listened for the answers—really listened—and it made her want to keep telling him more and more. And he even seemed to know just when, and exactly how, to touch her. Near the end of the night, he leaned across the table to Rita and gently pressed his lips over hers.

*Aaah, the first kiss!* He tasted just as smooth and delicious as Rita had imagined. Then came a second kiss, longer than the first, deeper.

# TEN

Billy and Rita were fast becoming an item, and the Lower Manhattan Precinct was buzzing with gossip about the in-house romance as if it were sweet nectar attracting swarms of hungry bees to a honeycomb. Rita had been on the force long enough to know that guy cops loved to gossip even more than proverbial washwomen. And from the perpetual grin beaming on her face, it was clear that Officer Del Vecchio was falling in love.

But while Billy and Rita's relationship was tightening, Rita and Franko's alliance was starting to sag. It was nothing she could put her finger on, but Rita could feel them growing apart. Maybe she'd been talking too much about *Billy this* and *Billy that* because whenever she did, she noticed lapses of silence between her and Franko. And no matter how she tried to fill the gaps, including goading and self-deprecation, her efforts fell short. Rita just couldn't seem to rally Franko. Even talk about the New York Yankees seemed strained. When gentle tact wasn't successful at rescuing him from the quiet broodiness that was taking him hostage day after day, her tone became one of exasperation instead.

"What is it? What's wrong with you? Talk to me, dammit!"

And he'd always reply, "I'm tired, that's all."

But after weeks of harping, she finally wore him down.

"I am tired," he told her. "But if you want to know the truth, I think I'm tired because I don't know how to handle this."

"Handle what?"

"You. I'm worried about you."

"Me? Worried? About what?"

"The absolute worst thing you could do is get involved with someone from our district. Too much pressure. Too much gossip. And when everything falls apart, you're gonna be a mess. Probably even transferred. Mark my words."

"Gee, thanks for the vote of confidence," Rita told him. "Here I think I've finally found *the one,* and you have to go and spoil it for me? Some friend you've turned out to be."

Franko dragged her by the sleeve of her jacket and whisked her away from the hubbub of a train derailment scene they were patrolling.

"*The one?* Please tell me you're not serious?"

Franko's tone was desperate and pleading. Rita, caught off guard, was stunned and afraid to answer.

"It's only been a couple of months," Franko said. "Billy can't be *the one.*"

"Why not?"

"Because you don't know him."

"I know what I need to know."

"Oh, no, you don't. Believe me." Franko let go of her arm and shook his head. "You're being starry-eyed and gaga. The whole mystique of the older man in uniform. What you're feeling for Billy isn't reality."

"So what are you saying? Love isn't a reality?"

"Love? You're not *in love.* You're just in love with the *idea* of love."

"Don't tell me what I am!"

"Rita, take it from one who has been around the block more times than a Yellow Cab. Love can be disorienting. If it's not real, it can be a trap. And if you fall prey, it can devour you."

"Gee, spoken like a true romantic!"

Franko tossed up his hands. "Look, I'm not going to wax

philosophical with you. It's just that you really surprise me sometimes. You're such a contradiction. You completely uprooted your life and managed to get through the rigors of becoming a cop. One part of you is as tough as nails, but another part of you is so incredibly naïve."

"It's called bliss."

"This isn't a joke."

Rita narrowed her gaze on him. "Where is this coming from? Why are you being like this?"

"I'm being like this because I care about you."

"Care? What you're doing is raining on my parade, Franko," she said. "A person can get a sense of things, have a gut feeling. And I'm happy with Billy. I'm really happy, maybe for the first time in my life."

Franko sighed and ran a rough hand along the stubble on his face and down along his throat. "Ree, I did a little checking. You don't know the same Billy Quinn that I know."

"Checking? You're checking up on him?" Rita was appalled.

"Billy has a dark side. He can be a hot-head and ill-tempered."

"So is every other cop on the force. It's called male bravado, the whole NYPD image thing. Billy might act that way with guys on the force, but with me he's an absolute sweetheart."

"A sweetheart?" Franko burst a loud guffaw as though he'd just heard the punch line of a clever joke. "Well, maybe you'd like to know that your *sweetheart* is a blowhard and braggart. Especially in the locker room. I've heard stories, how he mouths off resumes of women he's had. Conquests. And if that's not bad enough, there's even talk he's a dirty cop. On the take. Not to mention a racist thug."

"What?"

Franko's silence served to underscore his message. Rita didn't like it. She could feel heat rising in her face.

"Well, gee, Franko. Don't hold back. Don't feel you've got to use kid gloves with me or anything."

"Knowing you're getting mixed up with Quinn has been tearing me up inside. I'd be a lousy friend if I sugar-coated things," he said. "I'm only telling you this because I don't want to see you get hurt."

"Oh, yeah, that's a laugh. Hurt by whom?"

Franko's eyes darkened as though deeply wounded by the curtness of Rita's response.

She said, "I've always been under the impression that real friends don't begrudge or judge each other."

"Ree, that's not my intention. All I'm asking is that you hear me out—"

"I appreciate your concern." Her words trampled over his. "But I don't think it's fair to believe rumors and speculation. Actions speak louder, and the Billy I know is gentle. He's a good guy."

"Listen, Ree, I don't want to fight with you. And please don't kill the messenger. A red flag, that's all I'm waving here."

"That's enough. End of discussion," she told him, putting her hands over her ears. "I think I liked you better when you were tired."


Rita knew Franko well enough to know that he *was* looking out for her, but no matter how much her head tried to reason his intentions, her heart was hurt by his accusations. *Who does he think he is? My over-protective father? He was out of line!* Being unable to reconcile her thoughts and feelings, Rita continued to distance herself from her partner. It was the path of least resistance. That's not to say that she forgot Franko's warnings. In fact, everything he said made her take a closer look at things. But the Billy Quinn whom Franko described was nothing like the one with whom Rita was starting to spend every free moment. Since this seemed to disprove Franko's blatant misconceptions about Billy, Rita closed off that part of her life to Franko. But the blockade made their shifts feel endlessly dull and superficial. Soon Rita found herself eyeing her watch while they patrolled the subways, counting the minutes until she'd be off duty and able to see Billy again. The more time that passed, the greater the rift became, until it felt as though Rita and Franko were on opposite sides of a moat too wide to cross.

Billy became a bridge away from her disappointment with Franko, and she was eager to make that escape. Soon, Billy and Rita, the happy couple, became partners of their own. They started carpooling to work. But during their shifts, Billy made it clear that they both had a job to do, and they weren't to cross the personal-professional line when on duty.

In the precinct house or on their respective beats, Billy treated Rita as though she were any other officer. At first, Rita didn't appreciate Billy's coolness toward her, but after being in the company of men for all those months, Rita became something of an expert on all aspects of the fragile male ego.

When their shifts ended, Billy and Rita commuted back to the Bronx. Often, they stopped at the shooting range to take target-practice and afterward, Billy would wine and dine Rita, buying her flowers, jewelry and other little presents. There were movies and hand-holding long walks, trips to the park and the mall. Life had never been so wonderful, and love had never tasted so good. And the story of Rita Del Vecchio's own life was becoming even better—steamier and juicer—than those romance novels she'd once read by the stack.

It was the very first time that Rita had truly fallen in love, and not having much to compare it to, she savored every moment. Billy had won her heart, and she was convinced that she'd finally met someone with whom she had much in common, who listened to her and was attentive to her needs. Billy was someone who professed his love for her and really meant it.

They lived only a few blocks from each other, so they'd alternate between apartments during their off duty time together. On their three-month anniversary, it was Billy's night at Rita's. They ate dinner in bed, drank too much wine and made love for hours. The incessant roar and rumbling of nearby trains provided a vibrating soundtrack as they drifted in and out of sleep, cuddling together, until they finally dozed off. But when Rita stirred and looked at the clock, realizing that it was two o'clock in the morning, she quickly tried to rouse Billy.

"C'mon, time to go home," Rita told Billy, shaking him awake.

"Home? But I feel like I *am* home." He pulled her on top of him.

Playfully, she wiggled out of his grasp. "C'mon. You know the rule."

"Oh, you and your rules. Be daring and break them for once." Billy's kisses deepened as his passions increased. His touch was hard to resist—the way his hands raked hungrily over her body. But Rita drew away from him again.

"Billy, no. You can't stay the night. It's bad luck."

"Says who?"

"Me."

"Oh, c'mon," Billy protested "It's our three-month an-niversary. It's a special occasion. After the love we've just made, what's the difference if I stay the night or not?"

"It's the principle of the thing. I told you, I've always vowed that I would never spend a whole entire night with someone un-less we were married."

Billy groaned and pulled the pillow over his face.

When Rita peeled herself from the bed and slipped into her bathrobe, Billy leaned down to the floor and picked up his clothes. With deliberate slowness and drama, he stepped into his jeans and boots and thrust his robust arms through the sleeves of his t-shirt. He slipped on his shoulder holster and gun and threw on his denim jacket. Then he reached for her one last time.

"C'mon, let me stay," he said playfully, untying the sash on her robe.

"You know I want you to, but we can't. We shouldn't." When he pulled Rita to him and swept kisses down her neck, she pushed him away. "Stop. I told you. It's bad luck."

"Then let's just get married."

Rita's heart skipped a beat. She froze. "Married? Are you serious?"

"Yeah, what are we waiting for?" Billy said. "I'm almost thirty-five. I know what I know. And I know what I want. I can't get enough of you. So let's just spend the rest of our lives together."

"So is this a proposal? An *official* proposal?"

Billy nodded, grinning while he looked Rita in the eye. "Should I get down on one knee?"

On tiptoes, Rita reached up and with her small hands holding the sides of his face, she kissed him squarely on the mouth.

When they finally disengaged, Billy appeared breathless. "Should I take that as a *yes?*"

"Mrs. Billy Quinn," she said aloud, nodding. She flung her arms around Billy and interlaced her fingers behind his neck. "Mrs. William Morrison Quinn, the Third . . . Yes, yes. I like the sound of it."

Rita thought she'd crawl out of her skin, consumed by longing and the desire to be close to him again. She was convinced that their love would go on like this forever, that what she was feeling would always be fresh and new. Layer by layer, she shed all of Billy's clothes and her own robe until, recklessly and without abandon, they hurtled themselves at each other, fingers probing, kisses deep. They became lost in each other.

The next time Rita opened her eyes, the darkness of the night was already giving way to a fiery morning sun that was slowly easing up from an inky-colored sky.

The day-glow numbers on the digital clock read 6:20 A.M.

Rita's heart leapt. "Billy, get up!" she howled, shaking him awake and dashing to the closet. She yanked clothes from hangers and hurried to get dressed. "Get up! We're late. And you broke the rule—"

"We *both* broke the rule," he corrected, his gravelly voice filled with sleep. "C'mon. Come back to bed. Let's just take the day off."

"I can't. There's a subway terrorist training drill today. Then I'm supposed to head out to Jersey to have dinner with my parents."

"Then I guess we'll have to just pick up right where we left off again tonight?"

"No. Not tonight. I'm not going to be back until late," she told him, gathering her hair and sweeping it up into a ponytail. She dashed into the bathroom and pressed out some toothpaste. Before she started to brush, her words spilled out to the bedroom. "And what happened last night can't happen again. Not before the wedding."

"Why not? Your rule's already broken. Isn't the damage already done?"

"Oh, no, it's not. Someplace, somewhere in the world, morning's not yet broken. So if you look at it that way, we really didn't spend the *whole* night," Rita rationalized. She was determined that nothing, not even that silly rule of hers, would spoil their future.

# ELEVEN

"Dom, did you hear this? Dommy?" Rita's mother, Tina, screamed from the kitchen as if the broiler pan in the oven had suddenly caught fire. "Dommy, you better come in here. Quick."

But Rita's father, Dominic Del Vecchio, who was obviously employing his selective hearing, didn't budge from his favorite chair in the living room. He was deliberately keeping his attention on the television set, watching a rerun of *Everybody Loves Raymond* and pretending to be oblivious to his ranting wife.

"Can you believe this, Dom? We bring only one child into the world, and she's decided to marry the first guy who looks at her?" Rita's mother tossed up her hands in an I-give-up gesture. "A guy she's only known a few weeks?"

"Three months, Mother. *Three* months," Rita corrected.

"Three months, three hours!" Her mother's temper was brimming like a stopped up sink with the water still running.

"Does this mean you're not happy for me?" Rita asked.

"Happy? How can I be happy?"

Tina turned her back on Rita. She focused on the stove and continued frying the breaded chicken cutlets she had started before Rita dropped the bomb and delivered what she thought was great news. Prodding the meat with a fork, Tina let the chicken, sizzling in the hot oil, speak for her. She flipped the thin cutlets as if on one side was the love she felt for her daughter and on the other was the contempt she harbored for her daughter's announcement.

"Ma, I hate it when you're quiet. Say something, will you?"

"What do you want me to say? I've had head colds that have lasted longer than your relationship with this guy!"

"That's not what I wanted to hear." Still seated at the kitchen table, Rita twirled her curly, thick hair between her fingers. She had sat in this very chair at this very same table a million times, watching her mother prepare dinner to be served promptly at six-thirty each night. But they'd never before had *this* conversation.

"What kind of man proposes without a ring?" said Tina, as she started to pull the flattened, gold-colored cutlets from the oily fry pan and transferred them to a plate.

"He didn't propose exactly," Rita told her, reaching for a paper napkin and nervously starting to tear it. "It's something we talked about and last night, we decided to make it official."

"How *official* is it if he didn't give you a ring?"

"Stop with the ring. It's not about the ring." The napkin that Rita had been shredding was now ripped up into tiny, confetti-sized pieces—but so much for a celebration. "Ma, I'm sorry that you're not pleased with the way Billy and I got engaged, but that really shouldn't be an issue."

"You're right," Rita's mother said, tilting the fry pan and draining some of the hot oil into an empty soup can. "The issue is the marriage. And quite frankly, I'm not pleased that you've decided to marry a stranger."

Rita was perplexed. "A stranger? Billy's not a stranger." Then it hit Rita. The tip off was the word *stranger*. It was her Mother's code word for anyone who wasn't of Italian descent. "Tell me, Ma. This reaction of yours, does it have anything to do with the fact that Billy's Irish?"

Tina's silence spoke volumes.

"Ma, that incident with Mr. O'Shea was years ago. Please tell me you're not still holding a grudge."

"My mother was so sick. How could that man have fired my father when he knew how much we needed the money?" Some oil splattered up from the can and burned Tina on the arm. She cringed in pain.

"My God! You're a bigot, Ma. That's what you are!"

"You don't know what it was like." Tina flung the fry pan into the sink and lifted the faucet. The cold water singed and steam rose as it hit the hot pan.

"Ma, Mr. O'Shea was just doing what he had to do to run his business."

Tina opened the door to the freezer. She grabbed an ice cube and ran it along the burned part of her arm, near her elbow. "If that man didn't let my father go, my mother might've found a better doctor, a better treatment. She might still be alive today."

"So what you're saying is that Mr. O'Shea is a murderer? His actions tarnished the whole Irish race when he, quote-unquote, killed Nana?"

Tina's eyes welled up with tears. She turned from Rita, tossed the melting ice cube into the sink, and thrust her quivering hands beneath the water still flowing from the spigot.

Rita sat speechless at the kitchen table. She waited for her mother to regain her composure. Rita knew better than to continue the debate, especially since Tina was deep in the throes of menopause and her Vesuvius-like emotions had become even more erratic and unpredictable.

"I'm sorry. You're right. Listen to me." Tina's voice cracked. She wiped her moist eyes with the corner of a dish towel. "I'm like a damn elephant that doesn't forget. I admit it. I have had a hang-up about the Irish ever since Mr. O'Shea. But in truth, my concern for your marriage goes beyond all that."

Rita drew in a long, measured breath in preparation for the lecture that she expected would follow.

"Nana always used to say a girl needs to spend all four

seasons with a man before she says *I do*. And that's good advice. Three months isn't long enough to get to know a person, let alone someone with whom you're planning to spend the rest of your life."

"But I'm with Billy every day, at work and socially. This may sound hard to believe, but I think I know him better than I know myself. We're completely compatible, and we're totally on the same wavelength about everything."

*"Everything?"* her mother repeated skeptically. "I doubt that."

"Well, if not everything then *almost* everything. I've never met anyone like Billy. He makes me feel things I've never felt before. And I've never bonded so completely with another person in all my life."

"You're young."

"Ma, twenty-two is not *that* young."

"Do you love him?"

"Of course, I love him. And he loves me. He shows me in a million ways."

"Like buying you an engagement ring?"

"He's going to. He promised he would. And I believe him," Rita assured. "Ma, I can't describe it. It's not about the things he gives me. It's about who he is. He cares about me. I can tell him anything. He really listens."

"That's all well and good. Love's always wonderful at the start. But in marriage, the day to day stuff . . . well, that's a whole other ball game."

Rita frowned in frustration. What could she say? How could she convince her mother that the love between Billy and herself was real?

"I know you'll think that I'm being unfair, judging Billy based on the one or two times I've seen him," Tina said. "But the real problem I have with him is that he drinks too much."

Rita slapped her hand on the kitchen table. "Oh, great!

Dredging up Nana's death didn't cut it, so now you're going to play the stereotyping card—"

"He put away a whole six pack of beer last Sunday at dinner."

"You were counting?"

"Your father bought only one six pack that night. By the time you both left, all the cans were finished—crushed and tossed into the recycle bin."

"So Billy was a little nervous. He drank to take the edge off. It's not a big deal."

"Don't alcoholics do that?"

"Oh, Mother, please, stop." Rita tossed up her hands. "I can't believe you're going to do this. I can't believe you're going to pull out all the stops and try to knock him down for everything."

"I'm just telling you what I saw, what I'm feeling."

"No, you're passing judgment. That's what you're doing. No one is ever going to be good enough for me. Are they, Ma?"

"Rita, a mother knows. All I'm saying is give it more time. It's only been three months. Ninety days. Give him the four seasons. What's the rush?"

Rita could feel tears springing to her eyes. "I don't want to wait. I want to spend the rest of my life with Billy. And I want it to start as soon as possible."

"Ree, your father and I, we've been very accepting of your choices. I mean, how do you think I feel as a mother, knowing my little girl is going to work as a cop every day in the New York subways, especially after 9/11 and all those terror threat warnings? Yellow, orange, red. I can't even keep track." Tina let out a deep breath and leaned back against the countertop. "Your father and I only want the best for you. And I know I can't tell you what to do. If you want to marry this man, then you're going to marry him, and there's nothing I can really do to stop you. I just wish you'd wait a little longer, just to be sure."

"But, I *am* sure. There's no need to wait. Really. Trust me on this."

# Twelve

The world had already gone dark. Billy sat on the chilly front steps of Rita's apartment building and took the velvety ring box out of his pocket for the gazillionth time. He flipped it open. Even in the dim light of the streetlamp, the diamond sparkled. It was dazzling. But where was Rita? He was waiting to surprise her. What was taking her so long? And why wasn't she answering her cell phone?

Eight o'clock turned into eight-thirty.

Nine o'clock turned into nine-thirty.

*Where the hell is she?*

Billy couldn't sit still. And rather than let nervous energy get the better of him, he decided to head down to Finnegan's Pub for a drink.

*It'll take the edge off.*

But en route to the bar, Billy saw a drug deal going down just around the corner. He didn't like this type of action going on right in the neighborhood, so close to his home and Rita's. *I'll teach this little bastard to stay off my turf,* Billy thought, assuming the role of civilian and approaching the dealer.

"Hey, bro," Billy said, inching closer until he saw the whites of the dealer's eyes. He was a black kid. An African-American. He'd be an easy target to teach a lesson and at the same time, Billy could work off some of his angst. "You got any toot for me?"

The kid emerged from the shadows. He was small and

scrawny, wearing a knitted wool ski cap, pants three sizes too big with all kinds of pockets, and gold chains—*bling*—around his neck. On his feet were cloddy, expensive basketball sneakers.

"Sure, dawg. I don't see why we can't do ourselves a little business," the kid said to Billy. "Wait around the corner till I finish up here."

Billy didn't like to be told what to do. He didn't like this little prick's confidence. But Billy walked around the corner of the building anyway. Once he was lost in the dark alley, he slipped his police badge from the back pocket of his jeans and yanked his gun from his shoulder holster. He waited for the dealer to return.

"Now what you'd say you needed, dawg?" The white of the kid's bright smile glimmered even in the dark alley.

"You can start by giving me all you've got. Everything," Billy sneered, holding up the badge. "You're under arrest."

There was enough ambient light for Billy's police badge to reflect into the kid's stunned face. He tried to run, but Billy whacked the kid with the gun and wrestled him, face down, to the ground. Then Billy straddled the kid and did a thorough search of all those pockets.

"Looks like you've had yourself a pretty good night," Billy said, twisting the kid's arm backward more than should be humanly possible.

The kid howled in pain.

"Wow, you've got over a grand and still have a couple of bags left. You must be one helluva businessman."

The kid was crying, pleading.

"How about I just take what I need here, and we'll call it even? How's that sound, *dawg?*"

Billy stuffed the wad of money and the bags of cocaine inside the pockets of his denim jeans and jacket. Then he tucked his gun back into the holster under his arm.

"Just a little piece of advice," Billy said, rising to his feet and aiming the gun at the dealer, who was still writhing on the ground. "Next time, conduct your business someplace else. Stay outta my neighborhood." With the steel toe of his work boot, Billy kicked the kid in the groin. Then he composed himself and strode calmly out of the alley.

The drug dealer was in too much pain to fight back. But Billy, starting down the block, could hear the kid's angry words. They slithered around the building like the hiss of a snake. "I'm gonna get you, Badge Number 7-7 dash 5-7-7-2. I'm gonna get you back, good."

Billy ran his pointer finger beneath his nose. His nostrils felt on fire. It was cheap stuff he'd nabbed off that little junkie bastard on the street, and it pissed him off.

He wasn't even two steps into Finnegan's when he shouted to the bartender, "Gimme a double Johnny Walker Black, straight up."

His request for the Cadillac of scotches made the other men seated around the bar sit up and take notice.

"What'd ya win the lottery, Quinn?" a voice called out from amid the crowded bar.

Billy launched himself upon an empty stool and leaned over the bar, paying the remark no attention.

"Yeah, what *is* the occasion, Quinn?" the bartender asked, filling the glass tumbler with the expensive amber-colored liquid.

"Getting married. Hitched," Billy told him with little enthusiasm. He downed his drink, slapped the empty glass onto the bar and motioned for another.

"Gee, don't take it like a death sentence," said one of the patrons from other side of the bar.

"Na, tell him the truth. That's what marriage is, isn't it fellas?" The bartender looked to the others for support to validate his comment. But the onlookers were too busy sharing a laugh.

Billy felt the elbow of the guy seated next to him jab his ribs.

"Hey, Quinn. Is it that hot chick you've been bringing around here?"

*It?* Billy nodded and downed his refill.

The man went on, his words slurring. "Hell, I wouldn't mind spending the rest of my life with *her.* I bet she's good in the sack. One helluva lay."

Billy had had it. His temper triggered like a bomb explosion. He whacked the guy in the face and kept taking swings at him until the poor bastard fell to the floor. The other men jumped to their feet, along with the bartender, trying to break up the brawl, but Billy was hauling off, ripping the guy apart.

"Yo, lighten up," the man said, fingering his bloody nose. "Can't you even take a joke?"

"No. Not that kind of joke," Billy shouted. He thought his heart was going to pound out of his chest and slide right on to the shellacked bar, crashing into all the beer bottles and frosted mugs. "Give me another refill and keep 'em coming," he ordered the bartender.

*Damn you, Rita! Where are you?*

# THIRTEEN

Rita drove from her parents' house in New Jersey back to her apartment in the Bronx fuming. Why couldn't the people she loved the most be happy for her? First Franko, now her mother. Why were they trying so hard to undermine her decision and make her feel so insecure in the process?

As Rita walked from her car and approached her apartment building, she was surprised and relieved to see Billy waiting outside on the front stoop.

But when he greeted her with, "Where the hell were you?" his words stopped her in her tracks.

"At my parents. You knew that. Why? What's the matter?"

"I've been calling you?"

"You have?" Rita rummaged through her purse and pulled out her cell phone. The screen was dark. "Oh, my gosh. I forgot to turn it on. I'm sorry."

"What took you so long? It's after ten o'clock."

"I got out of there later than I thought. Then there was traffic on the George Washington Bridge. They're doing night-time construction." Rita approached Billy warily. She could tell he hadn't shaved. He had dark circles around his eyes and the whites looked bloodshot and glassy. "Is everything okay, Billy? Are you feeling all right?" Rita leaned over to give him a kiss. When he turned away from her, her lips brushed against his bristly cheek.

"I missed you, too," she told him. She slipped her arms

around his neck, trying to placate him. "How about a real kiss to make up for all the hours we were apart?"

The taut muscles on Billy's face softened. But as she planted her lips upon his, Rita could sense that he reeked strongly of cigarettes and there was the taste of liquor on his breath.

"So what did you do all night while I was gone?" she asked.

"Counted the hours till you'd come back. And bought you this," he said, handing her the small, crushed velvet box.

She *ooed* and *aahed* at the sight of the glimmering facets of the diamond. "I love it. Almost as much as I love you." She slipped the ring on her finger and stretched out her arm to admire it.

"Oh, how I wish I'd had this to show my mother tonight."

"Don't worry. You'll have forever to show her now." Billy pressed another kiss on Rita. The stubble on his unshaven face felt coarse as it grazed on her smooth skin.

# FOURTEEN

It was a blood bath at Grand Central. By the time Franko and Rita arrived on the scene, commuters were scrambling, trying to get away from the pandemonium. The victim was flat on his back, face up and unconscious on the cold tile platform. It was obvious that life was quickly draining from him. The tails of his tie were flung back over his shoulder, and the lapels of his suit jacket were parted like a curtain that revealed a bull's-eye of blood right at the center of his starched white business shirt. Papers that had spilled from a leather briefcase were strewn around the lifeless-looking body and sopping up the growing pool of blood.

"Freeze! Freeze!" came the shouts of Rita and Franko, who raised their weapons in order to corner three Latino men wearing leather jackets and holding switchblade knives.

"Drop your weapons. Now!" The commanding shrill of Franko's voice echoed in the terminal. The two men in the rear of the group did as they were told. They threw down their knives. But there was one hold-out—the pack leader, the guy heading up the trio. He waved a bloody knife in front of him, itching for a fight.

A spike of fear rose up in Franko. He stared into the man's face. The image of those wild eyes, his thick nose and taut lips seared into Franko's brain as he firmed his grip on his weapon, tight and damp, and ordered, "C'mon, man. I said drop it. Drop your weapon and put up your hands."

"But I ain't done nothing," the pack leader said. He had a well-defined V-shape to his body that made him appear the most muscular-looking of the three. He kept his feet firmly planted. He didn't blink. Perspiration was raining down from beneath the fringe of his black hair.

"Don't be stupid," one of the other men said, his voice rising from behind the group. "Just give 'em what they want. It's over."

The pack leader yelled something incoherent in Spanish that sounded like a bark.

Every muscle in Franko's body was tense, but he could feel his hand, his fingers wrapped around the gun, beginning to quake. Locked in this stand-off, Franko couldn't see a way out of this, but he tightened his bicep so that his arm might feel stronger.

*You're the one in control here,* spouted Franko's internal dialogue. *Keep your hand steady and your mind even. Finger on the trigger. Be cool. You've got this guy.*

With his piece still aimed on the defiant pack leader, Franko took a step closer and said, "Get against the wall." Franko could feel his adrenaline rushing, even through his eyes. "I said, put your hands up and drop your weapon."

The two men in the rear backed up toward the wall of the terminal. But brazenly, the pack leader stood his ground. He brandished the knife in front of him like a shield, ready for Franko's attack.

Franko kept his aim on the leader and again moved closer. One step . . . Then another. The perpetrator moved from side to side. He wouldn't back down. Rita, creeping alongside Franko, kept her own weapon drawn and followed Franko's lead. But as Franko took his fourth step toward the perp, Rita and Franko's police radios hissed and crackled with static. The sound must've jarred the man with the outstretched knife. He lunged for Franko.

*Pop!*

A bullet, a single shot, released from the chamber of Franko's gun. It echoed like the roar of a cannon. The assailant collapsed onto the platform. Franko had lodged a bullet into the man's leg.

The perpetrator looked stunned, and so was Franko. His arm was outstretched, and he kept the gun pointed straightaway. For a terrifying instant, a light, gauzy feeling filled Franko's head. Everything in the cold, desolate terminal looked and sounded muted, except for the bloodied knife-edge. The shiny part of the blade glimmered on the ground next to the perpetrator, and Franko saw it as clear as if he were holding it in his own hand.

"Franko, you all right?" Rita asked.

His hand shook, yet he couldn't speak. *Have I imagined this? Have I really just shot a man?* Franko could feel his face flush. He felt as though he'd just showered with his clothes on.

When the back-up team arrived, along with paramedics, the adrenaline of the scene finally began to drain from Franko. And on he went, business as usual.

The injured businessman, who'd been lying unconscious, was quickly put on a stretcher and rushed out of the terminal. After the victim's wallet was recovered from the pack leader, Rita and Franko discovered there was only one hundred dollars inside.

The two other assailants were handcuffed. They were read their rights and whisked away. As the wounded aggressor was being carted off on a stretcher, the medical crew worked hard to restrain him. But what they couldn't restrain were his words.

"I'll be back to get you, you fat pig," he wailed.

"Aw, I bet you say that to all your arresting officers," Franko chimed, trying to act nonchalant while a sick feeling shivered through him.

Through the barrage of paramedics and police, the aggressor

defiantly craned his neck. When he found Franko through the crowd, he raised his hand in a gesture of an imaginary gun.

"Bang, bang," he said, taking aim and firing a make-believe shot in the direction of Franko's head.

When Franko turned away, his gaze landed on Rita. He saw his own horror reflected in her pale face.

# FIFTEEN

## DISTRICT OFFICERS SAVE CONGRESSMAN'S SON

*Grand Central Terminal, February 22*—Officers Francis O'Malley and Rita Del Vecchio stepped into a robbery-in-progress scene involving James Thomas, son of New Jersey Congressman Patrick Thomas, at the Grand Central Subway Terminal at 42$^{nd}$ Street yesterday.

"Right in the middle of the mid-morning commute, three men confronted a male Caucasian en route to business," Officer Del Vecchio said. "In a matter of seconds, the exchange ended in bloodshed. One of the three assailants stabbed the commuter."

The two officers were able to secure the three men as rush hour commuters scrambled from the scene. Two of the assailants followed police orders. But one of the assailants, Santiago Ramirez, stood at the helm holding a bloodied knife.

"I had to size up the situation in an instant," Patrolman O'Malley said. "I told the assailant, 'Drop your weapon and put up your hands.' And he said, 'I've done nothing.' That's when I began to anticipate the worst."

Officer O'Malley tried to verbally persuade the suspect to drop his weapon, but the two remained at a stand-off. "I got a little scared because I knew that I was probably going to have to shoot this guy. He was so defiant, standing his ground."

"He was a big guy, very muscular," said Officer Del Vecchio of the assailant. "My initial reaction was that he was probably an ex-con doing his damnedest not to get caught again."

Officer O'Malley added, "My guess was that this guy was on parole. He was built like a parolee." Prisoners often spend their jail time lifting weights and their upper bodies are disproportionately developed.

When the suspect, Ramirez, lurched for Officer O'Malley, the officer was forced to shoot him, wounding him in the leg.

"The assailant left my partner no choice," said Del Vecchio. "Any other officer faced with the same situation would've acted similarly. I'm lucky to have Franko as my partner."

Santiago Ramirez, 29, who had served a seven-year term for rape, recently jumped bail on a drug-trafficking charge.

The two other suspects, Santiago's twin brothers, Chico and Puma, 23, will be arraigned today. Both have had prior arrests for drug possession.

Once apprehended, all of the suspects tested positive for drugs and alcohol.

James Thomas, a graduate law student at Fordham University, suffered a stab wound to the chest. He is listed in serious, but stable, condition.

When asked how it felt to be a hero, Officer O'Malley said, "I didn't have time to think about being a hero. I was only doing my job."

"So what do you think?" Rita asked Billy.

While he read the article in *The New York Post,* she could see his square jawbone flex. He was gritting his teeth.

"I'm proud of you, babe. And relieved you didn't get hurt," he told Rita. Right there, in a corner of the squad room, Billy crossed the line. The two officers leaned toward each other and hugged.

"Do you think all this attention is bad?" Rita asked him. "Ramirez did threaten to come back when he gets out of prison and settle the score with Franko."

Billy shrugged. "Oh, don't worry. Civic harassment is all in a day's work. People will say just about anything when they get busted. Besides, *you* didn't shoot the guy."

"I know. But what about Franko?"

"Franko's a big boy. He can take care of himself," Billy told her. "And don't worry. I'll protect you."

Rita didn't like Billy's tone. His response showed complete indifference for Franko. And his coyness and condescension only pointed up the fact that, through his eyes, she was being a naïve rookie. But who was he kidding? How could *he* protect her? The day before at Grand Central, she was completely on her own.

"Del Vecchio, come on!"

It was the blare of Franko's voice that interrupted Billy and Rita. When her partner poked his head around the squad room door, his face lit up in surprise. He obviously wasn't expecting Billy to be there.

"Hey," Franko said in greeting them both. "Sorry if I've interrupted—"

"If it isn't the hero," Billy said.

"C'mon, we've gotta go, Rita." Franko seemed to completely disregard Billy and focus his attentions solely on Rita. "I'll meet you outside. Later, Billy."

Franko left, and Rita slipped on her hat and tucked in her hair. "I'll see you in a little while," she said to Billy as she gave him a peck on the cheek and hurried off.

Billy's gaze trailed Rita as she left the room. He liked the sight of her hips as they wiggled in her tight, form-fitting police slacks.

After she was gone and the squad room emptied out, Billy took another look at that article in *The New York Post*. He stopped reading mid-stream.

" '*I got a little scared . . .*' " he read aloud, quoting Franko from the article and mimicking a whiny, girlish voice. "What a friggin' sap!" Billy howled a laugh while he stuffed the newspaper into the trash.

# SIXTEEN

Rita didn't want a bridal shower. She wanted a big party for *all* of their friends: husbands and wives and their children, boyfriends and girlfriends, coworkers. Rita and Billy invited everyone they could think of, even those whom they couldn't afford to invite to the actual wedding. Rita wanted everyone to be able to celebrate the wonderful news of her union with Billy. And Billy thought it was a great idea so he granted her wish. He spared no expense, financing the whole thing—*The Wedding Shower,* as she called it—at Finnegan's Pub.

"To Rita Del Vecchio, soon to be Quinn, my partner and friend for the past nine months, I wish you lots of love and happiness." When Franko held up his beer in salute, Rita thought she might cry. Franko had become her first and very best friend on the force, despite the fact that they still couldn't see eye-to-eye about Billy. "Please treat *our* girl right, Billy!"

Rita turned to look at Billy seated at the bar. He held up his beer in Franko's direction then chugged a big gulp.

Finnegan's was standing room only. Regulars, as well as the couple's friends, family and acquaintances crowded the room. Rita could not have been more ecstatic. She mingled with the well-wishers, rambling on about wedding arrangements: photographers, invitations, flowers, seating charts. Between chats, Rita stole several glances toward the bar. The fellas were watching a hockey game, doing shots, and having a good old time. But when Rita took a break and meandered through the crowds of well-wishers en route to getting another drink, she inadvertently stepped on someone's toes.

"Ouch!" came a shriek.

Rita stopped and found herself staring into the long-forgotten face of Sergeant Gary Hill.

"Well, well, well. If it isn't Officer Twinkle Toes of the Transit Division." Sergeant Hill smiled and laughed, his playfulness rising above the pumped-up volume of music spewing from the juke box. "What happened? A few months on the job, and you've already lost your ballerina-like grace?"

"Sergeant Hill? What are you doing here?"

"I never pass up a party with free food and beer, even if the party *is* for one of my sleazy, low-life coworkers." He lifted his bottle of beer and pointed it in Billy's direction. "How about you?"

"I'm your low-life, sleazy coworker's fiancée."

"Get out!" Hill's eyes seemed to bulge out of his head. "You? *You're* marrying Billy Quinn? *You're* the fiancée?"

She nodded.

"*Him?*" he asked, crooking his head in Billy's direction. "Gee, why would you ever get involved with someone like *him?*"

Rita bit her lip in an effort to maintain her composure. Who else was going to take potshots at Billy and her choice in marrying him?

"Gee, maybe I should've brought him down to the Police Academy for your stamp of approval first?" Rita mocked. It felt weird, yet somehow liberating, to no longer be a student of Sergeant Hill's.

"Well, I see the Transit Department has made you no worse for the wear, Del Vecchio. You obviously haven't lost your sense of humor. That's an accomplishment in itself." He held up his beer and toasted her. "But I hate to break it to you. You're gonna lose it real quick if you marry that clown."

*Clown? Look who's calling who a clown?* "Oh? Why's that?"

Gary Hill shook his head and frowned. He took a sip of beer as if to wash down his words. Then he said, "Aw. It's just that, between you and me, I think you could've done much better."

Sergeant Hill's fair complexion was suddenly brightening pink.

"Hey, you ain't flirting with my girl, are you, Hill?" Billy interrupted. Rita could feel Billy's arms slide around her from behind. Then he extended his hand over Rita's shoulder, toward Gary Hill.

"Hey, Billy. Congrats, man. I think you've got yourself a prize in this one."

"Oh, I know. And she's all mine," Billy said, as he and the sergeant firmly shook hands. "You having a good time?"

"Yeah, nice party. Good crowd. Must be costing you a fortune," Hill said.

There wasn't much more for Billy and the sergeant to say to each other. So after an awkward silence, Billy asked Rita, "Can I get you anything, sweetie?"

"I could use a refill," she said, holding up her empty wine spritzer glass.

Off Billy went.

"I read about the Grand Central thing in the paper," Sergeant Hill told her. "As a rookie, it must've been pretty frightening. How are you holding up?"

"Now that's it's over, I'm fine." Rita was surprised by his sensitivity and concern, even a little suspect. "Thanks for asking."

"Yeah, well, after you made headlines, I had big money on you and Franko hitching up. Traumatic things like that have a tendency to seal the deal between people. Too bad you and Franko had to go and spoil everything by being friends. I could've cleaned up in the betting pools."

Rita laughed. "Sorry to disappoint you," she said, grateful that Sergeant Hill had lightened the mood.

"Yeah, well, best of luck to you, Del Vecchio. Enjoy your wedding and honeymoon and all that nonsense. When you get back, stop down at the academy and see me sometime."

"Why's that?"

"I don't know. Just to say hello. I sort of miss you. Of all the recruits who pass in and out of that smelly gym, there's been nobody quite as much fun to pick on."

"Yeah, I bet," Rita said. She was floored by Sergeant Hill—and charmed. After he vanished into the crowd, Rita looked across the pub at Billy. The way he was watching her quickly snapped her back to reality. For a moment, she even felt guilty. But why? Maybe it was that sense of guilt that drove her to walk directly over to the bar and plant a wet kiss on Billy's cheek. She put her arms around him and crawled up, cuddling on his lap. She was determined to convince herself that the doubts Sergeant Hill sowed in her head were wrong. Dead wrong.

"Having a good time, hon?" Billy asked.

"Yes, great. But I can't wait until we can get home."

"Our wedding day will be here before you know it, Ree. We'll be together forever."

Billy pulled Rita closer and planted his lips on hers. But she cut their kiss short and clung to him, anchoring her head on his shoulder instead. This position left her a clear sight of the room—and Sergeant Hill as he headed for the door. When he realized that Rita was watching him, Hill gave Rita a nod and waved goodbye.

# SEVENTEEN

Rita turned from the window and looked at the clock. Ten minutes past one. Where was Billy? They were due at her parents' house in Jersey at one o'clock. Now they were late, and Rita was still in her Bronx apartment—waiting. In her mind, Rita could see her mother, pacing back and forth, near the picture window of the Cape Cod style house set on the sprawling suburban street. By now, Tina's face would undoubtedly be pressed up against the glass of the front storm door while she nibbled on a crust of Italian bread and grumbled over the tardiness of her dinner guests.

"The Caesar salad is soggy. The manicotti is dry. And the bread is stale," Rita could already hear her mother say.

The mere thought of a disapproving Tina made Rita regret that she'd accepted the invitation in the first place. And she feared that her and Billy's tardiness would only add fuel to the fire of her mother's apprehensions about their fast-approaching marriage.

When Rita finally heard the screech of car brakes squeal to a stop at twenty after one, she rushed to the window and found Billy's red Mustang idling in front of the building. Rita dashed out of the apartment and made a beeline for the car.

"Sorry I'm late, babe," Billy said, leaning over to give her a kiss. "I can explain—"

"Explain while you drive. Let's go. We're late."

Billy threw the car in gear then reached into his pocket. "I stopped at my mother's to get this," he told her, pulling out a small velvet jewelry box.

The rush of Rita's anger slowed as she focused her attention on the box. When she slowly inched it open, she asked, "What's this?"

"I know how busy you've been with all the wedding plans, so I decided to surprise you. It's one less errand we'll have to run."

Inside the box was a gold wedding ring. It was a simple band, in desperate need of cleaning and polishing. Even with Rita mentally trying to envision the ring sparkly clean, it was ugly. "Is this a joke?"

"A joke? No." Billy's tone made it clear he was taken back. "It was my great-great grandmother's wedding ring. Isn't it beautiful?"

*Define beautiful,* Rita thought, swallowing hard. She took the ring from the box. "It's your great-great grandmother's?"

"Yes. It's been in the family for ages. It has been passed down the line for generations."

*Yeah, well, it sure looks like it's been to hell and back.*

"The last one to wear it was my mom. Now it's your turn to carry on the tradition."

Rita's chin dropped. "My turn?"

"Look at the inscription," Billy said, turning the ring so she could see what was engraved inside.

It read: *March 12, 1879—All my love, Warren.*

*The inscription has never been changed? What in the heck do I want with someone else's ratty old ring?*

"What's the matter, Rita? Don't you like it?"

"Like it?" Rita repeated, searching for what to say. "It's not that I don't like it, Billy. It's just that I thought we'd decided to get a wedding band to match my engagement ring."

"But this is vintage. It's a priceless antique. It's got real sentimental value."

*For who? What is he talking about? The last person to wear this ring was his mother, and she was in a miserable, loveless marriage. A marriage that ended in divorce.*

"I know the ring means a lot to your family, but remember how I told you that I wanted to make my engagement ring become the insert for my wedding band?"

"But this ring goes. It matches," he said, taking it from her hand and moving it closer to her engagement ring. "See, they're both gold. They go together just fine."

Rita was speechless. He obviously wasn't getting it. She would have to tread lightly.

"Ree, it's one of a kind. It's a family heirloom. The tradition is that it goes to the first child in the family who marries, and I'm it. You should feel honored."

Rita tried to clear the frog from her throat. "Don't get me wrong," she told him. "The ring sure looks one of kind. And the history of it is really something. But I just can't accept it. I don't feel right about it."

"Don't be ridiculous. My mother wants you to have it. It's already been passed down for three generations. You'll be the fourth, and my mother's thrilled that you'll be the one to continue the legacy. She never had a daughter of her own, and you're her very first daughter-in-law."

Anxiety burned deep inside the pit of Rita's stomach. *How can I possibly get out of this gracefully?*

"Ree, what's the matter? You're not saying anything."

"I guess I just don't know what to say," she told him.

"Go on, try it on," he said.

She didn't want to hurt Billy's feelings, so she slipped the ring on her finger.

"See? It's a perfect fit," Billy said.

"No, it's a little tight." She was exaggerating.

"Don't worry. We'll have it sized."

*Lucky me!* The more Rita looked at the ring, the more disappointed she felt. Throughout the drive across the bridge and passing the sign welcoming them into New Jersey, she kept glancing at the ring, hoping it would grow on her. But it didn't. It wouldn't. This wasn't the ring that Rita wanted to wear for the rest of her life. It was somebody else's ring. Four other somebodies, as a matter of fact.

Billy was oblivious to what Rita was feeling. He took her ringed hand, brought it to his lips and kissed it as he kept on driving.

"I bet your mother's going to love it," Billy said.

*Like hell she will! She'll love the ring about as much as she will love our tardiness for dinner.* Rita knew this ring would only serve to solidify her mother's doubts, especially because Tina had already asked her Uncle Jimmy, a dear friend of the family and a jeweler, to see if he could get them a good price on a wedding band to match Rita's engagement ring.

When Billy finally flipped on the car directional signal and veered off the highway that led into Rita's old hometown, Rita slipped the ring off her finger. She placed it back inside the box. When Billy questioned her about it, she said, "We're not married, Billy. It's all right that I try the ring on, but it's bad luck to wear it before the wedding."

"Oh, no. We're back to the bad luck thing again?" Billy sighed.

Rita wished she could tell him straight out that she didn't want the ring. She didn't like it. But the last thing Rita needed right now was to fight with Billy before they arrived at her parents' house.

# EIGHTEEN

"I think your parents are being ridiculous."

Billy was doing seventy-five miles an hour in a forty-mile zone down Forest Avenue in Paramus. His emotions were more heated than the rubber of the tires burning upon the road. The carefree afternoon that Rita had planned to spend with her parents in Jersey had turned into a full-blown fiasco.

After smoothing over the fact that she and Billy were dreadfully late, the conversation inevitably turned to the ring.

"Go on, Rita," Billy urged. "Show your mom."

Rita timidly took the velvety box from her purse, while her mother slipped on her bifocals. She looked as serious as a jeweler about to inspect the authenticity of a diamond with a magnifying loupe.

"Oh, look at that," Rita's dad said. His response was just as Rita would've expected. But his opinion wasn't the one that mattered.

Time seemed to move in slow motion while Tina brought the ring box up close to her eyes. "Yikes, whose was this? Adam and Eve's?"

Rita was mortified.

Her mother moved the ring box farther away, keeping it at arm's length, as if hoping the ring might look better from a different perspective. When it was clear that distance wasn't producing the desired result, Tina slipped the ring out of the box. She read the inscription, *"March 12, 1879—All my love,*

*Warren.* Is this from a pawn shop?"

"No, it was my great-great grandmother's. It's been in my family for generations. Now it's Rita's turn."

"Oh, is that right?" Tina peeled off her bifocals and shot a confused look Rita's way.

Rita was relieved that her mother was at least trying to be tactful in her response. But from the droop of her mother's eyebrows and the flare of her nostrils, Tina's reaction was clearly no different from Rita's.

"What happened, Ree? Did you change your mind?" she asked. "I thought Uncle Jimmy was going to work on getting you a wedding band that your engagement ring could be inserted into so you'd have a matched set?"

Before Rita could answer, Billy jumped in. "Oh, no, Mrs. Del Vecchio. It's all settled. Rita will be carrying on a Quinn family tradition. Right, Ree?"

Rita forced a grin and nodded to appease Billy, who straightened up tall and proud. But she could see her mother eyeing her, suspect.

"Well, maybe Uncle Jimmy can take a look at it. Polish it up and re-engrave it or something."

"No, the tradition is to pass on the ring *exactly* the way it started."

"Really?" Tina shot Rita a look encouraging her to speak up and say what was really on her mind.

But not another word was spoken. Tina took her cue from Rita and backed down.

Throughout dinner, the conversation revolved around the wedding. Rita's parents, along with Billy, had their own ideas as to how the wedding should be planned, and who should—or should not—be invited. Rita felt left out and somewhat resentful. But in an effort to keep the peace, she remained silent and neutral.

As Billy pulled the car out of her parents' driveway to return home that night, Rita wished she'd never gotten out of bed that morning.

"My parents are not being ridiculous," she said to Billy on the drive back to the Bronx. "I wish you wouldn't speak about them like that."

"Well, they won't let me invite anyone from my side of the family."

"Hey, wait a minute, Billy. That's not true. My parents said that you can have seventy-five people from your side. If you want to invite more, you can pay for anyone above and beyond that number. I think that's fair."

"But they won't even pay for the bagpipers."

"That's because they're shelling out so much for the dance band. Having bagpipers in addition is your idea. If you want them so much, then you and I will just have to spring for that expense ourselves. It's not as if we don't have the money." *Especially now, since I'm stuck with this god-awful, decrepit ring, and we no longer have to buy the type of wedding band I had my heart set on.*

"If it's about the money, then I think they should just forget about that stupid idea of releasing bunches of helium balloons outside the church."

"But the balloons were *my* idea. And it's not stupid. It's a symbol of releasing our love, as man and wife, into the world."

Billy rolled his eyes. "You're obviously going to take your parents' side on everything, aren't you?"

"Well, they *are* paying the lion's share. I think we should be grateful that they're being as generous as they are with the wedding."

"Sure, and what about all those underhanded comments your mother made about the ring?"

Rita played dumb. "What comments?"

"The Adam and Eve remark. And who's Uncle Jimmy?"

"He's a jeweler. A friend of the family."

"Yeah, what's up with that? Why do you have a million aunts and uncles who aren't even blood related? And how is that they can all *cut you a deal* on just about anything?"

"It's an Italian thing," Rita explained, sloughing off his comment. "I had mentioned to my mother that I was going to try and stop by Uncle Jimmy's jewelry store to price out a wedding band to match the engagement ring."

"I picked out the engagement ring. Shouldn't I pick out the wedding band, too?"

"Not necessarily," Rita told him. "You might've asked me what I wanted."

Billy gripped the steering wheel with his outstretched arms with enough force to practically ram it straight into the engine.

"This is the way we do things in my family, Rita."

"But Billy, how you do things isn't exactly the way that I'm used to doing them." The uncharacteristic curtness of Rita's response halted Billy's side of the conversation. "Don't get me wrong," she said to him, attempting to soften her previous comment. "I love the engagement ring you picked out, but I also like the idea of having a choice as to what I'm going to wear as a symbol of our marriage for the rest of my life. You could have asked me, and we could have talked about things. We could've chosen our rings together."

"Rita, my family is just as important to me as yours is to you. The Quinn family has many traditions. This ring is just one of them, just like my first son will be named William Morrison Quinn, the Fourth."

Rita turned away. She looked out the passenger-side window and rolled her eyes. *Great. He's already planning our family and our children's names. Can't we get past the ring issue first?*

Billy veered onto the highway. His speed remained steady at

seventy-five in a now fifty-five-mile-per-hour zone. His rage and upset were being transferred to the road. He was weaving the car in and out of traffic on Route 4 almost as intricately as he was manipulating this argument in his favor.

When sirens sounded and flashing lights became reflected in the side and rearview mirrors, Billy finally slowed and edged over into the right lane.

"Damn these Jersey cops! They've got nothing better to do with their time," Billy roared. He pulled the car over to the shoulder.

As the officer approached the car, Billy held up his New York City Police badge. It flashed through the open window. Rita hated the way he used that shield to get him out of every mess. The Jersey officer gave Billy a warning, then the two men engaged in small talk. Rita couldn't believe that with cars whizzing by them on the highway, Billy and the other cop were shooting the breeze as though they were old drinking buddies. When the cop returned to his car, Billy returned his badge to his pocket.

They drove the rest of the way home in silence. The wedding was just a few weeks away, and tensions were mounting. Perhaps Rita could work on him slowly. Maybe given a little more time, she could change Billy's mind about the ring, along with the other Quinn family traditions. Or was this just wishful thinking on Rita's part? Whatever the future held was still unknown. But Rita did make one major decision, right then and there. Married or not, she would definitely not stop taking her birth control pills any time soon. One William Morrison Quinn in her life was more than enough for now.

# NINETEEN

The drug raid on Nick the Spic Zapato turned out to be one of the biggest heists of the year for the Gun and Drug Task Force. The team of McSweeney, Sanducci and Quinn earned high commendations not only from the commissioner, but they also scored high marks with the rest of the Mean Nineteen. It granted the select group of specialty cops more job security in the federally funded project. And now that the team was successfully implemented again in all five boroughs, the Mean (and Dirty) Nineteen was becoming quite the force with which to be reckoned. They were earning respectability and credibility within the NYPD, while they were also becoming better businessmen. While cracking down on guns and drugs, and making arrests when they had to build their cover, they were also fueling their own drug trades.

The greatest reward for the newly decorated trio of the Mean Nineteen—McSweeney, Sanducci and Quinn—was the ten thousand dollars apiece profit they skimmed off the top from the raid on Nick Zapato. Each officer was gradually filtering the money into his own personal bank account. Dirty Roy and Tony Sanducci were saving for college educations for their kids. And Billy Quinn was stashing away his share of the money to eventually put down on a house after he and Rita were married.

Since the heist, extra city funds were thrown back to the Special Task Force, but the team of McSweeney, Sanducci and Quinn was suddenly split up. The apparent rationale of the higher-ups was that the city would benefit most by spreading out the expertise of these three, courageous and heroic officers. But in actuality, the NYPD never liked their cops to get comfortable for too long.

Sergeant Roy McSweeney was routed into Spanish Harlem. Sergeant Tony Sanducci was stationed in Morningside Heights. And Sergeant Billy Quinn was re-assigned to the Hamilton Heights-West Harlem district. The men were instructed to continue working out of their current precincts until more permanent placements could be made.

Each of their prospective neighborhoods was tough, but *tough* was an insignificant term when you'd seen and experienced as much as these three officers. Once the new rotations began, new alliances would be formed and that meant that the Mean Nineteen might soon be growing in strength and numbers. And that would also translate into more dollars and cents.

"Pull over here, man," Sergeant Billy Quinn directed his new partner, Rudy Palumbo, as they cruised down Amsterdam Avenue near 145th Street.

Palumbo, a newcomer to the task force, slowed the squad car. "What do you make of this?" he asked Billy. A half-dozen or so punks, wearing oversized hooded sweatshirts and baggy pants, were loitering on the street in front of a row of dilapidated buildings.

A shiny, old white Cadillac, refurbished with black-tinted windows, was blocking a fire hydrant. When Billy saw the license plate marked with the initials *M. T.,* he recognized the car as one belonging to a drug dealer who used to work out of the New Bridge Avenue circuit, where Billy had once been stationed. As Palumbo cruised the patrol car past the Caddy, it was clear that the driver's side window was open. No one was inside, but Billy could see a pair of fuzzy dice hanging off the rearview mirror and plush, leopard-skin covers adorning the dash and front seat. The sound of cranked-up rap music spilled loudly from the car.

"I think this could be our lucky day, *Pal*," Billy said, calling his partner by his nickname. "I think we just found the man who might have our new weekly paychecks. God knows, I could use a little extra cash to finance my honeymoon."

From inside the squad car, Billy slipped his hand between the seats and fished out a bag bursting with white, powdery-looking cocaine. He stuffed it up the sleeve of his jacket.

"Now you just keep your mouth shut and let me do all the talking," Billy told his partner. "Radio for a tow truck and then follow my lead."

When Billy got out of the car, he kept one hand close to his nightstick and the other near his revolver. He walked around the Cadillac, inspecting it. Once Palumbo joined him on the street, Billy started in.

"Who owns this car?" Billy asked the cluster of street kids. Several of the gang members disappeared, vanishing inside the tenements. The ones that were left on the sidewalk greeted Billy and Palumbo with defiant stares.

"Somebody's got to move this car, fellas," Billy told them.

"We move the car when *we're* ready," one of the gang kids shouted.

"I think *we're* ready right now," Billy said.

Kids on bicycles quickly congregated. Tenants began opening their windows, curious to gain a look at what was happening on the street.

"Police brutality! Police brutality!" some of the onlookers started to chant.

Billy removed the nightstick from his belt and beat the hardwood against his palm. When the tow truck came lumbering down the street, it forced some of the onlookers to scatter.

An African-American driver emerged from the truck, and someone shouted, "Traitor!"

The man shrugged and said, "Hey, look, I'm just doing my job." Then he turned toward Billy and Palumbo and asked, "This the vehicle you want outta here?" pointing to the shiny white Cadillac.

As the tow truck driver lowered the boom and started to hook up the chain beneath the chassis of the Caddy, a dapper-looking black man in his early thirties, wearing a designer suit and dark sunglasses, emerged from one of the buildings. He hurried over to Billy and Palumbo who were standing near his car.

"Yo," he said. "What's going on?"

"Parked illegally—gotta move it," said Billy, as the tow truck operator jacked up the front end of the Cadillac.

"Big mistake," the driver said. "You should've left the ticket and walked away."

Billy gave the man a visual once-over from the lapel of his expensive-looking suit to the cuff hem on his pants. "Ticket or tow—it looks like you can afford to pay. But it seems like a shame, forking over your hard-earned money to this city. But I guess we all gotta do what we gotta do, right?"

In the midst of this exchange, Billy approached the Cadillac. Peering into the open driver's side window, he said, "Gee, what do we have here?" Billy reached into the car, onto the seat, and shook down the bag of cocaine hidden inside his sleeve.

"Holy Christmas, look at this. A magic eight ball. What's an eighth of an ounce going for these days, about three hundred bucks?" Billy held up the bag bursting with the white powder as if he were dangling a freshly captured mouse by the tail. "And what else, besides probable cause, have you got in this car?"

The drug dealer shot Billy a dirty look and offered a few choice words under his breath.

Billy didn't like it. He flaunted his power by stepping closer to the dealer and purposely invading his personal space. "Why don't you get rid of your fan club over there, so we can talk. Private-like."

The dealer hauled in a deep breath as though he were about to be plunged into a vat of water. Then he said, "All right. But cut my Caddy loose."

Billy waved off the tow truck operator. Once he packed up and left, the dealer hopped behind the wheel of his car and maneuvered it into a nearby alley. Billy and Palumbo followed. When the two officers popped the trunk, inside was a green, woolen army blanket. Beneath it were at least fifty guns—pistols, rifles, machine guns—along with shells and cartridges. There was also a box filled with heroin, crack and quaaludes.

"Boy, am I glad we didn't just leave our new friend here a ticket. Look at what we'd be missing out on now," Billy said to Palumbo, before turning to the drug dealer. "By the way, what's the *M.T.* on your license plate stand for?"

"My Territory."

"Not anymore," Billy cackled. "Not anymore."

From diagonally across the alley, a dark-skinned Latino man was sitting on an inverted milk crate alongside a garbage dumpster. The man was smoking a cigarette and fingering his rosary beads. He wore a backwards Yankees baseball cap and a big silver crucifix atop his soiled white t-shirt. His hands were clasped, and he appeared to be in deep spiritual concentration as he prayed the *Our Father*—half the words in English, half in Spanish. But he was only saying the prayer by rote. All the while his lips moved, he was actually paying more attention to what was happening with the two cops who were staring into the trunk of that Cadillac. Not only had Johnny the Jinx Delgado recently found Jesus, but he also had a hunch that he'd just found what the Department of Internal Affairs had been looking for.

# TWENTY

"Rise and shine."

Rita could feel the mattress spring beneath her. She rolled over in bed and rustled from under the bulky, flowered comforter. The scent of bacon, eggs and sausage frying told Rita she was home—in her parents' house. After the rehearsal dinner, she'd decided to crash in her old bedroom the night before the wedding. This way she'd be closer to the church. After she wiped the sleep from her eyes, she focused on her father seated on the edge of her bed. He ran his fingers along her brow and brushed her thick, brown hair away from her face.

"Is it over yet?" she asked him, her voice raspy and hoarse.

"Over? The day hasn't even started."

"What time is it?"

Her father looked at his watch. "About a quarter to six—in the morning. Are you having second thoughts?"

Rita groaned. "Is that any way to greet a bride on her wedding day?"

"You're not just *any* bride. You're my daughter."

Rita was never a morning person, and she wasn't up for having this conversation, not again. "Dad, please. Don't you remember when I was a little girl, how you used to say that when true love finally found me, I'd know? And how I'd go fast?"

He nodded. "It's just that your mother and I are concerned

that perhaps you and Billy haven't had a long enough courting period."

*Courting period? What is this, the stone age?*

"She still doesn't like him, does she?" Rita asked.

"We just want you to be happy."

"But I am happy. See?" Rita forced a super wide smile.

Even with his glasses on, she could tell that her father's eyes were misting up. "We're going to love you, no matter what," he told her. "It's never too late to change your mind."

"Dad, please. The only thing I need to *change* is into my wedding gown."

"Just remember that this will always be your home."

"I know, Dad. I know," she said, relieved when her father finally left the room.

When she got up and faced herself in the mirror, she was horrified.

"*This* is getting married today?"

Her face was lost in a mass of hair that was frizzy and tangled. She looked like a creature who had wrangled up from the depths of some dreary underworld. She pulled the locks away and revealed her pale cheeks. Then she tried to remove smudged traces of leftover mascara from the rims of her brown eyes.

She wondered why her father had chosen the morning of the wedding to have this talk with her. Where was her mother?

After the confrontation they'd had in the kitchen, Rita and Tina had never spoken again of her relationship with Billy. Rita got the feeling that her father had been sent in that morning as a last ditch emissary. It was his job to broach an issue that lingered like an invisible brick wall between mother and daughter.

*Parents never believe any man is good enough for their daughters . . . It's just the way of the world,* Rita thought.

"I do love him," she said to her reflection thinking of Billy.

But her own image suddenly blurred, and she found herself staring into the face of Sergeant Hill. She heard his voice again: *Oh, Twinkle-Toes, I can't believe you'd get involved with Billy Quinn . . . You could've done much better.*

"Rita, breakfast is ready." Her father's voice rippled from beneath the memory of Gary Hill's.

"Please tell me this is just normal, wedding-day jitters," she asked the reflection of Sergeant Hill in an attempt to keep her doubts from tamping down and taking root.

But he didn't answer. He simply shrugged. Then his image started to fade until it finally disappeared.

A chill of uneasiness consumed Rita. She could feel tears pressing up in her eyes.

"C'mon, breakfast is getting cold," came her father's voice again. "Get a move on, Rita Marie Del Vecchio."

"Yes, coming." Rita's voice cracked. "Be right there."

Hearing the sound of her own name—the name she would be giving up in just a few hours—made a fluttery sensation gnaw in the pit of her empty stomach.

# Twenty-One

In the sacristy of Saint Leo's Church, the photographer staged a few shots of the best man, Dirty Roy McSweeney, wiping the sweat-laden brow of nervous-looking husband-to-be, Billy Quinn.

It gave the guys, all cleaned up and standing tall in their black tuxedos and pink cummerbunds, a couple of laughs and diffused some of the anxiety swelling around the big day.

After the photographer packed up and left, Dirty Roy ran his fingers through the mousse in his hair, making a couple of strands stand up on edge, while Billy started to pace the small room in the back of the church. The priest's vestments, that were pressed and hung on the closet door, rippled in waves each time Billy trod his path.

"You nervous or what, bro?" asked Dirty Roy.

"Na, I think I'm ready."

"Take it from me. Once you say your vows, you're home free."

Billy straightened his tie. "Yeah, it'll be nice to finally cut loose at the reception."

"We can actually cut loose right now, if you want to, bro." Roy lifted the cuff of his tuxedo jacket and eyed his watch. "If your Rita's anything like my wife on our wedding day, she'll be late. How about I give you your wedding present right now?"

"Sure. What'd you get me?"

"A couple of grams of the best, purist stuff straight from

114

Columbia." Dirty Roy reached into the pocket of his tux and pulled out a bag of coke affixed with a tiny bow. He handed it to Billy.

"It's uncut and ready to blow."

"Gee, Roy. Thanks, man," Billy said, embracing his buddy with hard, grateful slaps on the back. "This is better than gold. Better than caviar."

"Well, you don't get married every day. Or at least I hope you won't," Roy said. "Shall we christen it right here?"

"Now?"

"Yeah, let's get up, up and away. It'll be a real trip seeing the angels and saints come to life in the stained glass windows while you're tying the knot."

The two guys howled with laughter, while Roy reached into his pocket and pulled out a tiny spoon.

"I ain't no Indian giver, but I assume you *will* share a toot with me. Right, bro?"

"Heck, yeah. No need to ask," Billy told him, inhaling a snort up each nostril then wiping a finger across the gum line in front of his teeth. "You just might be the very *best man* a guy could ask for!"

# TWENTY-TWO

"Bride! Bride! You're losing that pearly white smile. Give me some teeth. Cheer up. This isn't a funeral." The cheery photographer clapped his hands together like two cymbals and ran over to Rita, giving her cheeks a pinch to enliven them with color.

When the photographer stepped back behind his tripod-mounted camera, Rita took Billy's hand. It felt quivery in hers, and it only deepened her worries about him. He'd been twitchy and fidgety all through the ceremony. He seemed unable to stand still on the altar and when he fumbled his vows, he momentarily lost his composure. His anger and humiliation burned through his red face. Now, he seemed completely unable to stay put long enough for the photographer to get a halfway decent picture of them.

"You all right?" Rita said to Billy between her clenched smile.

"Sure. Fine. Never better. Why?"

"You seem more wired up than a mad dog."

"Cheese! Cheese! Over here. Smile people," came the photographer's order.

Rita did as she was told.

*Click!*

*Snap!*

Billy wasn't Billy. He was distant and aloof. *What happened?* Inside, Rita felt like a dressed up mannequin in a store window, posing next to the shell of a man who was her husband.

"Nice. Nice . . . Work with me, lovebirds."

Billy wrapped an arm around Rita's waist. He tickled her side until she giggled and lit up in a playful smile.

*Click!*

*Snap!*

*Flash!*

"Okay . . . Okay. It's a rap," said the photographer. "We'll have oodles of shots to choose from."

"Finally! I thought we'd be here all afternoon," Rita sighed. The muscles in her face hurt from forcing a smile for so long.

The newlyweds stepped down from the gazebo steps. And as they made their way out of the flower garden, Billy snuck up on Rita from behind. With both his hands, he held fast to her hips and steered the way he wanted her to go. When she realized that he was guiding her from the path that led back to the reception hall, she squirmed beneath his touch.

"What's with you, Mrs. Billy Quinn? You've been wearing a plastic smile, and you've been a bundle of nerves all day."

"Me?" Rita gathered her long train and bunched it into her right hand. Billy was navigating her across the manicured lawn, toward a row of tall hedges surrounding a small thicket. When she resisted the path he was taking, he stopped in the middle of the open landscape. He turned to face her and plastered his lips over hers.

Rita didn't enjoy the taste of cigarettes and alcohol. She wiggled away from him. "How much have you had to drink?"

"Oh, lighten up. It's our wedding day."

He clasped his hands around her face and locked his lips with hers again. This time, the couple was met with an unsuspecting shower of applause. The guests in the reception hall had obviously spied the playful-looking newlyweds out on the lawn and began clapping from the lanai of the elegant reception manor. Billy, feeding off the attention, took Rita in his

arms and dipped her body backward. When he finally maneuvered her upright, Billy took a bow. Then he snatched Rita's
hand and forcibly led her off again toward the nearby thicket of
trees.

"What are you doing, Billy? Where are we going?"

The hum of guests at the reception—the low hum of their
banter and laughter, ice swirling around cocktail glasses—slowly
began to fade. As Billy whisked her away, winding them among
the bushes and deeper into the shadowy woods, Rita could feel
the heels of her pumps sinking into the soft, springy earth.

"Billy, what are you up to? Where are we going?"

He stopped short suddenly and thrust her against the trunk
of a tree. She gasped as he turned her around to face him and
shoved his body against hers. He smothered her with a kiss.

"I want you all to myself," he murmured, his lips anointing
her neck and trailing beneath the wisps of her hair. His hands
bustled through the bottom of her gown, his fingers groping her
legs.

"Billy, stop. The guests, they're waiting."

"Let 'em wait." Billy fumbled with her garter and pulled at
her stockings.

Rita tried to push him off her, but he was too dominant. And
the more she tried to resist, the more his passion rose.

"Billy, no," she pleaded, now both angry and frightened.
When she heard the sound of Billy's zipper, she shrieked, "Billy.
No. Stop."

When he finally let her go, the two of them were breathless.
She looked down at her gown. The hem was covered with grass
stains and brown dirt. When she lifted it, her shoes were even
muddy.

"Look at what you did?" she cried.

Billy didn't seem to care. He fixed his pants and ran his
fingers roughly through his hair. "A man has needs. And you're

my wife now. Don't you forget it."

Rita looked into his glassy, bloodshot eyes. They bored through her as if taking dead-aim on a target. She felt chilled. *What's come over him? Who is this crazy person?*

"Wait until the honeymoon," he hissed.

"Is that a warning?"

Billy cackled, amused by her question. He started away from her. And all she could do was stand there in her soiled wedding gown, wide-eyed and slack-jawed, watching him, in his black tuxedo, move like a crow across the open, grassy landscape.

Franko swung his bulk out onto the balcony of the reception hall. He stood alone, sipping his gin and tonic. He couldn't be sure if the blinding sunshine was creating a mirage-like effect, but it appeared, from off in the distance, as though someone dressed all in white was running across the atrium.

*Is that Rita? What is she doing out there?*

Here Franko thought he would step out of the cocktail lounge for a breath of fresh air, yet the air and the aura he saw surrounding Rita seemed thickly foreboding. He watched as she scurried out of the thicket and ran through the white lattice of the gazebo. Her hair was all tousled and the once perky-looking flowers woven around her French braid looked droopy and skewed.

When she approached the opened French doors leading into ballroom, Rita wiped her eyes. Franko considered calling down to her, but in her obvious bewildered state, he decided against it. Instead, he stood just watching her from above. Rita took a long measured breath. She squared her shoulders in an effort to compose herself. With her head held high, she waltzed back into the reception hall.

# Twenty-Three

Rita played the role for the rest of the day and was careful not to spend another minute completely alone with Billy. She'd have that confrontation soon enough, but she intended to postpone it for as long as possible.

Outside of mingling with the guests, she'd danced her way through most of the reception. But now her feet were tired. She needed a rest. With her muddy shoes slipped off and dangling from one hand, the soles of her stockinged feet sank into the plush carpeting that bordered the dance floor. She made a bee-line for her parents' table. Her father was seated at the table with her Aunt Gilda.

When Dominic saw Rita approaching, he lit up. He appeared thrilled that the bride had come to rescue him from his usually glum sister.

"Finally, a moment's rest," Rita said, throwing her arms around her father's shoulders and giving him a peck on the check.

"Having a good time?" he asked.

Rita's throat felt tight and pressure built behind her eyes. "Of course," she said, reaching for her father's glass of red wine and swilling a sip in her mouth. Her body might have escaped the incident with Billy in the thicket, but not her mind.

"I think the day's been a hit," her father said. "Everybody seems to be enjoying themselves."

"Even Aunt Gilda," Rita added as a whisper in her father's ear.

Rita and her dad turned and looked at the silver-haired woman. Aunt Gilda was shimmying in her chair to the up tempo beat of the song, "Shake Your Booty."

Rita said, "Next time the band plays a slow ballad, why don't you ask her to dance?"

Her father opened his eyes wide and gave short shakes of his head in a firm gesture of "no." Everyone in the family knew that once anyone escorted Aunt Gilda onto the dance floor, she'd never let him sit down again.

"Make sure you save your old father another dance before the day is over. Okay, Ree?"

"Gotcha."

As Rita downed the last sip of her father's wine, she saw Billy out of the corner of her eye. He was on the dance floor. His tie was undone. He was gyrating around a tall, pin-thin, blonde-haired woman, someone to whom Rita took an instant dislike. And Rita didn't even know who she was.

"Rita, how about a dance?"

Rapt by the sight of Billy and the woman, Rita was startled by the question. When she turned, Franko stood before her, looking instantly apologetic.

"I didn't mean to sneak up on you," Franko said, easing a hand to Rita's elbow. She could feel herself tremble nervously beneath his touch. And she could also sense, from the way Franko had narrowed his eyes on her that her good friend knew something was awry.

Franko held out his hand in a courtly manner. "May I have this dance, Mrs. Del Vecchio-Quinn?"

Once on the parquet dance floor, the band slowed things down with a ballad. Rita welcomed the chance to be close to Franko. He reeked of so much aftershave it was as though he'd broken the bottle. But she felt safe with him, and she rested her head on his shoulder as they swayed to the music.

"Looks like your mother is handling all these drunken Irish really well," Franko joked.

Rita could feel him looking down at her, trying to gauge her reaction. She was careful not to make eye contact.

"And how very thoughtful of her to arrange transportation to an A.A. meeting right after dessert—for anyone who cares to jump back on the wagon."

Rita, in sheer amusement, firmed her arms around Franko and gave him a hug. "I'm so sorry about things," she told him.

For a beat, Franko stopped moving his feet. "What things?"

"Y-you know . . ." Rita stammered. "I wasted a lot of time, and I feel terrible about how things have changed between us with all the wedding stuff. I think we've been off track these past few months. I've really missed you. And I'm sure going to miss you the next three weeks."

Franko stepped it up and reclaimed the lead. "Yeah, right," he said. "While you and lover-boy are lounging on the dark, sandy beaches of Hawaii, I'm sure you'll be thinking of poor, pitiful me, choking on lethal doses of carbon monoxide in the subways."

Rita buried her face in his chest. "Your day will come."

"No, I doubt it."

"Why's that?"

"I'm just too much man for only *one* woman."

As he said this, Rita saw Billy and the blonde huddled closely on the dance floor. While Billy clung to the woman, he bore an agitated gaze at Rita and Franko. Hurt and anger were scrawled on her husband's face, a sense of betrayal and vengeance. It was a look that Rita had never seen before.

Franko must have witnessed the same sight. He said, "Wow,

did you see that? Did your husband just put an evil eye curse on me?"

"No. If he's put a curse on anyone, it's *me.*"

"You? His bride? On your wedding day?"

Rita visually trailed Billy and his dance partner as they intertwined, swaying together. She wanted so desperately to tell Franko what had happened earlier in the thicket, but when the song suddenly ended, Rita took it as a sign that maybe she shouldn't. It wasn't the time or the place. So she decided to end her dance with Franko before she'd be faced with more questions.

She and Franko walked off the dance floor. But before he let her wander away, Franko placed a firm hand around her arm in an effort to gain her undivided attention. "I know you better than you think, Rita Del Vecchio-Quinn. I know something's not right."

"It's just that the day feels so surreal."

Franko studied Rita. His eyes diligently searched her face as if trying to penetrate through to the unspoken thoughts in her mind. "Marriage is a very big adjustment," he told her. "Just remember, you can talk to me. You can tell me anything, anytime, twenty-four/seven. All right?"

"Thanks, I'll keep that in mind."

Rita was distracted by that woman's long blonde hair as it cascaded over Billy's broad shoulders. With their bodies pressed together, Billy slowly eased his hands down the blonde's back. When he reached her waist, he yanked the woman's pelvis closer. He clasped his hands together, resting them atop the smooth silk of the woman's cocktail dress, right on her derriere.

Rita stood there smoldering. She kept her eyes glued to the spectacle, balling her hands into tight fists around the taffeta of her gown. Her anger was sharply diffused by Aunt Gilda, who tapped Rita on the shoulder. But when her aunt's troubled face telegraphed toward the dance floor and she said, "I'd say it's high time for the bride to cut in," Rita was mortified.

She marched away from Franko and her aunt, boldly approaching the couple as though she were nearing the scene of a deadly crime-in-progress. She feared she was too late. The crime, it seemed, had already been committed.

# Twenty-Four

It was over before she knew it. Not just the reception, but all the idealism she'd brought to the marriage. How could that be, when the day had started out like something from the pages of a storybook? Rose petals were strewn down the aisle by the flower girl. Dominic lifted Rita's veil and bestowed a loving, farewell kiss. Tina blotted tears from her already swollen eyes. And a mass of pink and white balloons—perfectly coordinated to match the colors of the wedding party—soared high into the sky until they vanished from sight. Did all those inflated colors simply carry away the fairy tale?

The Irish bagpiper band arrived at the reception promptly at three o'clock. They played for a full hour—an hour where Rita's mother plugged up her ears with her pointer fingers (the bagpipe music was deafeningly loud), while Billy's mother and father (placed strategically at separate tables) were distracted long enough to forget their hatred for each other.

Aside from jamming a bulky chunk of wedding cake into Billy's mouth during the cake-cutting ritual, the newlyweds couldn't appear happier. Billy had more than a few too many and, with him in that condition, Rita wasn't looking forward to the challenge of trying to communicate with him after the festivities. As soon as they had waved goodbye to all the guests and closed the door to the limousine, Rita's smile finally sagged into a frown. Everything came to a head.

"This has been the worst, most harrowing, day of my life."

Tears rained down Rita's face. Livid, she began punching her fists into Billy's arms and chest. He collapsed in on himself to escape the unexpected blows. "I don't know what the hell you were trying to pull in the woods or with that display on the dance floor. But that's it. It stops here."

The force of Rita's words tired her out until she gulped back sobs. She could see the limousine driver's eyes shift toward the rearview mirror and widen on her. But that didn't stop Rita from continuing to blast Billy.

"Do you have any idea how much you frightened and humiliated me?"

Billy didn't answer. He firmly crossed his arms against his chest and stared out the window.

"You won't treat me this away. Not ever again! Do you hear me?"

"Yeah, I hear ya," Billy said, finally turning to her.

"And were you trying to make my whole family despise you? Or were you just trying to punish me because I was dancing with Franko?"

"I saw how he was looking at you all day."

"Why don't you stop?"

"Why didn't Franko bring a date?"

"I don't know. Maybe he couldn't get a date. Maybe he thought he'd meet someone at the reception. A lot of our friends are single."

Billy sneered at Rita as if her rationale were preposterous. "Why don't you just admit it? He came alone because he's in love with you."

"Honestly, Billy!"

"I've seen how he looks at you. He worships you."

"He *what?*"

"You heard me."

"That's ridiculous. If he's so *in love* with me," Rita said, putting air quotes around the words *in love,* "then what's taking him so long to express how he really feels?"

"Don't make a mockery out of this."

"Billy, it's *you* who's making a mockery—out of me *and* our marriage. What is wrong with you?"

"I don't want our sex life aired to the whole world."

*Does he actually think I told Franko about what happened in the thicket?* "Billy, our sex life won't be aired unless *you* start airing it."

"Then what were you whispering about while you were dancing with him?"

"If you think for one minute that I told Franko *anything* about what happened in the woods, you're crazy. It was too disturbing, and I'm still too shocked and enraged to even discuss it."

"You're my wife now. I won't share you with him or anyone."

"I'm not asking you to," Rita said. "Franko is my friend. But I married *you.* And what happens between us stays between us. What is wrong with you? Why don't you trust me?"

Rita took a much needed breath, but it couldn't release the tension that gripped every muscle in her body. She turned from him and got lost in the passing blur outside the window. *What happened to the bliss of a girl's wedding day? What happened to vows that would go on forever and always be fresh?*

Rita felt Billy reach for her hand. "I'm sorry, Ree," he murmured. "You know I love you."

"No, I don't know. I really don't," she said, jerking her hand from his. "At least not after how you've behaved today. You scared me. You really scared me, Billy."

"I'm sorry. It's just that everything leading up to this day has been so tense. It has kept me on edge. I needed a release."

"A release? So you attack me?"

"I didn't attack you."

"You went too far. People who love each other don't try to hurt each other so viciously. And especially not on their wedding day."

They had hit an impasse. After sitting on opposite sides of the bench seat for miles and miles of the drive back to the Bronx, Billy finally reached out and rested his hand softly atop Rita's. This time, she didn't pull away, and Billy slid closer. She stared at both of their wedding bands. Billy's was shiny and new; hers—the unmatched heirloom. She had thought the ring was going to be the biggest hurdle she would have to surmount in the marriage. But after today, she feared for worse than that.

"I'm sorry, Ree. I love you. I really do. I'll make it up to you, I promise," he told her.

She studied his face, searching it to see if what he was telling her was real, was true. His brow was wrinkled and his frown lines severe. He was obviously repentant. And the softness of his touch—the warmth, the gentleness—that had made Billy so lovable to Rita from their very first meeting had now returned. She collapsed into him, crawling inside his arms and pushing against him. For the rest of the ride home, over every bump and around every turn, he held her close. He cradled her as she buried her head into his tuxedo shirt, her tears drenching right through the fabric.

What other choice did Rita have but to give Billy a chance to live up to his promise? After all, they'd been married less than seven hours. In her mind, she reasoned away his behavior. *He's right. The day was stressful. Emotions were running high . . .*

When the limo driver glided the car in front of the apartment building and assisted the couple out of the back seat, he said to Rita and Billy, "Well, it's probably good you two lovebirds have already gotten your first fight out of the way. Now you can both enjoy the honeymoon. Best of luck."

*Luck? We need more than luck.*

Billy swooped Rita off her feet. He carried her up the stairs and over the threshold of his second floor apartment, which was now their home. *Husband and wife. Their first, official night together.*

When the door to the apartment swung closed behind them, Rita left her doubts and her teardrops outside, hoping never to reclaim them again.

# TWENTY-FIVE

Franko was hung over from the wedding, and the shrill sound of the phone, ringing out into the darkness of the night, wrenched through his head like an ax splitting his skull.

He cringed, and without opening his eyes, he picked up the receiver after the first ring.

"Hel-lo," he groaned into the phone.

There was dead air on the other end.

"Hello?" Franko asked again.

There was no answer, just a faint sound of breathing. Someone was obviously listening on the other end.

Franko hung on until the dial tone finally took over.

He looked at the Caller ID. It read *Private Name, Private Number.* He slipped the phone back onto the cradle. The digital numbers on the alarm clock read 2:37. Franko realized that he was still wearing his shirt and tie from the wedding. He must've collapsed as soon as he arrived home and had fallen asleep atop the bedcovers.

Franko slipped the phone receiver back on the cradle. He wiped his eyes, ran his fingers through his hair and then switched on the night stand lamp. Whenever the phone rang in the middle of the night, it played tricks on Franko's mind and left him to toss and turn. And ever since the incident at Grand Central—that Ramirez character and his searing threat—phantom calls like these were coming in several times a week. During the day, Franko tried to convince himself that the calls were probably from some crackpot who saw his name in the newspaper and had nothing better to do. But while the rest of the city slept amid the shadowy stillness of the night, reason wasn't strong enough to ward off the ghost of Franko's paranoia.

He unplugged the phone. Then he rolled out of bed, walked to the closet and pulled his revolver from the top shelf. He burrowed beneath the covers and slid the piece beneath his pillow. He decided to keep the light on. Wide awake, with his eyes closed, his still groggy mind spun with mounting fears.

*Enough was enough,* Franko thought. He'd call the phone company first thing in the morning and change to an unlisted number.

# Twenty-Six

"I told you. I ain't the old Johnny no more."

Internal Affairs picked up Johnny the Jinx ten days after he'd witnessed the incident in Harlem. This time, Johnny was panhandling as a blind man outside of St. Patrick's Cathedral in Midtown. "I would've come forward earlier, but I've been busy. And I ain't lying when I tell you that I've turned my life around, and I belong to Jesus."

"Yeah-Yeah, we know," one of the detectives said, growing impatient with the Jinx's born-again Christian routine.

"Spill it, Johnny. We want to know what you know—the rest of the story—and we want it now," another suit-clad detective broke in. "You know how it works. If you renege on our deal, then we send you upstate. You wouldn't want that, Johnny, now would you?"

The Jinx shook his head.

"So tell us again. You saw the police officers making the exchange in the alley and then what?"

"That's all I seen. That guy Leon—"

"You mean the guy who has the Caddy with the M.T. license plates?"

"Yeah, that's him. Leon Johnson. He traffics weapons and stuff around Harlem and Hamilton Heights. He's one bad brother, but he's in—and in real cool—with the cops now. He's been giving them part of his draw."

"And are you sure this is the cop you saw that day?" they

asked Johnny, pointing to a page in an opened book that sat on the table in front of him. The thick volume contained police identification photographs. The picture on the page was labeled with the name Rudolph J. Palumbo.

"Yeah, that's him. Tall, dark and as hairy as an ape."

"And who else did you see, Johnny?"

"I told you, I ain't seen nothing else. Nobody. Just him," he said, pointing a stiff finger at Palumbo's face and pushing the ID book away.

Johnny was only telling half the truth. The brothers from the Heights and Harlem, the Spanish and African-American neighborhoods, were never united. But they were in total agreement on one thing: *Never rat on Q or Queey,* as they called Sergeant Billy Quinn on the streets. He was considered one of the meanest, most hot-tempered, iron-fisted racist cops on the whole island. When Queey came for his cut, folks said he was usually stoned or hot-wired on free-base cocaine. He was too powerful and unpredictable to ever mess with. Johnny the Jinx knew he'd be six feet under if he so much as mentioned Quinn's name to the detectives.

"C'mon, Johnny. Don't hold out on us. What else do you know? Spill it."

"I ain't got nothing else," he told him. "Honest."

The Internal Affairs suits looked sideways at each other. Then one of the detectives leaned across the table and evened his face with Johnny's. When the two were eye to eye, close enough to inhale the same air, the detective drilled his gaze into the Jinx's and shouted, "What do you think? We were born yesterday?" The detective's words were so loud and raw that some of his spittle flew into Johnny's face.

It didn't take being a detective to know that the word *honest* wasn't an adjective one would ever ascribe to the likes of Johnny the Jinx Delgado.

# TWENTY-SEVEN

The balcony doors of the honeymoon suite at the Maui Princess remained wide open to brighten the days with sunshine and fill the nights with warm, cozy moonlight. For the entire first week, the *Do Not Disturb* sign remained affixed to the door. The newlyweds' cool water bed heated up with their passions, while the splashing sounds of the sea ebbed and flowed beyond the tangles of hibiscus flowers and muted metal drums that droned from down on the beach.

One lazy day mingled into the next, and Rita and Billy only allowed the world to reach them via three immense skylights and the luxury of room service. Billy was adventurous and splurged on edible delights like mango bread and seaweed-wrapped pork. Rita passed, opting for her usual burger and fries or even a plate of pasta. They took all their meals on the private veranda, watching cloud formations and the changing Hawaiian sky beyond the sway of silhouetted palm trees. With each sultry breeze that whipped in from the sea, it was as though the animosity from their wedding was blown away like grains of sand.

Rita was reassured by Billy's undivided attention. He caressed her softly and kissed her tenderly. He held and rocked her, satisfying her every yearning. The beast seemed long gone, never to return again, just as he'd promised. She couldn't help but believe him. Billy was sensitive and loving. How could she ever have thought he would deliberately hurt her? It was all just a bad dream.

On the seventh day, the couple ended their seclusion. Rita popped a few air-sickness pills and off they went to Oahu. A helicopter excursion air-lifted them above the shoreline of dark sand and whitecaps dotting the endless sea. There were volcanoes and the sight of surfers, who moved like specs through the dappled turquoise blue water at Waikiki Beach. Afterward, the helicopter sailed to the Canyon of Waimea, where the earth seemed to end and the ground opened up into an enormous pit that stretched big and wide. Rita clung to Billy as the aircraft soared and glided through the air then dipped inside the crater. From out the window, the multi-colored, jagged walls of the canyon resembled what Rita envisioned the bottom of the ocean would look like if all the water were drained away. The feel of Billy's arms around her alleviated her fears. She felt safe by his side. Never in all her life had she been so content and happy. She was living a dream come true, sharing life's splendor with the man she so loved.

When they returned to the hotel, their passions erupted once more.

"I'm the luckiest man in the world," Billy cooed, over and over. "Nothing can dissolve a love like ours. Nothing."

The days and nights went on in bliss for another whole week. They had no concept of time, only that this was the beginning of forever.

# Twenty-Eight

It felt good to breathe the fresh air of the city for a change. Instead of suffering through the scent of worn-out deodorant and nervous sweat from new recruits down at the police academy, Sergeant Gary Hill was relieved to be basking in the early spring sunshine and traipsing through the aroma of mowed grass in the Sheep's Meadow of Central Park. He relished being back in uniform and out on the streets of Manhattan again, back on his old rotation on the Upper East Side.

He couldn't have asked for a more stress-free patrol. And he didn't ask for it. It was his annual physical that detected a sharp spike in his blood pressure. The diastolic pressure, or the bottom number, would not come down below a hundred, even after he had taken medication for a month.

Gary Hill tried to slough the numbers off with the department doctors, promising that he'd cut out his addiction to burgers, fries and milkshakes. But doctors warned that the high blood pressure reading was a serious warning and not to be taken lightly. A change in scenery was suggested, so he took an imposed vacation, which he made a *stay-cation,* where he dilly-dallied and tinkered around at home, counting the hours until he could get back to work.

But when he returned to the force, he learned that he had been reassigned. *Temporary* was how it was posed. At first, the sergeant resisted, but he was given an ultimatum. Either take a Central Park detail or a desk job. It was a no-brainer. Gary Hill would rather give in to what many called a sissy-detail than be forced to sit inside all day and push a pencil. And why not? After all, he'd joined the force when he was just twenty years old, and he only had three more years to go until he hit the twenty year mark and retirement. Why drop dead from a heart attack before he had the chance to collect his hard-earned pension? And who could resist the lure of springtime in New York?

Patrolling Central Park was a real switch for Gary Hill, who'd been breaking the spirits of every new recruit who passed through the dreary four walls of the police academy during the past ten years. But it took only a few days on the new detail for his hard-line, take-charge attitude to soften and his level of stress to diminish. He wouldn't want this post permanently, but perhaps it *had* been just what the doctor ordered . . . the best thing for him. Of course, he would never admit his fondness for this patrol to any of his cohorts on the force. God forbid!

"Hey, Mr. Police Officer!"

Sergeant Hill heard a small, urgent voice and felt a tug on the seam of his slacks.

"Please. Please help me find Iggy." A little boy was staring up at him. He couldn't have been more than seven or eight years old.

"Calm down, son. Who's Iggy?" Sergeant Hill said.

"He's my iguana." The boy's voice cracked, his eyes spilling tears. He pointed into a nearby oak tree. "I was taking him to school for show-and-tell. I dropped his cage, and he ran out."

"Do iguanas climb trees?"

"Mine does. He's right up there. See him?"

Sergeant Hill glanced up in the direction the boy was pointing. Camouflaged amid the foliage and the bark was a four-legged, green animal, still as a stone.

"Don't worry," Gary Hill said, patting the boy on the head and setting off on the rescue mission. "If he doesn't run away, I think I can get him."

"Kids today!" Gary Hill mumbled under his breath. *Whatever happened to having a plain old dog or cat—even a hamster—for a pet?*

The little boy and his friend stood beneath the tree and watched as Sergeant Hill began his ascent. The limbs of the oak crackled and groaned under the weight of the officer. Gary finally climbed high enough to reach a hand around the little green monster.

"Work with me. Nice and easy there, little fella," Gary whispered. With great care and concentration, he tucked the creature under his arm like a football and started down the tree. When Gary's feet finally hit the ground, the two boys clapped and cheered the rescue.

The iguana felt solid. Outside of a ticking pulse and the blink of his eyes, Iggy looked and felt like a molded, assembly line toy in Gary Hill's hands. "Why don't you let me put Iggy inside the cage for you. This way we'll be sure that you all get to school safely."

As Sergeant Hill was about to release the iguana inside the plastic pet carrier, he noticed bold face type on the soiled newspaper that lined the bottom of the crate: *DEL VECCHIO and QUINN of Bronx, NY*

*No wonder Iggy tried to escape!*

"Here, let me get rid of this messy top sheet for you," said Sergeant Hill, appearing as though he were doing the kid a favor.

Gary slid out the first page of newsprint from the ten or so lining the bottom of the carrier. Then he placed the iguana inside, latched the metal grate door and made sure it was securely fastened.

After the boys and Iggy hurried off, Gary eyed the newspaper again, trailing the header entitled: ENGAGEMENTS/

WEDDINGS.

Sergeant Hill read and re-read the brief article about Rita and Billy's wedding. When he finished, he shook his head. "Oh, that poor thing," he said, thinking about Rita Del Vecchio. "How could she marry *him?*" He frowned, unable to peel away from the sight of Rita. She looked gorgeous in her gown. Her face was beaming. *What a beauty!*

Iggy had obviously left a little brown dropping right on Billy's left cheek. *That about sums up what that marriage is gonna be worth.*

Sergeant Hill carefully tore the paper around the image of Rita. When he had captured her, he smoothed out the crinkly, jagged edge of the newsprint and slipped her picture inside his wallet. The rest of the paper, the part with the marred image of Billy, he crumpled inside his fist and pitched into a nearby trashcan.

# Twenty-Nine

Three weeks passed quickly. Rita and Billy relished the beauty and flavor of each tropical island. Most of the time, they went off and explored things on their own, finding a private beach to laze away the hours and give in to their every whim.

Soon they flew back over the Pacific and reached the shores of California. They planned to spend a few days on the West Coast, transitioning back to reality, before returning to New York. They landed in San Francisco and spent the afternoon riding cable cars up and down the hilly streets until they disembarked near Ghirardelli Square, indulging in a sinfully delicious chocolate sundae before setting off for Fisherman's Wharf.

The rest of the evening was spent at a sports bar, where the San Francisco Giants got slaughtered by Billy's favorite team, the New York Mets. Watching a Mets game on TV with a bunch of strangers wasn't Rita's idea of a good time, but Billy thought it was fun. And it was only for one night. However, Rita became somewhat apprehensive when, after several glasses of straight-up scotch, Billy proudly announced that he was buying a round of drinks for everyone at the bar.

"Billy, are you crazy? What are you doing? There has to be at least fifty people here."

"Oh, lighten up, baby." Billy slipped his arms around her waist and sidled up close. "How often do we get to honeymoon? Why not let the whole world celebrate with us?"

*In Transit*

"But we don't even know these people," Rita said through clenched teeth. "They're a bunch of strangers."

" 'I have always depended on the comfort of strangers,' " Billy said dramatically in a drunken stupor. "*Street Car Named Desire*, Tennessee Williams. Wow, look at that. I really did learn something from all that crap they jammed down our throats in high school."

Rita firmed her arms tightly across her chest. She wasn't amused—or impressed. And it was *kindness of strangers,* not *comfort,* but she wasn't about to correct him, not in the state he was in. Instead she said to him, "But we really don't have this kind of money."

"It's just a few drinks—"

"A few drinks that will equate to a couple hundred dollars."

"C'mon, Ree. It's not a big deal. I've been working side jobs and doing overtime."

"But we're married now. It's not just your money anymore. It's *our* money."

"Rita, stop. You're being a tight-ass." The volume and curt tone of Billy's words turned heads around the bar. A hush descended.

When Rita looked at Billy in shocked, hurt disbelief, he took her hand and offered an apology. She let it go, sensing that Billy, having already had a lot to drink, felt a sense of power— and importance—being the only New Yorker in the place. She convinced herself that he was probably just sowing his oats, act- ing like a big shot, still on the high of being newly married. Perhaps once they got settled back home and into the routine of their marriage, he wouldn't be so impulsive.

The next day they set off for Los Angeles, and Rita capitalized on Billy's contrite humility about his antics from the night before. After much ado, she convinced him to take her to

Universal Studios. Being a movie buff was an extension of her love affair with romance novels, and she was totally enthralled touring the back lots of the motion picture wonderland. They went from amphitheater to amphitheater, learning about special effects in cinema and tricks of the trade. Rita was fascinated, but Billy yawned every step of the way.

They waited on line for the Interactive Film Lab attraction for nearly an hour. Rita was like a kid waiting on line for a roller coaster, and she was losing her patience with Billy's chronic complaining.

"It's too damn hot. Let's just go back to the hotel and cool off together," he said, running a smooth hand along her bare arm.

She was angered by his touch, so she eased away from him, determined that he would not daunt her enthusiasm. "But they might pick us. Wouldn't it be neat if they chose *us* to star in a film clip?"

"Well, they're not picking *me*. I don't want to be a movie star."

"But this could be our big break."

"You're a dreamer, Rita. It's never gonna happen. Look at how many people are on this line. It's a million to one that they'll choose us."

"Oh ye of little faith."

Billy rolled his eyes.

"C'mon, we could be like Brad and Angelina," she joked.

"No thanks."

"Hey, lighten up," she told him, swatting him in the arm as if to jolt him out of being such a wet blanket. "Last night, you forced me to sit in a bar, watch a Mets game and buy drinks for a room full of strangers. That was *your* idea of fun. Now it's *my* turn."

When a woman from the studio, wearing a photo identification badge, approached Billy and Rita and asked if they'd like to do a screen test, Rita beamed. Billy just made a face and shrugged his shoulders.

"If you could both just sign on the dotted line," the woman said, thrusting a clipboard toward the two of them. "It's a release form. Just a formality giving us permission to broadcast your screen test to the public."

"We're not doing it," Billy said.

"Of course, we're doing it," Rita told him. "C'mon, be a sport."

When Rita took the pen from the woman's hand and pressed the tip to the page, Billy grabbed her arm in an effort to stop her.

Rita looked at Billy. They stared each other down, while Billy put spaces between the words he articulated. "I. Said. *We're*. Not. Doing. It."

Rita clenched her jaw. She scowled at Billy's fingertips as they whitened around the tanned skin of her arm. What would it take to win him over? Should she try to keep reasoning with him? Be silent? Beg? Give in? Or was it time for her to resist?

"*You* don't have to do anything, Billy, but *I* am. This is a once-in-a-lifetime opportunity." Rita tore her arm away from his grasp. She took two steps from him and grabbed the clipboard from the woman. Rita quickly jotted her name and started away.

Escorted by the representative, Rita peered over her shoulder at Billy, who was left standing on the line. His arms were set firmly across his chest. He sneered at her, a severe disapproving look.

Rita's heartbeats clumped together. *Oh, my goodness, what have I done? He's pissed.*

Step by step, her feet kept moving her away toward the lure of the spotlight, while her head said she should turn around and go back to him, right that instant.

But as Billy's image grew smaller in her sight, she realized that her decision was already made. There was no turning back now.

# THIRTY

Rita refused to let Billy put a damper on her fun. She obliterated all thought of him from her mind during the film shoot. Nothing was going to obscure her moment in the spotlight.

After the production wrapped up, she changed back into her jeans and spaghetti-strap shirt, but she decided not to remove the make-up the stage cosmetician had applied. She wished she could have kept the costume, but that wasn't part of the package.

When Rita stepped out of the side stage door, Billy was standing there, waiting for her. At the sight of him, she felt her shoulders square and her heart begin to pound. Had he been waiting to ream her out?

When he walked cautiously toward her and produced a bunch of roses from behind his back, she got her answer.

"I'm your biggest fan," he told her, his grin widening until parenthesis seemed to form around his stretched lips.

She chose not to respond to him right away, hoping he'd get the sense that she was still not happy with him. He worked harder to get back in her good graces.

"I'm sorry I made such a big deal before," he explained. "It's just that it was too damn hot. I'm still a little hung over from last night, and we had been waiting on line for so long . . ."

Rita let him rattle off a litany of excuses. Now that he seemed more meek and humble, she intended to use it to her advantage.

"So what do you say? Peace offering?" he said, thrusting the flowers under her nose.

Inhaling their scent, she softened. He was becoming an expert at knowing exactly how to pierce her heart with hate one minute and win it back the next. When she took the flowers, he reached for her hand and stroked her arm. Then he moved closer and gave her a kiss. There was the fresh taste of cigarettes and alcohol on his tongue, but she didn't let that spoil the moment.

"So, how'd it go?' he asked, as they entered the large movie theater.

"You'll have to see for yourself," she told him.

Rita made a trip to the concession stand for popcorn. When she returned, her film clip was already being projected toward the big screen. Billy and the crowd seemed to be enjoying it. And she enjoyed it too. But watching herself as a silent-screen femme fatale on the wide screen added ten pounds to her petite frame. *I'll have to start dieting the minute we get home.* But in her nervous elation, she shoveled handfuls of popcorn into her mouth anyway. She sat in awe in the darkened theater as if watching someone else on the big screen. Was that really her? A brunette-looking Mae West-type, strutting around a saloon in a flowing red dress and a fluffy red boa?

She loved it. The audience loved it. It was a riot. Her afternoon in front of the camera seemed the perfect way to round out her fairytale honeymoon. But when flirty-Rita dropped her derriere onto the lap of one of the poker-players in the scene, and then she proceeded to flaunt her wiles and tease the other men with her on-screen persona, she feared the gauge of Billy's reaction. His smile sagged like a rubber band that had suddenly lost its elasticity.

It was as the end credits began to roll and the letters of her name popped across the screen that Rita realized, in her haste and hurry, she had signed the release form as *Rita Marie Del Vecchio* instead of *Rita Marie Quinn.*

"What the hell is that?" Billy said, his words aimed on the screen.

Rita played dumb. "What?"

"What the hell name did you put up there?" he roared again, this time loud enough to gain the attention of other people in the vicinity.

"It was a mistake—"

"You're damn right it was a mistake."

Rita kept her voice calm and low. "Billy, please. Don't make a scene—"

"Don't tell me what to do." His face became pink and puffy, his breath short. His anger was visibly uncoiling. "I'll make a damn scene if I want to."

"You're blowing this out of proportion. It was an honest mistake."

Billy grabbed the bouquet of roses from Rita's lap. He whacked the bundled arrangement against the top of the seat in front of him, decapitating some of the young, tight colorful buds. With the blossoms that hung on, he ripped his fingers down the thorny stems, severing the buds from the ends until they bounced upon the sticky, butter- and soda-laden floor.

"There. I'm making an even bigger scene now. How do you like that?"

Rita couldn't take her eyes from his red-soaked hands, the lines of blood that oozed along his fingertips where the prickly thorns had cut him. Some of the woody spines were still embedded in his flesh like nails driven into his skin.

"Damn it, Rita. You're a Quinn now. You're not a Del Vecchio anymore."

Rita was stunned. She couldn't get her mind around what was happening.

"You're my wife!"

The way he blasted her made her jump. "Billy, I'm sorry. I'm sorry. I'm just not used to the name yet—"

"Well, you better get used to it."

Billy stormed out of the theater, leaving Rita to sit there amid the rows of seats, feeling empty and hollowed out inside.

The half-eaten hamburger and fries were cold, sitting on a plate at the edge of the bed. She thought eating might help her feel better, but she had no appetite.

After two hours of waiting by their rental car parked in the lot of Universal Studios, Rita decided to take a cab back to the hotel. And now, with dinner half-finished, along with a host of empty boxes in the daily crossword puzzle from the *Los Angeles Times*, there was still no sign of Billy.

Rita picked up the phone and started to dial her mother.

"I shouldn't be doing this," she said, punching in her mother's number anyway. "She's only gonna say 'I told you so.' "

With the three-hour time difference, it was only seven o'clock on the east coast. The phone rang and rang and rang. When no one answered, Rita realized it was Monday night. Her parents must have forgotten to turn on the machine. They were probably over at Church Bingo, hoping to make a killing in order to pay off the wedding.

Unable to reach her mother and afraid to call her friends and dump on them so soon after the wedding, Rita began to question herself and everything people had tried to tell her about Billy before the marriage. Was she wrong? Had she been naïve and foolish? Had her love for Billy made her blind to his glaring faults?

What a way to spend the last night of her honeymoon. Maybe three weeks was just too long in the company of any one person, even a spouse. And especially a moody, unpredictable husband like Billy.

Rita listened to the clock ticking in the empty hotel room all night long. She tossed and turned.

But when she heard the door key jiggle in the lock at five in the morning, Rita kept her eyes closed and feigned sleep, her heart pounding beneath her chest. The mattress ebbed beneath the weight of Billy as he crawled into bed fully clothed. He gently touched the back of her hair, twirling it around his fingers. Fumbling beneath the covers, she could feel the coarseness of his hands on her skin and how scabs had already formed. He kissed her neck, her shoulders, the small of her back. Why had he reacted as he did? Why had their marriage become such a strain on his moods?

When she flounced around to look at him, his face was racked with sorrow.

He eased up on his elbow. "I don't know what came over me, Ree. I'm sorry."

Rita's fingertips covered his mouth. She didn't want to hear it. She didn't want to talk. She didn't want to smell the alcohol and cigarettes again on his breath. She just wanted to be with him and feel as she did all of those other nights of their honeymoon.

Rita reached for Billy's hands and pressed her lips upon his wounds. She longed to claim something real, something solid, something true.

The low whisk of her breath whispered, "Just love me," as she cried and cried, their bodies entwined in the dark.

"I love you," he pronounced, ravishing the pain of their love until it was made exquisite.

# THIRTY-ONE

At roll call on Rita's first day back, a department memo was read:

*A rise in civilian threats and brutality against police personnel now requires all officers to wear bulletproof vests while on duty. Newly designed, high-impact vests will be distributed to each officer after roll call. The lightweight, concealable vest features extra body coverage and can deflect higher velocity weaponry. It can and should be worn under the police uniform. Please note this initiative is mandatory until further notice.*

The precinct room erupted with groans. There wasn't a cop on the force who was keen on the idea, least of all Rita and Franko. The concealable vests, with a slew of Velcro accoutrements, were cumbersome and hot. A real nuisance. Wearing a vest seemed to add twenty pounds to Franko's already-wide girth. And because Rita was shorter, she thought it made her look even worse. Franko begged to differ.

"At least I don't have a waif for a partner anymore. You look like you've finally got some meat on your bones," he told her. "Love must be sating your appetite better than pizza these days, eh?"

The duo strapped into their armor for the first half of their shift, but by midday they stopped back at the precinct house and liberated themselves from *life support,* as they coined the vest.

"They hinder our movement," Rita rationalized. "How can we possibly live up to our heroic reputations if we can't act spontaneously?"

"Exactly. We're targets every day. It comes with the job. When it's our time, it's our time. Why mess with fate?" Franko added. "Besides, even with the vest, they can still get my brain and the family jewels. What's the point of living if those are kaput?"

"It's settled then. It'll be our little secret." Rita and Franko shook hands to seal the deal.

As the two of them burst through the doors of the precinct house and out onto the street, Franko thrust out his arms wide. He announced, "Officers O'Malley and Del Vecchio at your service. Take your best shot."

"It's Officer Quinn now," Rita corrected.

"Ooh, I forgot," he said.

"Easy mistake. I did the same thing on the honeymoon. Billy practically handed me my head."

"Oh?" Franko's tone flared with interest. "That doesn't sound too good."

Rita hesitated, unsure whether to tell Franko about the experience at Universal Studios. But maybe a male perspective could help reconcile her feelings.

"It was a bigger scene than he made at the reception," she told him.

"Aha. So something *was* awry between the two of you that day. I knew it!"

Rita kept talking while she and Franko descended the steps that led into the subway. She opened up, recounting the ugly, sordid details from the reception and the last days of the honeymoon.

"My God. He's a piece of work," Franko said when she'd finished telling him about Billy destroying that arrangement of roses. "And it's hard for me to be objective and give Billy the benefit of the doubt—"

"You'd actually do that?"

"It's not for Billy, sweetheart. It's for you. And after the scolding you gave me last time, what other choice do I have?"

Rita smirked.

"Don't get me wrong. I'm still not nuts about Billy. But like I told you at the reception, marriage is an adjustment. A biggie. And the whole wedding thing, it's taxing. Maybe Billy, a hothead to begin with, just got too wound up from being in the pressure-cooker. And he probably blew his stack in California because he was stressed, anticipating that you were going to have to leave paradise and come back to reality."

"You think so?"

Franko shrugged. "I'm no Dr. Freud—or Dr. Ruth—but hey, it's possible. I just hope that you hold your ground, Ree, and you're able to nip that explosive temper of his in the bud."

"Bud? As in *rosebud?*"

Franko shivered as if in fear. "No. No pun intended."

"Well, things have been fine between us since that last night in Los Angeles."

"Let's just hope that everything stays that way. I'd hate for him to fly off the handle and physically hurt *you* someday."

Rita's heart raced. Billy's maddened face from those heated moments invaded her mind. But she desperately tried to rationalize away those images. "Billy's intense," she told Franko. "But he isn't like that."

"Oh, right. He's just the crazy, jealous husband type."

"Don't make me regret having told you all this."

"Just don't let him bully you," Franko said. "If he gets out of line again, you tell me, and I'll straighten him out." While Franko pulled imaginary punches in the air, an old lady, a bag lady, shuffled down the platform. Franko stopped shadow boxing and reached into his pocket. He walked toward the woman.

"Here, Maggie," he said, handing a few dollars to the disheveled-looking lady, "you look stunning today."

"Are you still on that kick?" Rita asked him.

Franko nodded a proud *yes* as the two of them boarded a train. The pneumatic sound of the door closed, and off they went. Rita yawned. She felt tired and sluggish. She clung to the cold steel bars to keep her balance as the subway glided in sonic speeds, through shadows and light, swaying down the tracks. A few straggling commuters were texting on their cell phones or reading the early morning paper, iPods in their ears. Rita was just as lost in thought. She was thinking about Billy, how much she loved him but how frightened she was by his mood swings.

When she and Franko finally exited the train and emerged back on the platform, Franko waved a hand in front of Rita's face. "Earth to Rita. Come in, Rita. We're back on New York time."

"Listen, do me a favor," she asked. "Whatever I told you before . . . Billy would kill me if he knew I was airing our dirty laundry. Please don't tell anyone."

Franko reached for his lips. He gestured as though he'd locked them closed and tossed the key away. Then he twisted his arm and gazed down at his wrist watch. He leaned toward the digital face and spoke into it, "Come in, Billy. Billy, come in. Disregard what Rita just said, boss. Scratch it. It was all off the record. You weren't intended to hear any of that."

They both laughed. Then Franko held up his right hand. He looked earnestly at Rita. "You have my word. I hope you know how much I love you, Ree. I'd never break your confidence."

*Love? The L-word? From Franko?* Had she heard him correctly?

In her hesitation, Franko's face turned tomato sauce red. When he realized what he'd just said—and what Rita had just heard—he jerked his watch toward his mouth again and spoke playfully, nervously.

"Clarify, boss. I love her like *a sister,* and if I wasn't gay, I would've married her long before you, macho man."

*Gay?* His comment stopped Rita in her physical and mental tracks. But Franko was a beer-guzzling Irishman. She thought he hung out with a bunch of crude, good old boys.

Rita was tongue-tied. "You? Are you?"

He nodded.

"Are you *really?*"

"You can say the word, Rita."

"Gay?"

"Disappointed?"

"No. Not at all," she said, still flustered. "It's just that . . . I mean, I never would've guessed. You don't look like . . . I mean, you don't act . . ." Rita caught herself. She knew she was sounding ridiculous. "Why didn't you tell me?"

"We never played true confessions before today," he joked. "Billy would just die if he knew, wouldn't he?"

They both howled, doubling over with laughter.

"Yeah, he'd burst more than just a blood vessel, that's for sure," Rita told him. Her stomach muscles hurt from laughing so hard.

"I'm still in the closet, at least at work. So tit for tat. We're even now. Let's just keep this between us, okay?"

Rita mimicked Franko's earlier gesture of locking up her lips, then asked, "Is that thing off?" pointing toward Franko's wrist watch.

When he nodded, she leaned in closer to him. She gave him a pat on the arm and whispered, "Thanks for telling me. And I love you, too."

# THIRTY-TWO

Before the car door even closed, Billy unleashed a world-class verbal assault. His words laced into her with, "How dare you, Rita!"

She was still feeling guilty about her very candid conversation with Franko. But Billy could not have known about that, so what would explain his fit of rage?

"I want you off the beat with that lard-ass."

Billy rammed his foot against the gas pedal, and the car peeled away from the station house. It seemed as if Rita, getting inside and closing the door, had tossed a match into a line of gasoline that was heading toward an already-raging inferno.

"Billy, slow down. What are you talking about?"

"You know damn well what I'm talking about."

"No, I don't."

Billy gritted his teeth. She could see his chiseled jaw bone flexing in anger. "I don't want you working with O'Malley anymore."

Rita rolled her eyes. "I thought we were through harping on all this?"

"I got word today that your partner was reamed out by the captain for not wearing his vest. I bet you went along with him on that, didn't you?"

"Billy, stop driving like a maniac. Pull over so we can talk."

"Answer me."

"Why the hell should I wear a bulletproof vest? I'll get killed simply by riding in this car with you!"

"Cut the crap, Rita. Tell me you wore that vest."

"I wore the vest. All right?"

"Don't you lie to me."

"I wore the stupid vest. Now stop." In the midst of all the excitement, Rita didn't even blink at not telling Billy the truth—two times. "For God's sake, Billy. Pull this car over and let me out."

Billy slammed on the brakes. He stopped the car, right in the middle of the road and in cross-town traffic.

"You're lying." Billy's face, including his ears, were beaming red. "I found your vest in your locker. You were already out on your tour."

"Since when do you go into the ladies' locker room?"

"Since I heard Franko removed his vest halfway through his shift."

"How dare you!"

"No. How dare *you*. You're my wife. I care about you. You're not some low-life, beer-guzzling loser who hasn't got a thing to live for."

Rita couldn't take anymore. She lunged across the seat and slapped Billy in the face. It was enough to cause a ceasefire between the two of them. But the gridlock spilled well beyond their idling car. Billy's Mustang was blocking the traffic, caught in the throes of rush hour. Car horns and curse words erupted all around them.

"You should know that I've pulled some strings. You've been reassigned to City," Billy told her. "I don't want you working in those subways anymore. And I sure as hell don't want you working with someone who isn't qualified to offer quality protection."

Rita thought her head would explode. "You bastard!"

Before Billy could throw the car in gear and get them moving again, Rita undid her seatbelt. She flung out the car door and burst through it. He screamed at her to come back, but she ignored him and kept on going. Weaving around and dodging cars amid the pileup of traffic, she headed across the street, disappearing into the crowds milling about Central Park.

# THIRTY-THREE

Beneath an underpass off the West Side Highway, Billy Quinn slipped into the passenger's seat of Officer Tony Sanducci's brand new pickup truck.

"Hey, how's the missus?" Tony asked, chomping on a wad of gum as he shook his old partner's hand.

"Already nagging at me like we were an old married couple," Billy told him. "Maybe once I stash away enough money and buy her a big house with a white picket fence up in Westchester someplace and give her a couple of kids, she'll chill out with me."

Tony laughed. "Soon as they get that ring on their finger, they really start to show their true colors, don't they?"

Billy nodded. "I was wondering, Tone. How come we're meeting tonight? Business okay? You got my share from those weeks I was away?"

"No. Actually, I don't got nothing. None of us do."

"What are you talking about?"

"We're out of it, Billy."

"Who? What you mean *out of it?*"

"Me and Dirty Roy. We don't think we should do business for a while. There's talk of a rat."

"A rat? Who?"

Tony shrugged.

"Is it a uniformed rat?" Billy asked.

"Nobody knows. Dirty Roy heard it might be a couple of

undercover dealers. But that's not confirmed," Tony said. "All we really know for sure is that Roy and me, we've got mortgages and kids. We can't take the risk anymore."

"Yeah, I hear you," Billy told him. "Who else could be the stoolie?"

"I only know what Dirty Roy told me, which ain't a helluva a lot. I thought I should warn you as soon as I heard. We've all gotta watch our backs now."

Billy stared through the windshield, sorting through a sea of faces in his mind, hoping to recollect which one might be the Judas.

"Yeah, thanks for the heads up," Billy told him, still in a fog. He was mentally trying to run down all the gun and drug runners that might have it in for him. The list was longer than he'd realized. "You guys be careful, too."

"I'm sure it'll blow over. You know Internal Affairs and their grandstand plays. Probably just flexing their muscles. I'm sure once things die down, we'll be back in business," Tony said. "I guess you'll just have to make the missus wait a little longer for that picket fence, eh?"

Billy Quinn hated being back-stabbed. He started up his car after the meeting with Sanducci and cruised toward Broadway. But he slammed on the brakes when he spotted a sleek Monte Carlo with dark tinted windows parked outside the Cotton Club, right near the access ramp to the West Side Highway.

*How the hell could Nick the Spic be back on the streets already? Did he cut a deal?*

Billy was about to find out. And, if need be, he'd settle the score.

# THIRTY-FOUR

Rita kept walking until she came upon the Italian Gardens tucked away in Central Park. She sat for a long time on a wrought-iron bench, until her hot, shallow breaths started to become more slow and steady. Fresh cut grass and the scent of flowers filled the air. The limbs of weeping willow trees draped over the pathways, shading the area and making it appear as narrow as a tunnel.

She stayed there for nearly an hour. When she felt calmer, she set off again on foot. It had been a long time since she'd been a civilian in Manhattan and not forced to look out for the safety of Frisbee players or dog walkers or even lone joggers. And it had even been longer since she'd noticed how a rich harvest of greenery filled this part of the city this time of year. Why did it take having a fight with the man she loved to awaken her to the beauty that was around her?

It was already getting dark, and Rita knew that she'd wandered too far when she heard the sound of violins and flutes as they echoed from nearby Tavern on the Green. Tiny white lights, like twinkling stars, dotted the perimeter of the gastro-nomic oasis tucked within the park and the bustling city. Her feet were killing her, so she sat down on a bench in front of the restaurant. She decided that she'd hail the next cab and go home. While she waited, she pulled out her compact and saw a horror story reflected in her face.

"Miss, it's getting dark. You might want to get out of the park while there's a few minutes of daylight still left."

When Rita looked up, she found Sergeant Gary Hill, in uniform, standing before her.

"Twinkle Toes?" he exclaimed. "I thought it was you. What are you doing here?"

Rita's heart skipped a beat. "I was about to ask you the same thing. You're not walking a beat, are you, Sergeant Hill?"

"Yeah, I needed a change," he told her. "And by the way, I think the statute of limitations is up. Now that you're a full-fledged member of the NYPD, you can drop all the sergeant stuff and call me plain old Gary."

Rita was touched by his offer, but she couldn't bring herself to call him plain old Gary, at least not on such short notice, so she simply skirted calling him anything at all. "I can't believe you gave up the academy. How long did you work there?"

"Ten years. Ten long years of being trapped inside—doing my damnedest to skirt every new case of Athlete's Foot that plagued the locker room. I put in for a transfer a few weeks ago. It's been a nice change of pace," he told her. "You back from your honeymoon already?"

"Yeah, the honeymoon's over," she told him, adding in her head *in more ways than one.*

"I thought Quinn would be keeping you home, and you'd be making babies for him already."

"No, not yet." *Thank God!*

"Well, you got plenty of time for that. You're young," he told her. "What are you doing in this neck of the woods, anyway?"

"Running away from home," Rita said.

"Well, I guess the honeymoon really *is* over. But that doesn't sound too good. You want to talk about it?"

Rita took a double-take at him. *Is he kidding? Sergeant Gary Hill—plain old Gary to me now—actually wants to talk? To me? I thought he only had two speeds, yelling and belittling? Does he really know how to talk? How to communicate like normal people?*

When Rita didn't answer right away, Hill must've sensed that he'd caught her off-guard. He put up the palms of his hands as if under arrest. "None of my business. I just thought that if I'm going to grab some dinner, maybe you'd want to join me. It seems as though we could both use the company right now."

Rita sat there, shocked by his proposition.

"Not Tavern on the Green or anything," he said. "Just a slice of pizza at the place around the corner."

Rita gratefully accepted. It was the best offer she'd had all day.

# Thirty-Five

"I don't know why I'm telling you all this," Rita said to Gary Hill, while she took a paper napkin and blotted oil off a second slice of pizza. "Ever since Billy and I got married, I just can't figure him out."

It was as though Rita had cut a vein. Everything that happened that day seemed to be gushing out of her: anger, frustration, rage, confusion. All the while she kept talking, a little voice inside warned that she should stop telling him so much, but he was a surprisingly good listener, and it was like she couldn't help herself. After what happened in the car, she needed to vent and get things off her chest, and Gary Hill was the closest ear.

"Let me ask you this," Gary said at a lull in the conversation. "How would *you* feel if Billy had a female partner? One who was as friendly with him as you are with Franko?"

He had her there. "Whose side are you on?"

Hill smiled. "I just think that anyone in Billy's position would feel jealous. It's a typical male reaction."

"Oh, and it's a typical male reaction to go flying off the handle, too?"

"Actually, yes. It happens to the best of us. It's not easy being married to a cop—"

"You don't need to tell me."

"No, I don't. But it's different for guys. I mean, there's a helluva lot of stress in general, but it's even worse when your wife's a cop. Believe me, I know."

163

While Rita sifted through the implications of what he'd just revealed, he went on to explain. "I'm not proud to admit it, but I lost it more than a few times with Johanna."

Rita eyed him quizzically. "Johanna?"

"My wife."

"I didn't know you were married."

"I'm not. At least not anymore," he told her. "I'm widowed."

For Rita, this information cast a whole different light on Sergeant Hill. She felt terrible for going on about her problems. They seemed minor in comparison.

"I'm sorry," Rita said. "I had absolutely no idea."

"She was killed seven years ago. Car chase across town that ended down near Penn Station. She was a detective. Went the way she probably would've wanted, dying in the line of duty. And in truth, I think she loved being a cop more than being married to me. In retrospect, I can't say I much blame her."

Rita didn't know what to say. Her uncertainty created a large gap of silence that encouraged Gary to fill it up by telling her more.

"I wouldn't admit it back then, but I couldn't deal with it. I couldn't deal with her being on the force. I was jealous, I think, and I gave her a really hard time. That included my being temperamental and a hot-head. And I kept tabs on her, too, just like Billy's doing with you."

After the way Sergeant Hill had grilled and berated her while she was at the police academy, it wasn't really hard for Rita to picture him treating his wife the way Billy was treating her. But the tender, vulnerable side he was now revealing made it difficult for Rita to imagine that her former sarge could ever be as erratic as her husband. *Did all male cops have a dark side? Was that just how it worked?*

"But you live and learn. And you do better next time. At least that's what my father used to tell me." Gary Hill took a last sip of his soda then wiped his mouth. "You didn't ask for it, but you want some advice?"

"Sure. What have I got to lose?" she said.

"Go back home. You and Billy have both had time to cool off. Speak your piece and then consider his. And take the new job. You'd be foolish not to. Sooner or later, everyone in Transit gets promoted. Your rise is a little premature, but Franko's is long overdue. I can't make any promises, but if you want, I'll see what I can do for him. Franko's a good guy. Maybe I can make a couple of phone calls and see about getting you both reassigned to a City detail."

Sergeant Hill was matter-of-fact and orderly in divvying out his advice, and hearing how neatly he sorted through the whole mess made Rita feel as though all her troubles would now be manageable.

"Don't let this get you down, Del Vecchio."

"It's Quinn now."

"Right. Right," he told her, nodding his head in remembering. "I forgot . . . *Quinn.*"

"I really appreciate your listening to me babble on and on," she told him.

"It's all right. I'll send you my bill." Gary Hill stuffed a couple of crumpled, used napkins atop the nibbled-off crusts sliding around his greasy paper plate. He was about to stand up, but midway he changed his mind and leaned across the table. Rita had never been this close to Sergeant Hill before. She had never looked into his eyes, really looked, until now. They were a deep hazel and flecked with shades of green. Laugh lines were embedded in the corners.

"Just between you and me, I haven't been wearing my vest either," he said. "A lot of cops are choosing not to and taking their chances. But do yourself a favor and make your life a little easier. Do whatever you have to in order to keep the peace."

# Thirty-Six

Nick the Spic Zapato didn't know how good he had it until after he had his walking cast removed. Having his heel and the bones of his ankle artificially reconstructed was a nightmare. But once the bone fusion was deemed a success, the doctors said he could try and resume normal activity, with a leg brace and a cane. Now all he had to do was get up three flights of stairs in the tenement where he lived and conducted business without suffering a lung collapse first.

He made it.

Huffing and puffing, he slipped the key into his apartment door. But before he even reached through the pitch dark to pull the chain attached to the overhead light, Nicky sniffed the air inside. *Cigarette smoke?* He scanned the room and knew by the glowing, orange pin-hole of light that he had company.

He pulled the light chain. The room brightened and il-luminated a face he'd never forget. Standing there was that damn cop who'd shot him and made him temporarily disabled.

"You watching your back, Nick?" Officer Billy Quinn flipped his cigarette to the floor and crushed it beneath the sole of his work boot.

The two were locked at a stand-still. Billy was armed with his .38 revolver and Nicky was armed with his cane. The light bulb on the chain kept swaying between them like a pendulum.

Nick the Spic stared confidently into the barrel of Billy's gun and said, "Yeah, I am watching my back. You watchin' yours?"

"You know, I really hate it when people answer a question with another question. It gets on my nerves. And a bad case of nerves ain't a good thing when you're holding a loaded piece."

Billy fired a shot, taking target practice on the floor around Nicky's feet. Nicky jumped.

"What do you want?" he asked Billy.

"I want to know how you got out of the pen so fast."

"I did my time. Fair and square."

"Then what does that make you? A rat?"

When Nicky didn't answer, Billy said, "I don't like rats. They skeeve me." Then he fired off another shot.

"Look, man. I ain't no rat, but I'll empty out the safe," Nick said, backing away from Billy and hobbling over to the big steel unit that sat on the floor beneath his desk. He cracked the combination and pulled out a few bricks of money. "Go on, take it. I got more where that came from. I'll give you anything you want—"

"What I *want* is for you to tell me what you told them."

"I didn't tell anyone anything. I've got just as much to lose as you do."

"You bet your life, scumbag. But I can't afford to take any more chances."

Nicky must've moved too fast. When he reached for the gun stuffed inside the rear waistband of his pants, Billy took another shot. This one nabbed Nicky, shattering right through the anklebone of his good foot.

"You son of a—" Nicky wailed, his body dropping to the floor. "They gonna get you and string you up by your—"

Before Nick the Spic could finish the sentence, Billy finished it for him—with one single shot smack between the eyes.

When he heard the gunshots, Johnny the Jinx Delgado knew it

167

wasn't good news. He darted off the sidewalk and crouched low in the gutter. He got down on his knees. He blessed himself from forehead-to-chest, shoulder-to-shoulder and looked up at the square of light emanating out from the third story window. Johnny had been coming to welcome Nick the Spic back to town and see about doing a little business with him when the staccato sound of the gunfire rang out.

*Pop.*

*Pop.*

*Pop.*

The Jinx had been around long enough to read the finality of each shot. When silence finally settled again over the neighborhood, Johnny's eyes watered and an eerie feeling oozed over him like a despairing wave. *Bet Nicky's in the Lord's hands now.*

Johnny Delgado knew better than to rat out the most powerful cop in the neighborhood. But as he watched Officer Billy Quinn exit the building and hop into his Mustang, screeching the tires as he peeled away, the Jinx had a sudden change of heart . . . more like an epiphany. After all, it sounded to him like that dirty cop just killed Nicky Z., one of the Jinx's and Harlem's most beloved and powerful Latino brothers. Someone had to avenge Nicky's death and Johnny felt that, being at this place, at this time, a higher power was urging him to finally take action.

# THIRTY-SEVEN

Rita could see the glow of the television set through the second floor window of the apartment building. The light flickered out to the street like a colorful fire during a windstorm. *Billy's obviously home,* she thought, climbing the front stoop and preparing, with each anxious step, for the scene that might follow. After she slipped her key into the lock and wedged open the apartment door, a thin cloud of cigarette smoke streamed through the shadowy light source, making the air look frightfully foreboding. Billy had been something of a closet smoker, very considerate, while they were courting. But since they had gotten married, he'd been sparking up more heavily, whenever and wherever he pleased.

After she closed the door behind her, she saw the rounded crest of Billy's head. The waves of his hair were illuminated over the top of the sofa as he sat in front of the TV. He was brooding again; she could feel it. Coming home after her dance classes some nights, she'd catch him sitting like a catatonic, holding a glass of scotch and staring blankly through the screen. His wallowing in the dark was becoming a habit where he seemed too immersed in the intensity of whatever emotion had him in its grasp. Rita feared that he was drifting farther and farther away from her reach.

Rita pulled her leather badge case from her pocket and threw it next to Billy's on the foyer table. She slid off her pocketbook, jacket and gun holster and stashed everything in the hall closet.

She was stalling for time, trying to plot out some sort of strategy about how she'd handle him. She wasn't sure which Billy she'd face tonight or how short his fuse would be—or hers, for that matter.

When she inched closer to the parlor, she saw a half-started bottle of scotch on the coffee table. It stood tall and uncapped, rising up between Billy's sock-clad feet. *No glass. I guess he's going for the gusto tonight.*

"Where have you been?" Billy's raspy voice struck like a match. He didn't turn around.

*Oh, great. He's gonna make this difficult, isn't he?* She stared over him and saw that he was obviously watching the Mets game on TV.

"Took a walk. Tried to sort some things out," she told him. "I think we need to talk."

"Yes, we do. But first you need to apologize."

"*Me* apologize?"

Whatever placidness Rita felt after her conversation with Sergeant Hill was quickly dissipating.

"Yes, *you*. You lied to me, Rita."

"I only lied because of your craziness in the car."

"I had every right to be crazy."

"Nobody has a right to be crazy. Not as much you are," she told him, the tone of her voice escalating. "You're a loose cannon, and I don't know who you are sometimes. You're irrational."

"If we're talking rational here, then how *rational* was it that you decided not to wear your vest, especially after the warnings the department has issued?"

Rita knew nothing she could say right then would marshal a substantial enough defense. So she kept her mouth shut. Billy used the quiet to further his case.

"And how rational was it that you looked me in the eye and

blatantly lied to me?"

*Guilty.* He had her on that one, too. She couldn't deny it, but she did her best to try and make a point anyway. "You could've approached this differently, Billy. You could have come to me. We could've talked, rather than your throwing a tantrum in the car and our having a screaming match."

"Okay, so neither of us handled it great," Billy conceded. "But we're married now, Rita. We're a team. We're supposed to be in this together. No secrets."

*Secrets?* Rita's conscience flared. She swallowed hard. What a switch that Billy was holding the cards to this argument and dealing with this situation without becoming explosive. Maybe that cooling-off period was beneficial in some way.

"I know I have a bad temper, Ree, and it's something I need to work on. But please don't shut me out. Don't punish me and push me away. I love you. You're my world, and I don't know what I'd do if something ever happened to you."

Billy patted the seat of the couch next to him and motioned for Rita to sit down. She slowly approached, knowing that as this tender side of her husband once again re-emerged, compromise would be needed. It was the right thing to do.

"I'll wear the vest," she told him, "even though it makes me look as big as a horse."

Rita stood in front of Billy, watching how a warm, reddish-orange hue spilled over him from the stream of light cast by the television.

He reached for her and gently eased her onto the couch next to him. "I'd rather you look like a horse and be alive than to be faced with the alternative."

"And speaking of horses," she said, capitalizing on Billy's mood and taking the pun a step further, "I don't want to beat a dead one, but I still don't like that you pulled strings to change my work detail."

"It's not a big deal—"

"Yes, it is. To me, it is."

"Well, a buddy of mine owed me a favor. And after I heard that a couple of old-timers just retired from City, I thought the timing was right. It'll be a good opportunity for you, Ree."

"That's not the point," she told him. "It was the way you went about it. And we both know that part of this fuss had to do with Franko."

"You should've heard the way the captain reamed him out about the vest."

*He's changing the subject.*

"And now that Franko's in hot water, chances are the department would've split you two up. You probably would've been assigned a new partner, anyway."

Rita was tired. Too tired to hash through this with him anymore. And what could be gained? The paperwork for Rita's new detail was probably already being processed, and the powers that be were probably already giving their stamp of approval. So she took the easiest, shortest way to make her point and maintain this semblance of peace between them.

"What's done is done. I guess it's too late to do anything about it now," she told him.

"But, Ree, don't you see. This is really great news for you. You're getting a promotion."

"I know. But my career is *my* career, Billy. I don't need you to cash in favors for me. I make my own decisions, and I also take responsibility for those decisions."

"Okay, okay. I hear you," he said.

It was probably the closest she was going to get by way of a concession or even an apology from Billy, and after the confusion of the day, she took it as a small comfort.

# THIRTY-EIGHT

While she was signing in at the precinct the next day, Rita felt a sharp tug on the sleeve of her jacket.

"We need to talk," Franko said, whisking her off into the arrest questioning room and closing the door behind them.

Rita draped the clear plastic bag covering her dry-cleaned police uniform over the interrogation table and sat down. "You don't need to tell me. I already know you got reamed out for not wearing your vest."

"Yeah, and they're going to use *me* to set an example," he told her. "But that's not the whole reason why I dragged you in here."

"Oh? What gives?"

"You know those heavy-duty threats that put this whole vest policy into effect—"

"Yeah, what about them?"

"Well, it appears that some wing-nut with a bug up his wazoo has it in specifically for me."

"You?" Rita gasped out loud. "Is that why they're making such a fuss that you didn't wear your vest?"

"Bingo."

"Is it Ramirez?"

"Who?"

"You know, the guy," Rita told him. "The one from the bust. At Grand Central."

"Could be. But nearly offing a congressman's son? He'll be

singing the blues behind bars at Sing-Sing until long after we retire."

"You sure of that?"

"Yeah, I'm sure. I checked myself. Especially after I started getting prank phone calls in the middle of the night. It's been hell sleeping with the lights on and a piece under my pillow."

"When did that start?"

"When you were on your honeymoon," he told her. "I thought once I changed my telephone number, I could put my paranoia to rest. But then a written threat came into the precinct for me yesterday."

"What did it say?"

"You know, very *Hardy Boys*. A copy of a death certificate with my name typed on top."

"Yikes."

"Yeah. It might be nothing, but it's serious enough for precautions to be taken. We better wear those vests, especially now that they're splitting us up."

"I know. I heard."

"You did?"

"Yeah, from Billy." That was all Rita offered. Franko had more than enough on his plate right now. "When do you think our re-assignments will go into effect?"

Franko looked at his watch. "In about two minutes, at roll call," he told her. "It sucks that we're not going to work together anymore, but it's probably for the best. I wouldn't want you getting caught in the line of fire if somebody really *does* have it in for me."

"It's probably just a hoax." Rita tried to downplay things with Franko, but her heart was heavy. It was bad enough losing him as her partner, but the idea of his being in danger made her feel even worse.

"That's the bad news. Now you want to hear the good?"

Franko asked, changing the subject.

Rita nodded.

"Believe it or not, the two of us are actually moving up in the world, Ree. We're out of Transit. We've been reassigned to City. We're finally gonna see the light of day."

*Gee, Sergeant Hill must truly be a man of his word. He didn't waste any time, did he?*

"We'll be in different precincts, but at least we're staying in the same division. So it's not like we're never gonna see each other again."

Rita swallowed a brick of sadness lodged in her throat. *Who's he kidding? We both know our partnership is over. It'll never go back to the way it was.*

"Don't sweat it, Ree. We'll meet up like people in California now. It'll be a perfect excuse for us to meet and *do lunch,* as they say." Franko was trying to lighten the mood and look on the bright side, but she could hear a forced quality in his tone. "Maybe we should be really daring and Californian and not even wear socks with our police boots. I'm game if you are."

At the end of her first shift without Franko, Rita returned to the precinct and discovered that a note had been left for her at the front desk.

*A note?*

When the dispatcher at the desk handed her an envelope, she took it gingerly in her hands, suspect. Her legs felt wobbly as she carried it into the locker room. Maybe it was a *Hardy Boys* threat intended for her this time?

But when she slipped a finger beneath the seal, she found a hand-printed note inside with an odd-shaped, 14-karat-gold charm taped to the middle of the page:

*You may think this is a little sappy, Ree, but I saw this in a jewelry store where we answered a call today. I had to buy it for us. I figured with the two of us being die-hard Bronx Bomber fans and our lives so embroiled in this city, a heart with the "NY" logo of the New York Yankees etched inside was apropos. I had the jeweler split the heart in half, right down the middle, so we can still patrol the city together. You'll always be my good luck charm. Franko*

Rita smiled, tears springing to her eyes. She leaned back against her locker and re-read the letter, again and again and again. Then she traced the impressions engraved in the charm: the raised gold lettering from half of the "NY" logo; the curvy, rounded side of the heart versus the straight edge where the charm had been split in two.

Rita peeled off the tape and lifted her half of the charm from the page. She folded Franko's note in quarters and tucked it inside the leather wallet case that held her police badge. It fit perfectly behind her police identification card that was covered in protective, clear plastic. Once the note was fully concealed, she took the gold charm and slid it atop the picture of the Statue of Liberty embossed on her I.D. card. The distinctive shape of that charm was visible on top. It glimmered over the torch held by Lady Liberty and sat directly opposite the shiny, nickel silver of her patrolman's shield.

# THIRTY-NINE

"So tell us, Rudy. Just when exactly did you decide to cross the line between cop and criminal?"

Rudy Palumbo knew Internal Affairs had him by the balls. He sat in an interrogation room and listened to two agents broadcast a recording of his own voice, over and over, as they kept hitting play and reverse. Rudy was going off to another cop about some uncooperative folks in one of the drug-infested neighborhoods infiltrated by the Mean Nineteen, and how he felt the monies collected were not being divvied out fairly to each officer. It was a conversation that Rudy remembered having in a squad car that must've been bugged. *How sloppy! How foolish!* But even after three hours of sitting in a room no bigger than a closet and breathing the same recycled air as the agents, Rudy still wasn't ready to budge.

"The only way we can break down some doors and nab these drugs dealers is if we get some back-up. Now are you ready to start talking or what?"

"I'll only talk if we cut a deal."

"Fine. You tell us what you know about Billy Quinn and his involvement with you and this drug ring. Then we'll see what we can do."

"No. You put your cards on the table first. Then I'll start talking."

"That's not how it works, Palumbo. We're in the driver's seat here."

"I'm not saying another word without an attorney present."

"Who said anything about an attorney?" The affairs agents settled back in their chairs and loosened their ties. "How many kids you got now, Palumbo?"

Rudy swiveled his sights between the two suits. He was tired, too tired to maintain the vigilance needed to stay a step ahead of these guys. "I've got two boys."

"How old are they?"

"Four and seven."

"Good ages. Good kids?" asked the first agent, playing good cop.

"The best," Palumbo told them.

"Yeah, but sometimes good kids can go bad," said the second agent, bad cop.

"Wonder how they'll react when kids at school start calling their daddy a dirty cop. A jail bird, no less."

"And the missus. I bet she'll find somebody else while you're stuck doing time."

The two agents suddenly changed their tactic. Now they were playing devil's advocate in an effort to wear Palumbo down.

"Be a damn shame if those boys of yours start showing loyalty to some other daddy. A daddy living free and clear on the outside."

A clammy wave of sweat broke out under Rudy's armpits and on his brow. The I.A. officers had finally hit the nerve they'd been searching for.

"All right, all right," Palumbo said, his voice cracking. "Let's get this over with. What do you want to know?"

# FORTY

Officer Walter Adamsky proved to be as stiff as a slice of frozen pizza. He curtly corrected Rita when they were first introduced and she referred to him as, "Wally."

"You can call me Officer Adamsky," he told her.

*No wonder everyone on the force tells bad Polish jokes about him behind his back.*

Working eight hours alongside Walter Adamsky felt more like a double shift. He was a short, Napoleon-complex male chauvinist who, at first, wouldn't dream of allowing Rita, a woman, the chance to *man* the patrol car.

"It goes against the forces of nature," he'd told her.

But after a few weeks, when she finally cajoled the car keys from him and positioned herself behind the wheel, he acted as though he were being chauffeured around by a blind man.

For Rita, working alongside Walter Adamsky took as much getting used to as working aboveground and in daylight. Rita learned that in the evenings, Adamsky was studying forensic science over at John Jay College of Criminal Justice. "Just for fun," he'd said.

*Some fun!*

And by day, Rita discovered that Adamsky was a vigilant *germaphobe,* unheard of for a cop walking a beat in the overcrowded Petri dish called Manhattan. He would spend most of the shift diligent in his use of hand sanitizer, determined to disinfect the dash, wheel, console, vinyl seats and knobs of the squad car. Once, she'd even caught him putting a prophylactic dab of the stuff on the tip of his nose. Rita was convinced that his humorlessness was a direct result of brain cells damaged from his continued exposure to the alcohol fumes of the sanitizing product. But rather than engage Adamsky in a lengthy discourse about germ warfare, Rita figured the only way to deal with the likes of him and not lose her cool was to simply let him become a source of amusement. This served as a perfect antidote and soon, the two of them forged an alliance. It wasn't quite like the union she shared with Franko; it never would be. But it became a bond filled with their own unique brand of shorthand, where regulars on their beat came to expect them around their neighborhoods.

Rita had been on the force long enough to have learned that each enclave of New York City was really a small town at heart. Everyone seemed to know everyone—neighbors, cops, shopkeepers, street vendors—and most of their business, too. And working the streets, cruising along in a patrol car and answering calls about robberies, car accidents and suspected drug transactions was like being promoted from a cubicle to a corner-office job as compared to working the dreariness of the subways.

It was amazing how one could adjust to change and how new routines could ultimately settle into new patterns and a new status quo. But was being comfortable a good thing? It was for Rita, and comfort was something she sought regularly from the string of one hundred degree weather days that filled the month of July. The source of her greatest discomfort came from having to wear a bulletproof vest. Even after being strapped into it for so many months, it still irritated her. And now, many weeks later, she was convinced those threats were merely a hoax. Rita toyed, once again, with the idea of liberation. Amid the sweltering summer heat wave, she felt like an ear of corn wrapped in foil and placed over blazing hot coals on a barbecue. The only thing holding her back from removing the vest was the prospect of getting caught.

Every day before roll call, Rita strapped on the cumbersome vest like every other officer in the NYPD and concealed it beneath her uniform. But a half hour to an hour later, Rita would ask Adamsky to pull over so she could make a pit stop at the closest hotel. They had the cleanest restrooms.

When Adamsky, a wanna-be detective, began to recognize this as becoming a regular habit for Rita, he offered some unsolicited advice. "Drug companies have stuff on the market that can help you, I bet. It's nothing to be ashamed of." Adamsky presented her with oodles of information he'd downloaded from the Internet, lists of prescription medications for overactive bladder. Rita feigned interest and humored him for a while, but her propensity for migraines worsened when he took on her cause and spent hours of their shift spouting hosts of potential side effects.

Passing through the revolving doors of any hotel establishment became for Rita like telephone booths for Superman, where he changed into—or out of—his cape and red boots. However, for Rita, once inside the stall of the ladies' room, she'd undo the Velcro straps of the vest and stuff the bulky, itchy Kevlar fabric into her purse, which was the size of a duffel bag. With her body feeling ten pounds lighter, she'd return to the car, toss the bulging bag into the trunk of the patrol car and off she and Adamsky went, business as usual. For all of his exacting and forensic propensities, Rita was astounded how Adamsky never put two-and-two together and recognized Rita's daily transformations.

It made Rita eager to share the anecdote with Franko during their first attempt at *doing* lunch.

On the day they were to meet, Adamsky and Rita split up. He went for a bite at a Thai restaurant in Bryant Park, while Rita set out to meet Franko at a pizzeria over by the New York Public Library. Just as Rita was approaching her destination, she spotted the cushiony round of Franko's gut. He was loitering on the sidewalk in front of the pizzeria and talking to someone who looked like a panhandler. Rita heard him say, "Ramona, you look marvelous," and then he slipped a couple of bills to the woman.

"Well, if it isn't the Mother Teresa of Midtown," Rita greeted him.

Franko's face lit up at first sight of her. He lifted his slacks and revealed hairy legs and bare ankles rooted inside his police boots.

They both howled with laughter.

"Well, at least *one* of us is daring enough to lunch like a Californian," he said, rushing to meet her.

She planted a wet kiss on his flabby cheek, and he swooped her off her feet in a Teddy bear hug.

It felt good being in Franko's company again. They managed to pick up right where they'd left off. They had a lot of laughs, chatting about the Yankees' winning streak, their new partners, "the old days" and spewing gossip they'd heard from around the district. All through the lunch, Rita noticed how Franko kept fiddling with a gold chain around his neck. He kept toying with it, pulling the chain around and around until the clasp showed in front. The claw anchored his half of their shared good luck charm. Rita smiled when the gold shined back at her.

At the end of the lunch, Franko gave Rita a parting hug. As his arms tightened around her and he patted her on the back, he said, "Hey, where's your vest?"

"In this heat, wearing that stupid thing makes the temperature feel like a million degrees."

Franko shook his head. "Not good. Not with police-hating wackos still on the loose."

"*Wackos?* Plural? They haven't said a word about any threats in weeks. I just assumed that things had died down."

"Well, don't assume," he told her. "I hear threats are still racking up, and they're being aimed directly at other officers in our district. It's no longer just me."

"Who else do they have their sights on?"

Franko's momentary hesitation made Rita press, "Tell me."

"Billy hasn't mentioned anything?"

"About what?"

"It's just rumors, Ree. It might not even be true."

"Stop backpedaling. Tell me what you know."

Franko started to spout off a couple of names. But as one name in particular slipped from his lips a chill went down Rita's back. Why was she the last one to know?

# FORTY-ONE

Rita interrupted Adamsky just as he was cleaning his plate of Thai green curry.

"Gimme the keys," she told him, her outstretched palm beneath his nose.

Adamsky wiped his mouth with a napkin. He asked for an explanation, but when none was offered, he simply held up the car keys. Rita ripped them from his fingers and told him that she would come back to pick him up later. Then she drove directly to the precinct house.

Police cars were angled every which way in front of the building. Rita had no choice but to double-park. And the instant the car lurched to a stop, she hopped out and stormed past her co-workers, not acknowledging the many officers who greeted her with their usual, cheerful ribbing and banter.

Without knocking, she burst through Captain Stueben's office door and interrupted his lunch.

"What is all this about someone threatening to harm Officer Quinn?" she asked, her voice quivering breathlessly.

The balding captain was seated behind his desk. He was reading the ingredient label from a microwaveable entrée box and inhaling steaming spaghetti from a pre-fab, disposable plate. At Rita's sudden appearance, the captain stopped chewing and glanced up. He fixed his gaze on Rita, standing in front of him with hands on her hips. Long strands of noodles dangled from the captain's mouth until he sucked them in with a slurping sound, and they disappeared through his puckered lips.

"I prefer to eat my lunch alone," he told her, wiping his mouth and setting down his fork. "And I don't like cold Pasta Bolognese."

The captain's tone translated to Rita the magnitude of her actions. The gravity and boldness of her disrespect was a mistake. But it was too late to turn back now. She would have to follow through on her impulsive course of action.

"I'm sorry to barge in like this, sir," she told him. "But I was just floored to learn that an Officer Quinn from this district has been receiving harassing threats. Why wasn't I told?"

"Because we don't think *you* are the Officer Quinn who is the target."

Rita froze at the implications.

"How long have you been on the force?" the captain asked.

"Nine months, sir."

"Lucky for you, you're still a rookie. You've obviously got a lot to learn."

It was clear from Captain Steuben's words and the way he reclined in his chair that he wasn't just referring to the idea of the threats, but also the brazenness of Rita's action. He laced his hands together and threw his short arms behind his head. His elbows were outstretched like wings that revealed two round perspiration stains under his armpits.

"We never minimize the seriousness of threats. We check each one out thoroughly, and usually, nothing materializes. However, we've gotten numerous calls in the past couple of weeks specifically threatening Officer Quinn."

"And how do you know the threats *aren't* directed at me?"

"Because detectives are conducting a thorough investigation, the details of which I'm not at liberty to disclose. But I can tell you that there seems to be a correlation to your husband. This might be something for you to take up with *him*."

Rita could feel her eyebrows cinch. She was dumbfounded. "Is he aware of the threats?"

"Yes, of course. He's been working alongside detectives to get to the bottom of things."

"For how long?"

"A few weeks." Captain Steuben stood up and walked around his desk. He motioned for Rita to pull up a chair. Sliding his derriere atop the edge of the desk, he looked down at her and said, "As police officers, we live with the knowledge that some deranged character may decide to single out any one of us for whatever reason—a personal grudge, hatred for the force in general, his own amusement. You take precautions. You watch your back. And then you get on with it. It's part of the job."

"Why didn't Billy tell me?"

"In truth, that might be my mistake. I should've followed protocol and called both of you in together, but I made an exception with Billy," the captain admitted. "He asked special permission to break the news to you himself. He's a decorated cop, so I took him at his word. Maybe he didn't want to frighten you and get you upset."

"Well, it's too late for that."

"I can't help what you feel," he told her. "I've been on the force for twenty-five years, and threats like these are a dime a dozen. Ninety percent of the time, they fizzle into nothing. So if I were you, I wouldn't lose too much sleep over this."

"I understand," Rita told Captain Steuben. But the only thing that Rita understood just then was that she had more than a bone to pick with Billy.

# FORTY-TWO

It took Johnny the Jinx Delgado only twenty minutes to run down his sins in the darkened confessional of Saint Paul's Roman Catholic Church. Kneeling in front of the Blessed Sacrament, saying his penance of twenty-five Hail Marys and twenty-five Our Fathers, Johnny was a little annoyed that the priest showed so little mercy. After all, the worst sin Johnny had confessed to committing in the past week was robbing a blind panhandler. How big a deal was that?

"Not for nothin', but I don't think what I did was so bad, padre," the Jinx tried to explain to the priest after he'd dispensed Johnny's penance. "After all, I was hungry. We've all got to eat, don't we?"

Seated on the other side of the mesh confessional screen, the shrouded priest said, "Son, I'm sorry, but penance is non-negotiable. Go in peace. Repent and serve the Lord."

"*. . . Holy Mary, Mother of God, pray for us sinners, now and at the hour our death, Amen.*"

Johnny lost count, so he decided to skip ahead to the twentieth Hail Mary. Halfway through the prayer, he felt a tap on his shoulder. From down on the kneeler, the Jinx turned around and eyed a black kid sitting in the pew behind him. A chewed toothpick dangled from between the white teeth of the kid's smile. The Jinx wondered why on earth that kid was wearing a knitted ski cap on his head when it was a hundred degrees outside.

187

"I was told I'd find you here, bro," the kid said.

"Can't you see? I'm sitting with the Lord right now."

The kid looked on either side of the Jinx as if expecting to really see the Savior, Jesus Christ, sitting there in the flesh next to Johnny.

Annoyed by the interruption, the Jinx turned back around. He put his hands together, closed his eyes and returned to his prayers. But when he heard the kneeler next to him being lowered and saw the kid drop down next to him, he scolded, "I've found Jesus. Now beat it."

"Well, if you could find Jesus, then I bet you can find just about anyone," the kid said. "I hear you're the best eyes and ears in all of Harlem."

The Jinx stopped praying. "Who you looking for?"

"Badge Number 7-7 dash 5-7-7-2. Bastard cop owes me some money."

"A cop? No, I can't help you there," the Jinx said, turning back to the altar. He called the Hail Marys a rap and moved on to the Our Fathers.

"Maybe this'll help," the kid said, revealing a couple of one hundred dollar bills wrapped around a vial of crack cocaine.

*"And lead us not into temptation . . ."* muttered the Jinx, before he eyeballed that stash in the kid's hand. *Maybe this is the answer to my prayers?*

"Aaah, hell." Johnny took what the kid was offering. Then he peered up toward the crucifix hung above the altar. Jesus, in bloodied agony with his arms outstretched, seemed to be looking down on Johnny in complete disgust and exasperation. Johnny shrugged. "Cut me some slack, will ya?" he said, humbly bowing his head to the Savior. "We've all gotta eat."

# FORTY-THREE

"Who told you?" was the first thing Billy asked Rita when she got home that night and had it out with him.

"It doesn't matter who told me. What matters is that *you* didn't tell me."

"It was Franko, wasn't it?"

"How could you keep something like this from me?"

"So it *was* him."

"Stop making this about *him*. It's about how I made a complete fool of myself in Captain Steuben's office. How could you humiliate me like that?"

"*You*, humiliated? What about *me?*"

"Why does everything have to be about you and *your* ego all the time?"

Rita and Billy paced the perimeter of the living room on opposite sides like fighters dancing around a boxing ring.

"You had lunch with him today, didn't you?"

"*Him* has a name. It's Franko. And yes, I had lunch with him. So what?"

"Dammit! That's just like him. He always tries to drive a wedge between us. He's ruining our marriage."

"No. It's you, Billy. *You're* the one ruining our marriage."

"Are you having an affair with him?"

Rita stopped pacing long enough to say, "What?"

"You heard me."

She lifted her hands into the air as if reaching for heavenly intervention. "You're a broken record. This is like an obsession with you. When are you gonna stop?"

"Not until you tell me the truth."

Billy lumbered across the living room like the ugly bear he was. He headed to the table in the foyer where Rita always tossed her police shield wallet. He retrieved the wallet and flung it out toward Rita.

"Tell me what this is," he said, pointing to the little piece of the gold twinkling on her police ID card. "Does Franko have the other half?"

"What is it with you? Do you rummage through my things while I'm sleeping?" With anger flaring, Rita tried to swipe the wallet from Billy's grasp, but he yanked it away and kept it just shy of her reach.

"Answer me, dammit," he said. "Who has the other half of this 'I love you' charm?"

"It's not an 'I love you' charm. It's a New York Yankee charm. It's my good luck charm."

"Yes or no, does Franko have the other half?"

"Yes, he does," Rita finally blurted. "But we are *not* having an affair."

"Liar," Billy screamed, pitching the wallet like a fast ball across the room. Then he lunged for Rita and whacked her across the face.

The impact of Billy's hand blasting into Rita made her spin around, completely disoriented. Her cheeks stung with a lasting vibration. She pressed her fingers to the numb feeling in her face. *Did he just hit me?*

Billy turned from her. He walked over to the counter that separated the kitchen from the living room and reached for the half-empty bottle of scotch towering above the other liquor bottles on the counter.

"Get out!" Rita said.

Billy poured himself a double. He lifted the glass with the amber-colored liquid and in one quick, smooth motion he threw back his head and drained the contents of the glass into his mouth. Then he wiped his lips with the back of his hand.

"I said, get out!" Rita repeated, this time louder.

When Billy started to pour himself a refill, Rita howled in a fury. She charged, pushing him against the counter. When he dodged away from her, she took both of her arms and knocked over all the liquor bottles, whisking them off the counter in one fell swoop. The sound of breaking glass roared beneath her shrieks.

Billy headed for the door. When it slammed closed behind him, Rita collapsed into a heap on the floor, sobbing.

Two eyes peered out from the darkened alley across the street from the Quinn's apartment and fixed on the light that glowed through the opened second story window. The couple's silhouettes moved in shadows through the screen and the sound of raised voices, a heated argument, spilled down in waves to the street. *Trouble in paradise?* When Billy Quinn suddenly emerged from the building, bursting out the front door, the two eyes aimed upon Billy's tall, hunched frame as he headed down the street. No doubt, he was en route to the local watering hole, Finnegan's Pub. The eyes left the alley and trailed after Billy. Someone was moving in closer while the Quinns were being torn apart.

# FORTY-FOUR

Billy didn't come home that night or even the night after. In fact, Rita hadn't seen or heard from him in almost a week. She did see his car parked outside Finnegan's Pub on her way home from work. And it was still there when she came home from dance class each night. Perhaps he was sleeping under the bar. In the store room? Rita didn't know, and she tried not to care. But that wasn't easy, especially when Billy started to leave messages, humbly seeking forgiveness, on Rita's cell phone and on the answering machine in the apartment. When she didn't respond, his recorded voice began to sound less meek and more urgent. He switched gears and made the calls under the pretext of giving her updates on the threats regarding the welfare of Officer Quinn that continued to be received at the precinct house.

He was pushing her buttons, all the right emotional buttons, and it was slowly wearing Rita down. She was concerned about Billy and the threats. But her feelings were still raw. Although she had taken great pains to conceal the large black-and-blue bruise on her left cheek with two coats of base make-up, one look in the mirror was a glaring reminder of Billy's abuse.

On the day that she and Franko were supposed to meet for lunch again, Rita called Franko at the last minute and cancelled.

"Can't make it," she said, her words terse and brief.

"Well, let's do lunch tomorrow then," Franko suggested.

"Can't. Gotta be in court for an arraignment."

192

"Maybe a drink after work?"

"No. Terror alerts are back on high, so I'm doing some overtime. Why don't we just touch base again next week?"

"Next week? What's going on, Ree? This doesn't have anything to do with that bruise on your face, does it?"

Rita's pulse quickened. "What bruise?"

"The one I understand you've been trying to camouflage with Maybelline all week."

"It's Clinique. And I didn't think it was that obvious."

"Well, Adamsky said you don't need a forensic ultra-violet light to root it out, so that sounds pretty obvious to me. Did Billy hit you?"

"No." Rita knew that she'd answered a little too quickly. So she laughed, hoping that forced levity might overshadow the nervousness of her response. "Yeah, I hate to admit it, but klutzy me took a little tumble at dance class the other night."

"Really? I guess all those pirouettes and grand-plies can get a little tricky sometimes?" It was clear from Franko's tone that he wasn't buying the story. "C'mon, Ree. Tell me the truth."

Rita's heart winced. She really could have used a friend right now, but she didn't want Franko to know that her fight with Billy had all to do with him finding her half of the charm. She didn't want to upset Franko. And the last thing she wanted was to hurt him. So Rita continued to hedge until she finally caved under the pressure of his interrogation.

"Look, Billy had too much to drink and things got a little rough. You know how he gets," she conceded, evading the details. "But, it's okay. And *I'm* okay."

"Are you? Are you *really* okay?"

"Yes, I am. But I'll feel a lot better once this bruise heals and Billy calms down."

"That bastard!" Franko blurted. The line went dead for minute. "You know, if he hit you once, he'll hit you again—"

"Franko, please. If you're my friend, then don't lecture me. That's not what I need right now."

"Then what *do* you need? C'mon, let me help you. What can I do?"

"If you really want to help, then just give me a little time. There's a lot I need to figure out."

When Rita finally disconnected the call, her head was swimming. She was still smarting from the physical impact of Billy's blow, and now, feeling even more isolated and alone after the call with Franko, it felt as though Billy had just inflicted another. Even after she'd thrown him out, he was still calling all the shots, controlling people and circumstances. She hated him for that.

*Billy, that louse!*

That night, Rita returned home to the empty apartment. It was early still—six-thirty—and she looked forward to the peace and quiet, along with a little TV, a glass of wine, then early to bed.

But when she pressed the play button on her answering machine, she found three messages from Billy. His words were modulated, forcibly contrived to sound steady and emotionally even, as though he were reading a script. "We need to talk, Rita. It's urgent. Please. Call me."

She toyed with the idea of caving in. After all, enough was enough. Maybe she should look him in the eye, without makeup, and force him to see the still-gaping wound he'd inflicted.

But she dismissed that thought and decided to take a little more time to clear her head. With a low-fat frozen entrée defrosting in the microwave, Rita poured herself a glass of Chardonnay and kicked her bare feet up on the coffee table in the living room. She clicked on the television via the remote control and, multitasking as usual, she took a few sips of the *vino* and flipped through the pages of *The Daily News* in search of the crossword puzzle. In the background, the anchorman from the six o'clock news reported the top stories of the day. Rita wasn't really paying attention, but when she heard the TV broadcaster say that an inmate had escaped from Sing-Sing Prison in upstate New York and was suspected to be prowling the streets of Manhattan, she looked up from the newspaper. A picture of a familiar face flashed on the television screen:

*"It is believed that Santiago Ramirez escaped during the inmate's daily exercise session. Ramirez is serving consecutive sentences for robbery and the attempted murder of James Thomas, son of Congressman Patrick Thomas. There is reason to believe that Ramirez may be armed and dangerous . . ."*

*Oh, my God, Franko!* The chilled, sweaty glass of wine in Rita's hand trembled. She grabbed the phone and dialed Franko's number. When she got his answering machine, she left him an urgent message to call her back. Then she dialed his cell and his pager. No answer. She left messages there, too.

Five minutes became ten minutes . . . became thirty minutes. She moved the fork around the microwaved dinner, picked at the peas and the mystery meat that was drowned in too much brown sauce. She had no appetite. When Franko still hadn't called by eight o'clock, she flung her gun holster over her arm and fastened the straps. Then she grabbed her purse and badge wallet and rushed out the door. The only thing to do was to find Franko—fast.

# Forty-Five

It was the third time that Rita had cruised her car along Fifth Avenue. She finally came upon a police squad car idling near the Frick Gallery.

When she pulled up alongside the shiny black and white, she rolled down the window. Sergeant Gary Hill was seated behind the wheel.

"Twinkle Toes! What are you doing here?" His voice and his face beamed from amid the dark shadows filling the patrol car. "Why aren't you dancing tonight?"

"I'm actually looking for a friend."

"Anyone I know?"

"As a matter of fact, yes. Frank O'Malley. I think he's in this district. Have you seen him?"

"No. But I think he works the day tour."

"He does. But I thought he might be doing some overtime tonight?"

"Don't know about that," Gary Hill said, scratching his close-cropped, wheat-colored hair. "You want me to try and get him on the radio for you?"

"Could you?"

Sergeant Hill picked up the handset and radioed headquarters. Rita could hear the dispatcher say that they would check on Franko's whereabouts and radio back.

"You know, I never thanked you," Rita said, while they were waiting, talking to each other through the opened car windows.

"I'm really grateful for everything you did. And for all the advice."

Hill's forehead became a mass of wavy lines. Rita feared that maybe he could see the black-and-blue bruise on her face. "Everything work out okay?"

"Sort of," Rita said, relieved when static from the radio interrupted the conversation, and Sergeant Hill answered the call.

"Well, looks like your buddy's off tonight. There's the big subway series between the Mets and the Yankees. The second game of the doubleheader is over at Citi Field. I bet O'Malley got tickets."

"Yeah, maybe," Rita said, frowning and biting her lip.

"You in some kind of trouble?"

"Have you heard anything about that prisoner on the lam from Sing-Sing?"

"You mean that Ramirez character?"

Rita nodded.

"The department's on the lookout. There's an A.P.B. out on him."

Sergeant Hill lifted a photograph of the suspect from the passenger's seat and handed it to Rita. The sight of Ramirez's mug shot, his unshaven, rodent-like face, stabbed Rita with terror. It was definitely the same perpetrator she and Franko had held in that stand-off all those months before. Rita would never forget his face.

"He's the guy Franko and I arrested at Grand Central," Rita explained. "He attempted murder on that congressman's son."

"Yeah, I remember him."

"He made a threat against Franko that day. An ugly, intense threat. I just wanted to give Franko a heads up. Haven't been able to reach him by phone."

"Don't look so glum. Every cop in this city is on the lookout. If Ramirez is smart, he's miles away from here by now. But if not, we'll get him. Don't worry."

Sergeant Hill got a call on the radio again. "I better go," he said.

"Anything serious?"

"Nah. Looks like some 9-1-1 call. A bunch of kids acting up. You gonna be okay?"

"I hope so," she said. "But if you hear anything about Ramirez, would you give me a call?"

"Sure. But I don't have your number."

"Do you have a piece of paper?"

Sergeant Hill fumbled around the inside of the patrol car. "I lose everything. Just tell me the number, and I'll jot it on my hand." He held a pen in his left hand and opened his right palm, waiting for her to rattle off the numbers.

"A lefty, eh?"

"Yup, a southpaw."

"Me, too," Rita said.

"See that? I always knew that, deep down, we had something in common."

As Rita spouted off her telephone number, Gary Hill scribbled it across the bottom half of his palm, from his pinky toward the wrist. "I'll never be able to wash this hand now. You know that, don't you?"

Rita chuckled. "It might be easier, and a lot more sanitary, if you just take a cell phone picture of your hand for posterity's sake."

Gary's smile glimmered. He winked at Rita and drove off. She soon followed. But as she slipped her car in gear, she was oblivious to the vehicle trailing a short distance behind her. If she'd glanced up into the rearview mirror, she would've noticed that someone had been watching her and Sergeant Hill's meeting, taking it all in from afar.

# FORTY-SIX

He made a deal with his new friend, Steve, a younger guy he'd met at a club in Midtown that if he'd join him for the second game of the doubleheader over at Citi Field then afterward, Franko would go to the Village to meet some of Steve's friends at Chumly's Pub.

The Mets lost both games of the doubleheader to the Yankees. And it was midnight by the time Franko and Steve ordered two frosty beers at the tiny, dim-lit bar that at one time was a speakeasy. Now it looked more like a frat house. Crowded in among tables of young, well-dressed intellectuals from NYU, Franko reached inside his shirt and fingered his half of the New York Yankee heart. He moved the charm, his talisman, back and forth along the chain. It had become for him a nervous habit.

*What the hell am I doing here with all these smarty-pants people?*

But Chumly's was a safe place where no one from the NYPD would ever recognize him. For in fact, the life Franko lived prowling the streets was a far cry from sitting there listening to a bunch of bookworms rattle off names like Byron, Keats and Hemingway and toss them around like baseball trading cards. But Franko dug his heels into the floor beneath the table and decided he'd give Steve and his friends a chance. Life in the city was lonely, especially when you were a gay cop still in the closet.

By one-thirty and two pints of Guinness later, Franko knew this just wasn't going to work. He waved goodbye to Steve and headed for home. His date was essentially a bust, but for some reason Franko felt completely carefree and happy, even when the skies rattled with thunder and rain began to fall. He didn't mind getting wet. He welcomed the drenching, soaking rain to cool him off while he walked to his apartment near Madison Square Garden, in the Chelsea section of Manhattan. Franko whistled, and the high-pitched sound echoed amid the empty streets where car headlights and the harsh yellow glare of street-lights reflected off the wet pavement.

When he started down the block toward his apartment, he saw the neighborhood bag lady, a woman he'd nicknamed Sophia, huddled on the sidewalk in her usual spot, under the awning in front of the liquor store. Franko immediately recognized her familiar red and white checkered blanket. The pattern resembled tablecloths he'd seen in second-rate Italian restaurants. It was wrapped around the woman's shoulders. He wondered why she was all bundled up in the blanket when the night was so sticky and hot. Maybe it was sheltering her from the rain, which had since tapered off to a mist.

As was Franko's custom, at the sight of Sophia, he reached a hand into the tight pocket of his jeans and pulled out a clump of bills. The smallest he had was a ten.

"Aw, what the hell," he said, his gut sagging over his belt buckle and shaking as he laughed, giddy, to himself. "I'm feeling generous tonight."

When Franko approached the woman, she rose to her feet and flung the blanket, draping it over her head. Franko couldn't understand why she was hurrying away and running toward the alley.

"Hey, Sophia. Where are you going?" he called, following after her. "And it's like two hundred degrees out here. What's with the Eskimo-look?"

Sophia turned the corner, swallowed up by the shadows filling the alley.

"Crazy skel," Franko mumbled. He squinted his eyes, staring into the dark narrow passage in search of the woman. He heard what sounded like a distant cry.

"Hey, Sophia. You all right, hon?"

When she didn't answer, Franko tensed. He drew his weapon and stood in the forefront of the alley. Lured by the prospect that something was wrong, he took a few tentative steps. When something stirred, it stole Franko's breath. He almost fired. But when he realized that it was only the powerless cry of a stray kitten near a garbage dumpster, Franko was relieved. He lowered his gun.

"What's up, Sophia? What's with all the cat and mouse tonight?" he said, when suddenly, emerging from the darkness, there it was: the blanket, those red and white squares. The shrouded figure blindsided Franko, colliding into him. The sharp blade of a knife ripped into the ample flesh of his belly. Stunned, Franko gulped down his pain. His finger tightened in reflex on the trigger of the gun, but the bullet escaped its target and got lost in midair. Franko's warm, flabby body collapsed until he landed face up on the pavement. With his eyes opened wide on a shadowy face hanging above him, Franko could feel his pockets being picked. A pair of gloved hands fumbled around his neck and ripped off his gold chain. But then the pressure stopped. The tension released. The weight was lifted. Franko coughed. He touched his abdomen: warm blood, a knife protruding from his gut like a marker. Through his groans, he could hear his attacker's footsteps quickly retreating, lapping through wet puddles. A whisper of wind howled through the dark night air. A hot, humid breeze streamed into the alley and stirred Franko's thin black hair.

# FORTY-SEVEN

She decided to sleep with the television on. And when her head hit the pillow, Rita's mind swirled with the sights and images of the day. All those calls from Billy. The mysteriously silent and missing Franko. Seeing Sergeant Hill again. Things blurred one into the next until she slipped under the power of sleep . . .

She was on the flowery set of the *Dating Game*, the popular, syndicated game show from the sixties and seventies. She was seated behind a partition that hid four bachelors perched atop high barstool-style chairs. Although she couldn't see them from her placement on the set, she had the benefit of unlimited dreamer perspective, as though she were a fly on the other side of the wall.

Seated in the row of high stools was Billy. He was dressed in the same black tuxedo with pink cummerbund that he'd worn on their wedding day.

Franko sat next to him in a red, Mae West-style dress, the same one that Rita had worn for her photo shoot at Universal Studios. Franko, in his comical style, threw the boa around his neck. He batted his eyes, winked and blew Rita a kiss.

Alongside Franko was Sergeant Hill. He was wearing white tights, a baby-blue tutu and matching ballet slippers. He didn't look happy.

And last was Brad Pitt, the movie actor. With his chiseled jaw bone and his hair slicked back, he looked as irresistible as ever.

"Which bachelor will it be?" the distinguished voice of the announcer asked. "Will it be Bachelor Number One? Bachelor Number Two? . . ."

Rita told herself that it was a no-brainer. *Brad Pitt, of course.* But her head and her heart were completely out of synch. She was overwhelmed with confusion.

"Which one will it be?" the announcer's voice rang out again.

Rita felt flushed with perspiration. She knew what she wanted, but for some reason she couldn't articulate the choice. And then, from her dreamer's perspective, she realized that Franko was in distress. The boa he'd been wearing was suddenly choking him. He was trying to loosen it by wedging both his hands between the red feathers and the skin on his neck. But the long, fluffy scarf was growing tighter and tighter and cutting into his flesh. Blood began to spurt out as though an artery had been severed. *Someone help him! He needs help!* His eyes bulged wide. His face was growing pale, cold and gray-looking.

"Pick me, Rita. Pick me," Billy hollered, completely disregarding Franko's struggle. "I'm your husband. There should be no question. You're supposed to pick me."

As Billy tried to rise from the tall stool, the floor beneath his feet had become so slick with the blood pouring out of Franko that Billy slithered down to the ground—

Rita's eyes popped open. Disoriented. *Where am I?*

The glow of the television set permeated the darkened room and illuminated Billy. He was sitting on the edge of the bed, shaking her shoulders.

Rita leapt from his grasp, her heart thrashing.

"Get your hands off me," Rita shouted. "Get away from me!"

When Billy firmed his grasp, she stopped thrashing, realizing that she'd been dreaming.

"What are you doing here?" she said, staring up at him. He reeked of liquor and cigarettes. His hair was falling into his eyes. And his unshaven face looked moist, as if marked by tears.

"I've been pounding on the front door. Didn't you hear me?"

"What time is it?"

"A little after four."

"What are you doing here? What's the matter? What happened?"

Even though Billy's eyes were bloodshot, compassion and true sorrow bore into her gaze. "It's Franko," he told her. "He's dead."

"What? What are you talking about?"

As he tried to convey the details, the news cut through Rita like a nail hammered into a heart made of glass. She took swings at Billy, a demon in the night. Her fists beat savagely against his chest. She screamed and cried, wanting to crush his heart to equal the shattered mess of her own, until her madness was diverted into a wild flood of tears. When she finally surrendered, she was rescued by the stinging comfort of Billy's embrace.

# FORTY-EIGHT

The days seemed to drag on long and endlessly after Franko's death, and Rita felt numb. On the morning of the funeral, Rita, having spent many sleepless nights, rose at five. She showered and washed her hair. Then she tiptoed through the apartment, the sound of her footsteps traipsing softly over the creaky wooden floors as she fixed herself a cup of tea.

Billy was asleep on the sofa. She had let him back in the night he delivered the news about Franko and ever since, she didn't have the strength to ask him to leave again. At least not yet.

Armed with her tea, she closed the door to the bedroom and settled herself into the recliner chair by the window. She pulled her silky robe around her seeking its softness. The city seemed like a ghost town at dawn, and it had been a long time since Rita had sat and watched it awaken. The only thing that would offer her heavy heart a cure would be a good long talk with Franko, like the ones they used to share while working the Lexington Avenue Line. But those days were gone, so she resorted to the next best thing. She dialed her mother, knowing she'd already be awake.

Tina was always early to rise and her sleepy, "Hello," gave Rita some comfort.

"Why did this have to happen?" Rita cried into the phone, blotting her tears. "If only I'd been able to track him down that night, maybe he'd still be alive."

"If only. If only. You can't keep blaming yourself. It's not your fault that Franko was killed. We all have to die of something. Some disease, some accident—"

"But it wasn't an accident. It was murder. A gruesome murder."

"All murder is gruesome. To be taken before your time, in such a horrible way . . . I'm so sorry, Ree," Tina said, a catch in her voice. "Any news on them finding that escaped convict yet?"

"Yeah, they picked him up late last night in Queens. Charged him with the murder. He's probably already on his way back to Sing-Sing, where he belongs."

"Let's hope they keep him there, so you can sleep easier. You are sleeping, aren't you?"

"Hardly."

"Well, you have to try. You have to keep your strength up," her mother said. "I know you're overwrought, but I've been meaning to ask you, how do things stand with you and Billy?"

"I really haven't had time to think about it, Ma."

Rita had been wondering how long it would take her mother to start grilling her with questions. Amid the shock of Franko's death, Rita, in her vulnerability, had finally slipped and told Tina that she and Billy had separated for a while. Her mother seemed genuinely troubled to learn the news and surprisingly, she had yet to pass judgment. But then again, Rita didn't offer details, and she never mentioned that Billy had hit her.

"Are you planning on taking him back?"

"He came with me to the funeral home both nights, but I was scarcely aware of his presence. I mean, he's here, but we're not discussing our marital problems right now."

"Maybe it's better. One crisis at a time," her mother said. "Has he been spending the night?"

"Sleeping on couch."

"No more arguing?"

Rita was lost in thought. Even though Billy had stood by her side the past few days, she'd paid him very little attention outside of noticing that he'd been smoking and drinking too much and keeping his distance. In the past that had bothered her no end. But now, it didn't even seem to matter.

"Mom, I think it's over," Rita said.

"Over?"

"Please don't give me a litany of *I told you so,* but I think we're headed for divorce."

Rita took note of Tina's unusual silence.

"Ma, are you there? Doing cartwheels in the kitchen?"

When her mother still didn't respond, Rita said, "Ma, could you say something?"

"I don't know what to say. I had no idea things were this bad," she told Rita. "Why didn't you let on? Why didn't you tell us sooner?"

"Because I didn't want to worry you and Dad."

"We're your parents. It's our job to worry."

"All I know is that since the day we got married, this relationship has taken everything out of me. And right now, I'm tired of trying to make it work."

When Rita heard Billy knock on the bedroom door, that familiar rush of fear and dread returned. She hadn't missed it.

He wedged open the door and slipped his head through. When he saw that she was on the phone, he pointed toward the bathroom and mouthed, "The hallway door is locked."

Rita nodded and motioned for Billy to come in. The apartment had only one bathroom, but access could be gained through either of two, lockable doors. One door was off the living room and the other was inside the bedroom.

"Listen, I better go, Ma."

With a towel draped over his shoulder, Billy quietly walked

through the bedroom and closed the bathroom door behind him.

"Is he right there?" her mother asked.

"Billy just got up. We're gonna have some breakfast before we head out to church. I'll talk to you later."

Rita hung up the phone. She heard Billy turn on the squeaky faucets of the shower and the water blast on. With steam rising from beneath the door, she sipped her tea and kept her sights out the window. She gazed down at the children's park on the corner. Beyond the sway of lonely looking swings and the dull finish that darkened the curve of the slide loomed the elevated subway tracks. As daylight burned away the dawn, Rita could hear the train cycles already starting. Whistles blew in the distance, and the noise grew louder as subway cars thundered by on ruthless schedules. As each train approached, she could feel a vibration beneath her feet and see sparks from the rails sprinkling down onto the blighted little shops and the shadow-filled streets below. It had been a long time since Rita had stopped and watched and listened—really listened—to the rumbling siren calls that awakened the city each morning.

In all the months that she'd been working in Transit, she must've become immune. This time of day, the elevated tracks were etched like dark silhouettes against the brightening morning sky. The wrought iron structures, with intricate arrays of joists and cross beams, looked like complicated pen and ink drawings—ink-blot Rorschach tests. From day to day, the configurations always looked different, depending on the light and Rita's mood. Sometimes, the structures took on the beauty of an abstract sculpture. But today, they more nearly resembled the bars of a stark, cold prison cell that seemed to be holding Rita captive.

# FORTY-NINE

Rita's knees knocked behind the altar pulpit. She stared down at the words she'd written for Franko's eulogy. The index cards quivered in her fingertips, but glancing at the notes was simply an idle gesture. It wouldn't have mattered if the cards were blank. She knew what she wanted to say. She'd dredged the words from her soul and had gone over them countless times in her mind. But now, she wondered if this moment was real. *Is this me? Am I here, standing before this full-house congregation? Am I really preparing to say goodbye to my former partner, my mentor, my friend?*

She peered over at Franko's casket in the center aisle of Holy Mother of God Church located in Breezy Point, the Irish section of Queens. She stared out into the pews, where rows of police officers were outfitted in their dress blues and white gloves. *How am I ever going to get through this without breaking down and losing it?* Before she began speaking, she reached toward her neck, searching for the chain that held her half of the New York Yankee heart. When her fingers found the charm, a sense of peace descended upon her as if Franko's spirit had lifted her burden of fear.

"My first day riding the rails as a Transit cop, Franko gave me three pieces of advice. Number one: always look like you know what you're doing. Number two: never take yourself too seriously. And number three: don't ever think you're going to change the world. It was good advice and wisdom I've actually drawn from in preparing this eulogy for my dear friend. However, I see now that Franko had it partly wrong. For in fact, you can change the world. Franko changed the world. Maybe not the whole world, but he changed *my* world. And I know he changed the world of so many others who knew and loved him."

Word by word, Rita gained strength, and staring out into the sea of grief stricken faces, she felt as though her friend were standing right there beside her. What fun she and Franko would've had gossiping after the fact about who showed up and who didn't, and who sat next to whom.

Franko's parents were in the first pew. Rita saw a red-headed woman with tears steadily streaming down her face. Beside her was a portly man with slicked back hair who looked strikingly like Franko would have looked, had he lived to see his sixties.

Seated behind them, before the orderly rows of blue-outfitted policemen and women, was one long pew filled with well-groomed and manicured, neatly dressed men wearing designer suits. Rita suspected that these men were the only other people walking the face of the earth who were privy to Franko's well-kept secret.

"I don't know why things turned out the way they did for Franko. I can't believe it was his time to bid us farewell . . ."

Rita's voice trembled. When she glanced up, she continued with the eulogy, but her thoughts were diverted by the intensity of Billy's stare, which had always been a barometer of love for Rita. The once clear blue of his gaze now appeared murky, and as she tried to swim through a riptide of her thoughts and emotions—the Billy of before versus the Billy of now—she suddenly held a clearer vision of him. The love she once felt for Billy filled her chest. But that love was now diluted by pain and hurt. She realized that an undercurrent of fear and loathing had become embedded at the core of their relationship. Her heart lurched; it ached. She knew that all that had come between them could no longer be lightly erased. And with Billy now a distance apart from her, Rita wondered if that's where he should stay. Perhaps things that look good at a distance should stay at a distance. Once you move in too close, all the flaws and imperfections become more glaringly real.

"Franko once said, and I quote very loosely, 'When my time comes, it comes, and I'll do my best to be ready to go. After all, if the good Lord has a beer waiting for me with my name on it, I want to drink it with Him in Paradise while it's still ice cold— and on the house.' "

In sharing Franko's words, Rita had opened an emotional pressure valve that allowed the mourners to come up for air. She joined them in a hearty laugh, and as she wiped some stray tears, her vision stumbled upon Gary Hill. His flaxen hair was shining like gold in the sun-drenched church. When he winked at her, it gave her the strength and support she needed to finally wrap things up.

"I think I'll miss the laughter the most," Rita said, directing her words toward Franko's casket. "Cheers, Franko. Have one for all of us. And save one for me."

Gooseflesh rose up like a rash through Rita. She gathered her cards and stepped down from the lectern. The hard part was over.

# FIFTY

Billy left for the station house immediately following the church service. At least one of the Quinns had to report for normal duty that day, and Billy offered to do so without Rita having to ask. The district had been very accommodating to the far-reaching implications of the tragedy, and Rita was able to switch shifts—three in the afternoon until eleven at night—so she could go to the cemetery and attend Franko's repast.

A procession of bagpipers played mournful Irish hymns while the pallbearers carried Franko's casket from the church to the cemetery up the street. After the gravesite service was over, Rita waited for everyone to leave to say her final farewells. Staring at Franko's casket and inhaling a scent of flowers and fresh-turned earth, Rita thought she was alone, until she felt a soft hand on her shoulder. She turned. It was Sergeant Hill.

When he said, "You paid your friend a fine tribute today," Rita stiffened and started to cry.

"I'm sorry," he said. She could tell he felt awkward, especially by the way he tried to stretch a comforting arm loosely around her shoulder. "You've got to get it out. It's the only way you're going to deal with this and heal."

When Rita finally pulled herself together, Gary Hill let her go, and they stood a step apart. She dried her eyes with a tissue and wiped her nose.

"Where's Billy?" he asked.

"He went into work. It's better he's not here."

"Why's that?"

"Don't pretend like you don't know," she said. "I'd imagine that my faltering marriage has been hot gossip around the district."

"Yeah, well, there has been some talk." Gary twirled his police hat in his hands, revolving it as though he were slowly turning a wheel. "It's just that when I saw you with him at the wake, I wondered if you two were back together."

"No. We're not." Rita's tone was adamant. "I don't know what we are, outside of going through the motions. I'm still too numb about Franko to sort out my marriage."

"I know it probably doesn't feel like it right now, but things will settle down again. The dust will clear, and you'll figure everything out." Gary offered a consoling nod. His short golden hair swayed softly in the breeze like a field of wheat in an open, restful prairie. "And although I could never fill Franko's void, if you need to talk, I'm a pretty good listener."

"I know," she told him. "Thanks, Sarge."

As Rita and Sergeant Hill started away from the gravesite, someone was loitering in the cemetery, smoking a cigarette, obscured behind a nearby grave statue. The monument was tall and capped with a solemn-looking concrete angel whose wings were broken off as if they'd been clipped.

Billy hadn't gone in to work, nor was he planning to. Deep down, he'd secretly thought that with Franko gone, he'd be rid of his nemesis, his competition, once and for all. But now it seemed as though the good sergeant was already stepping in to fill Franko's void. How could Rita do this to Billy? To them?

When she and Gary Hill were far enough away, Billy walked over to Franko's gravesite and deliberately tossed his smoldering cigarette down upon the temporary grave marker. He twisted the toe of his boot, grinding the sole upon the marker, until the cigarette was stamped out and flattened. The time for watching and waiting was over. Billy decided he'd had enough. It was time to take action.

# FIFTY-ONE

Rita soon learned that an Irish repast is much different from an Italian repast. She swiveled her sights around the plain, wood-tone country kitchen with floral wallpaper at the O'Malleys' family home and knew that if her mother were present, she would've had a stereotyping field day.

At an after-funeral gathering, Italians usually have a table laden with food—pasta, meatballs, chicken parmigiana, salad, bread and desserts galore. Maybe a jug or two of red and white wine would be thrown into the mix. But the Irish did things differently. The centerpiece of the feast was the dining table, which was laden with liquor bottles in various shapes, colors and sizes, many of which were already empty, even at eleven-thirty in the morning. Rita seemed to be the only one who fixed a plate of food, and she wasn't even crazy about corned beef and cabbage. Billy had forced her to try it once, and she'd thought once was enough. But when you're stressed and famished . . . any port in a storm, Rita thought.

"Here you go, Twinkle Toes," Sergeant Hill said, handing Rita a white wine spritzer with a cherry resting in the bottom of the glass. Although it was just the two of them huddled on a couple of folding chairs set away from the crowd, he held up his beer and asked her to make a toast.

"To Francis O'Malley," she said. "One of the best of New York's finest."

"To Rita Del—" Hill caught himself and quickly corrected

215

his faux pas. "To Rita Quinn. And to justice—for all!"

The two sipped their drinks. Then Rita turned her attention to the plate on her lap and started to cut up her corned beef. It was much tastier than she had remembered.

"I was a real bastard with you in the academy, wasn't I?" Gary asked.

Rita swallowed and blotted her mouth with a napkin. The laugh lines around Sergeant Hill's eyes stayed deeply etched in her mind. She was beginning to really like this soft, lighter side of him.

"Aw, it's all right, Sarge. I knew you were just doing your job."

"Yeah, but I really busted your chops. I gave you such a hard time. I just want you to know that I'm sorry about that."

Rita put a hand over her heart as if his words had just knocked the wind out of her.

Gary appeared greatly amused by this.

"Apology accepted," she told him. "If it wasn't for you, I wouldn't be here right now. And I would never have met Franko . . ."

Rita stopped herself. Maybe it was because it was still so raw, but would she ever get used to the idea that Franko was no more? *Was he really gone?*

"It's funny how things happen, isn't it? How life can change just like that." Gary snapped his fingers to emphasize his point.

Rita said, "It must've been hell for you when your wife died."

"Well, it wasn't easy, that's for sure," he told her. "In the beginning I went on all kinds of guilt. I blamed myself for a lot. The wasted time and all that. You never really get over losing somebody you love, but life goes on. You'll see."

Gary Hill stopped talking when Rita's new partner, Officer Walter Adamsky, interrupted.

"I know this is a big imposition, Ree, but any chance a couple of the guys and I could crash at your place? They've jockeyed things around for us to do a graveyard shift. It's a long way back to Long Island, and we have to report to the station in a few hours. Maybe we could get a couple of winks at your place?"

"Sure," Rita agreed. "Billy's at work. So if you guys don't mind the sofa and a lumpy old pull-out, it's yours. I'm gonna leave in a little while, so you can all follow me back to the Bronx."

After Adamsky thanked her, he left Rita and Gary Hill to pick up where they left off.

"You get along with everyone, don't you?" Hill said.

"Just about everybody. Except Billy."

"Don't go by him," he told her. "Ever since 9/11, Billy's changed. He's been more moody and erratic. Everybody knows it."

"9/11? But he wasn't on the front lines."

"No, but he lost some buddies, like we all did. And just the idea of being on the force during the terror attack—it changed a lot of cops. The whole mortality thing. Some guys just can't deal with it. All that post traumatic stress disorder. The horror stories from Ground Zero, they spooked a lot of guys. Enough that some went off the deep end, trying to escape with gambling, sex and drugs. In Billy's case, he drinks too much. He always did, but ever since 9/11, his reputation for not holding his alcohol has gotten even worse. And I guess you could say he already had a strike against him. Alcoholism is in his blood. It runs in the family."

"How do you mean?"

"If you thought Billy was bad, his old man was probably ten times worse. A real firecracker. From the time I was a kid, my father always warned me to stay away from Mr. William Morrison Quinn, the Second."

"Your father?"

217

"My dad and Billy's dad were on the force at the same time. In fact, Billy and I went through the academy together."

"I didn't know that."

"Yeah, we've known each other a long time, since we were kids. We grew up on the same block in the Bronx, but I wouldn't exactly call us *friends*. Lots of skeletons in the Quinn family closet," he told her. "Billy's dad was a mean drunk. Didn't give a damn about his wife or their five kids. If he wasn't at work, he'd be at the bar. Story goes that one night, Mrs. Quinn had enough. She got so ticked off, she locked the front door on him. Well, when he got home and couldn't get in, he went nuts. Shot the lock off and beat up on the missus. Held the whole family at gunpoint and wouldn't let anybody in to take her to the hospital. One of the neighbors called the cops and my father hightailed it to the scene. Billy's dad had gone completely berserk, and it took hours to talk sense into him."

An eerie chill swept through Rita. "What happened after that?"

"Wife panicked. Didn't press charges. She couldn't, really. Things went back to normal, at least *normal* for the Quinns."

"What did the department do?"

"What could they do?" Gary shrugged. "They gave Billy's dad a slap on the wrist, kept a lid on it and waited for things to blow over. Police have a habit of protecting their own."

Rita was quiet for minute, mulling over what Gary Hill had just told her.

"What are you thinking?" he asked.

"What a nightmare. And Billy's poor mother. Why did she stay with Billy's father all that time? They were only divorced a few years ago, weren't they?"

Gary nodded. "Sometimes you get used to things, even if they're lousy. But the longer you hang in there, the harder it is to get out."

Rita bobbed her head and wondered about all that Gary Hill had said. Was he warning her?

# FIFTY-TWO

Rita did a double take when she drove past Finnegan's Pub and saw Billy's red Mustang parallel parked in front.

"What the hell!" she murmured aloud in the car. She was heading back to the apartment, grateful that the other guys were following in cars behind hers and couldn't see or hear her.

Billy had lied to her. He had obviously not gone in to work. He was probably drinking himself into oblivion. That seemed his regular pattern lately. And being reminded of that again, Rita felt that it was official. The plug on her marriage had been pulled. Now it was just a matter of time until their relationship stopped breathing on its own.

When they arrived at the apartment, she settled Adamsky and the other two officers on the couch and the pull-out in the living room. If they were spared interruptions, they might all get at least two solid hours of sleep. It was better than nothing.

Rita closed the door to the bedroom and dropped the blinds. She changed into her nightshirt, crawled beneath the covers and pulled a sleep mask over her eyes. But she couldn't wind down. She couldn't relax. She kept replaying what Sergeant Hill had told her about Billy and his family. *How violent? How disturbing? Maybe it's in the genes?* She tossed and turned, flipping over her pillow, trying to find the cool side. She finally gave up, ripping off the sleep mask and sitting up in bed. She kept thinking about Gary Hill. He had been so caring and tender about her loss. She wanted to hear the steady, disciplined cadence of his voice again.

She reached for the phone.

When she got his machine, she left a message: "Just wanted to thank you for everything, Sarge. It's been a tough couple of days, but it's good to know there are people out there who understand and care. I'm going to try and get a few hours of sleep, but I'd like to take you up on that offer to talk. It might help clear my head. Could we meet later? Maybe grab a bite at that pizzeria. Give me a call when you have a chance."

Rita hung up the phone and tried to settle back down, but she continued to toss and thrash about in the empty bed. She was finally starting to doze when the phone rang.

When she picked it up, Gary Hill was on the other end. He lightened the mood and joked, telling her that when she called, his cell phone lit up with the stored image of her number scrawled on the palm of his hand.

"I had forgotten that I'd taken the picture, so I didn't realize at first what I was looking at," he said, the two of them sharing a laugh as they agreed to meet. They set up a time and confirmed the place.

But Rita's plans were about to change. Billy's red Mustang was parked in front of Finnegan's Pub, but Billy himself was not there. Through the tiny crack of the slightly opened bathroom door, Billy fixed his eyes on his wife. She was resting like Sleeping Beauty. In his warm, sweaty hand, he palmed the cold steel of his revolver. The fairy tale was about to end.

# FIFTY-THREE

She didn't know how long she had been sleeping, but when she awoke, she did so with a start. It felt like a body had fallen headlong from the ceiling and landed atop hers. Instinctively, Rita tried to sit up, but a great weight kept her pinned down. She could feel the cold steel barrel of a gun jamming smack, dead-center into her forehead.

Her sleep shield was ripped off. Rita found herself staring into Billy's crazed, mottled red face. His wet hair was plastered against his sweaty forehead. His pupils were pinpoints, and the whites of his eyes were blazing pink.

"Damn you, Rita. You bury one and then you start a whore-house!" Billy slammed his fist against Rita's face. White noise, like static, filled her vision. "This is *my* apartment."

"*Our* apartment," she screamed as Billy's legs caged her body. He pressed his free hand roughly over her mouth.

He yelled, "Shut up! You can stop your screaming. No one can hear you." His foul-smelling breath smashed into Rita's face like another blow. "I've already taken care of your little boyfriends in the living room. They bailed on you."

Rita wiggled her body from side to side beneath Billy's, desperate to free herself. But she was trapped.

"And now you think you're gonna sink your claws into Sergeant Hill? Well, I've got news for you."

Rita's heart banged in her ears. She flashed her pulsing eyes wider in silent plea. Her injured face was throbbing, hot.

"What? You're gonna tell me you're just friends? That's bull! How much is he gonna like his little girlfriend now?" Billy took the gun and slammed it into her face, right into her nose.

Everything started spinning into a swirl: Billy, the bed, the windows, the walls. When it all stopped, Rita felt a cold, numbing sensation in her face and then warmth. She was bleeding. And with that realization came a surge of energy that ramped up her adrenaline. With all her might, she broke one of her arms free. She flailed at Billy, striking the gun out of his hand. He grabbed both of her arms and pinned her onto the bed.

"We're still married, Rita. Don't you forget you still have *my* ring on your finger."

Rita gasped for breath under the weight of him. He thrust his mouth against hers and pried open her lips with his tongue. The taste of him repulsed her. He was swallowing her up, practically smothering her. In desperation, she sank her teeth into his tense, furtive tongue. When she bit down, it was like a mousetrap snapping shut on a frozen pat of butter. But it worked. He jerked away and when he raised the back of his hand to take another swipe at her, his grip loosened enough for her to break free.

She scrambled out from under him. She leapt out of the bed, into the hall, until she stumbled through the living room and swung open the door. It shattered against the wall behind it.

Taking three steps at a time in a single arc, she burst through the foyer of the apartment building. Daylight. Back on the street. While she hurried down the front stoop, Adamsky and the two other officers sprang from crouched positions alongside the building, their weapons drawn. They grabbed her, trying to hold her back. It felt like a million gangly arms were reaching out to save her, but in her mind Rita kept running and running and running. She never wanted to stop.

# FIFTY-FOUR

"I'm pressing charges this time. No ifs, ands, or buts," Rita said from her stretcher in the emergency room.

"I understand how upset you are. And you have every right to be. But just hold your horses." Captain Steuben pressed his opened palms toward the floor in an effort to calm Rita. "Before you do anything, I need to check with Internal Affairs to figure out how they want us to proceed."

"Internal Affairs? What do they have to do with a domestic dispute?"

"When both parties involved are cops, legally possessing weapons, the rules change."

"Oh, yeah? In whose favor?" Rita winced as the doctor clasped both of his hands around her face. He was working hard to anchor it steady so he could tend to the numerous contusions, broken bones and blood vessels.

"Look, I'm not minimizing what's happened here," Captain Steuben said, hedging. "But there are extenuating circumstances at work."

"Like what?"

"Like your husband in hot water. He's in over his head. He has more serious problems than either of you are aware of."

"What kind of problems?" Rita's head was trapped between the doctor's hands as if in a vice, and she was only able to shift her eyes toward the captain.

Captain Steuben shot Rita a look that indicated he wasn't

about to discuss this further in front of the doctor and the other emergency room personnel. He waited until they finished, then pulled the curtain around him and Rita, who was hooked up to intravenous antibiotics.

"I'm not at liberty to go into details, but I will tell you that Billy has been named in a police corruption probe. I.A. has been looking into it."

"Well, what did he do?"

"It's what he's *accused* of doing. He's only a suspect for now. But because I.A. is embroiled in an on-going investigation that might implicate Billy and others, they're in charge. For now, my hands are tied. That's why I'm going to have to ask you to be patient."

"Patient? Take a look at my face."

"I know, but as awful as this is for you, Billy's actions today might only be the tip of the iceberg."

The gravity of Captain Steuben's words and his tone suddenly curbed Rita's defensiveness.

"Now here's what I propose we do. First, you'll give me a statement, and as soon as I.A. gets back to me, we'll see about pressing charges. In the meantime, I'll place you on temporary disability. Go to Jersey and stay with your parents. I'll be in touch in a few days, and we'll take it from there."

"But what about clothes? My purse, my weapon?"

"Adamsky's already at the apartment. He's getting some of your belongings together, and he'll drop them off before you're discharged. If I were you, I would stay away from the apartment, at least until things cool down."

Captain Steuben was take-charge and matter-of-fact. He had obviously deliberated over this situation and had devised what he believed was a solid game plan. But that didn't stop Rita from continuing to question him.

"But why am I being forced out? Why should I be punished?

What about Billy? What if he tries to kill me again?" Rita spouted these questions in one long stream, without taking a breath.

"There's already a temporary restraining order against Billy. And for now, he's in our custody. I'm going to question him myself. And believe me, after I get through with him, he won't come within a millimeter of you."

"How can you be sure?"

"You've got to trust me on this, Rita. I'm looking out for you. We all are. Now just sit tight and get well. And I will have to ask you to stay mum on the situation with Billy. What I've shared with you today is strictly confidential. If word gets out, it could ruin the whole I.A. investigation."

Captain Steuben turned on his heels and pulled open the curtain with a loud *swoosh!* After he disappeared, Rita picked up the mirror from her tray table and gasped at her own reflection. The teardrops that escaped felt like acid burning the cuts on her face, and the pain only made her cry harder.

# FIFTY-FIVE

Seventy-two hours after the assault, Rita's father and her Uncle Mike offered to go to the Bronx and pick up the rest of Rita's things. But when they arrived at the apartment and tried Rita's key, they discovered that the lock on the front door had already been changed. When Rita called Captain Steuben to see what he could do on her behalf, he told her that Billy was not responding in the way they'd hoped.

"Legally, he's within his rights. Possession is nine-tenths of the law," the Captain said. "Unfortunately, we're going to have to wait and see. I'm banking on the fact that once I.A. finally sits down at the table with Billy, he'll show his cards and start cooperating, across the board."

"And when is that gonna be?"

"Hard to say," Captain Steuben told her. "But I can assure you, we're all working on it."

For now, *wait and see* seemed the only recourse left for Rita. She had no idea that when she'd fled the apartment, she'd left her home for good. And while part of her was angry, another part was relieved to simply let go and leave the past, and everything from it, behind.

Maybe her feelings were colored by her captivity in New Jersey. The suburbs became a stress-free oasis where Rita slept, sometimes twelve hours at a stretch, and indulged in brainless TV. She was relieved that her mother was there to help change her bandages and cook three square meals a day. And all the while, Rita remained grateful that the phrase "I told you so" never once passed between Tina's lips.

Amid her perpetual state of healing, Rita kept in touch with Adamsky every few days and asked him to keep the troops informed about her progress. He was eager to help the cause. But when other calls started pouring in, including several from Sergeant Hill, she just didn't have the will to answer. She felt too emotionally wounded and humiliated to talk to anyone—to keep rehashing details and explaining what had happened. With so many important decisions to make about what would be next for her life, she needed room and time to think.

Whenever she started to feel overwhelmed, she'd reach for her badge wallet and, as if venerating some sacred relics, she'd finger her half of the Yankee charm and slip out Franko's note. That small, folded piece of paper had been read and re-read so many times that the creases were worn and splitting. Somehow holding the note in her hands and trailing the sight of Franko's handwriting on the page restored a sense of calm and peace.

It was after the bandages were removed that Rita finally decided it was time to file for divorce, so she paid a retainer and an attorney started to work on her behalf.

One morning about two weeks into her sojourn in Jersey, Rita heard the doorbell. She was still in her nightshirt, lounging in bed and on the phone, going over preliminary details with the paralegal from the lawyer's office, when she heard a familiar voice talking to her mother in the vestibule.

"Oh, so you work with Rita. How nice of you to drop by and see her."

"I feel so bad about what's happened. I've tried to phone numerous times, but she hasn't returned my calls. I hope you don't mind that I've just shown up like this."

*Is that Gary Hill? Sarge? What's he doing here?* The paralegal was saying something about making a list of assets, but Rita was too busy trying to hear the conversation happening downstairs.

"I'm sorry, but I have to go. I'll call you back," Rita said, switching off the phone and leaping from bed. She wedged the bedroom door open a crack and tried to listen.

"I was in the area and thought that maybe I could say a quick hello. I promise not to tire her out or anything."

*In the area? He lives in Long Island and works in Manhattan. Who is he kidding?*

Rita's heart flipped somersaults when she realized that it was, indeed, Gary Hill talking to her mother. She hightailed it to the mirror and ripped a brush through her hair, trying to corral the frizzy, unruly mess. Then she sat at her dressing table and applied a thick coat of base make-up. This time her efforts were futile. The make-up only drew more attention to the assortment of bruises and scabs on her face and the black-and-blues encircling her puffy eyes.

When Rita heard a knock on her bedroom door, she said, "Come in."

"There's someone downstairs to see you," her mother said. "Another Irishman, I think."

"Irishman?" Rita felt her eyebrows knot.

"Not *the* Irishman. He'll never be welcome in this house again," she said. "Some other Irish guy. Gary somebody."

"Hill?"

Her mother nodded

"Ma, he's not Irish. Hill's a British name. Isn't it? Look at that comedian that you and Dad used to love, Benny Hill."

"No, I can spot a meat-and-potatoes-man a mile away," she said. "Who is he? And what's your relationship with him?"

Rita had been wondering when this overly inquisitive side of her mother would finally re-emerge. Tina had more adept interrogation skills than some detectives.

"I work with him," she told her.

"Is he the reason Billy beat you to a pulp?"

Rita shot her mother an appalled look. "What exactly are you insinuating, Mother?"

"You know what I'm insinuating."

Rita put up her right hand. "He's a friend. That's all. Nothing else."

"You're not divorced yet. Don't add to the confusion in your life."

"Yeah. I hear you, Mom," Rita said, turning her off.

"Then I'll tell him you'll be right down."

Rita sighed at her reflection in the mirror. She thought she might cry. "How can I see him? Look at me?"

"If he can't deal with the way you look, then that's *his* problem. Besides, what difference does it make how you look? I thought he was just a friend."

"He is. But you can be concerned about your appearance with your friends."

Tina scowled, then shot Rita a look that telegraphed, "And I was born yesterday," as she left the room and closed the door behind her.

Rita flung off her lived-in nightshirt and searched through a pile of clothes on the floor for something to wear. She jumped into a pair of jeans ready to be washed and unraveled a tank top that had been rolled into ball. She took a whiff. A slight tinge of deodorant, but she threw it on anyway.

The idea of Sarge being in her parents' house, just a few feet away, flipped a switch inside Rita that resurrected her wounded spirit. But she didn't want to appear too anxious or happy to see Sergeant Hill, either to him or to her mother. So she curbed the rapidity of her footsteps as she descended the stairs. But while she consciously forced her exterior to remain cool and calm, her heart skipped several beats when she caught sight of Gary seated at the kitchen table. He looked so different in street clothes, wearing jeans and a polo shirt. When he turned in his chair to greet Rita, his jaw dropped and the color suddenly drained from his face until it matched the white of the Formica tabletop.

"Oh, my God. What the hell did he do to you?" Gary rose to his feet. Flinging his arms open wide, he hurried toward Rita and smothered her in a long, tight hug.

Being close to him, inhaling the musky scent of his aftershave and a trace of minty toothpaste, was the safest Rita had felt in a very long time. But while she stood in his warm, muscular arms, she could see her mother staring suspiciously at them. She was puckering her lips in judgment and no doubt reading something into their embrace.

"Can I get you something to drink, Mr. Hill?" Tina conspicuously cleared her throat in an effort to interrupt them. "A cocktail? A beer?"

"I go by Gary," he told Rita's mom, glancing down at his watch, a big diver's watch. "And no, I don't usually drink before lunchtime."

Rita smirked at her mother, irritated by her baiting.

"But a cup of coffee would be great," he told her.

"Would you like some Bailey's Irish Cream in it?"

Gary looked from Mrs. Del Vecchio over to Rita, perplexed. "No, I'm a purist. I always take my coffee black."

When her mother turned, Rita rolled her eyes and motioned for Gary to follow her to the living room. En route, he said, "Oh, I almost forgot. These are for you." He pulled out a kitchen chair on which sat a generous arrangement of sunflowers. He handed them to Rita.

"Gee, they're beautiful. Sunflowers are my favorite," she said. "Ma, do you think you could put these in a vase for me?"

Tina appeared thrilled to have something to do, and Rita was relieved to have her mother out of her hair for a while. As she led Gary over to the sofa, Rita could tell he kept studying her face. It made her feel self-conscious, and she tried to move her hair in such a way that it might conceal some of her injuries.

"So any idea when they'll let you come back to work?" he asked.

"I hope soon. I'm starting to go a little stir crazy."

"I'm so sorry he did this to you." Gary reached over and with a gentle hand, he brushed some of Rita's long, unmanageably curly hair from her eyes.

The slight touch of his fingers sent a shiver through Rita. When she looked away from him, he said, "I don't know if you've heard, but they've ordered a psychiatric evaluation for Billy, and he's been suspended, without pay, until the results are analyzed."

"It's about time," Rita said.

"Have you pressed charges?"

Rita swung her head. "There's a restraining order against Billy, but no. No charges have been officially filed, not yet. Captain Steuben has advised against it for now."

"Why's that?"

"I don't know. It's complicated. And I can't really get a handle on his motive—if he's really trying to help me, if he's protecting Billy or if it's just c-y-a. I heard a rumor . . . It's just a rumor," Rita said, careful to adhere to the promise she'd made to the captain. "Something about red tape because of an Internal Affairs probe."

"Yeah, well, that rumor is always going around. For as long as I've been a cop, I.A.'s always investigating *something*," Gary told her. "Department bureaucracy, police brutality, corruption. You name it. The problem is that I.A. often moves at a glacial pace. They won't take serious action until they've got all their ducks in a row. That can take forever sometimes."

"Have you heard anything about a probe? Anything about

Billy maybe being in trouble?"

"Well, Gun and Drug Task Force Cops are always top of the list when it comes to I.A. investigations. And after some of the beats Billy has walked over the years, you never know. A lot of cops, even good cops, see too much. The power goes to their heads, and they think they're untouchable. It happens more often than you'd think."

Rita shook her head. "Billy always said that he could never talk about his assignments with the Task Force. I respected that and took him at his word. But now that I've heard the rumor, I'm beginning to wonder if maybe he does have something to hide."

"Well, if the talk is more than just a rumor, you'll know soon enough. For now, you should probably just focus on yourself and what's next. And what *is* next?"

"Oh, I don't even know where to start." Rita sighed and ran her fingers through the tangles of her hair. "I'm filing for divorce. I have to find a new place to live. And the way the department seems to be walking on eggshells with Billy, I have a hunch that when I finally do go back to work, I'll be given a transfer and a whole new rotation."

"Would that be such a bad thing? It might give you a fresh start."

"But why do I have to be the one who is uprooted when everything stays status quo for Billy? I'm the victim here, and yet I feel as though I'm the one being punished."

"I know. It's definitely not fair," he said. "But look at it this way. If I.A. is really onto something, and they very well might be, then they've gotta move slow. Billy has been a cop for a long time. He knows a ton of people. He probably has a slew of favors he could cash in, and that's going to give him leverage in the system. He's not going to be easy to tag and take down."

In the midst of Gary sharing his thoughts, Tina walked into

the living room carrying a tray with coffee and cake. Rita was actually glad to see her. Her presence lightened the mood and kept Rita from suddenly feeling too overwhelmed.

"Let's try to talk again soon," Gary Hill said before he left that day. "It would be nice if you answered the phone or even called me back once in a while."

"I'll work on that," she told him.

His thick, broad arms firmed around her, and she wished she could hang on to him and that feeling of comfort forever.

*Life is so strange.* Rita stood at the storm door, waving to Sergeant Hill as his pickup truck pulled away, cruised down the street and then turned the corner. *Whoever thought that he would be so caring? Whoever thought he'd turn out to be such a nice guy?*

But as Rita began to close the front door, she gasped. A sporty, red car was making a three-point turn up the block.

*Is that a Mustang? Is that Billy's car?*

She stood there trying to get a better look, listening to the distant rev of the engine, its roar filling the air. The driver gunned the transmission. The tires squealed, and the car took off.

*Don't be paranoid. It's just a coincidence. That's all it is,* she reassured herself. When the door clicked closed, she double-checked to make sure the deadbolt was engaged.

# FIFTY-SIX

A few weeks after the divorce papers were filed, Rita signed a lease on a small, one bedroom apartment in New Rochelle and moved in. It was a breadbox compared to the apartment she'd shared with Billy in the Bronx. But it was close enough to the city and just far enough away from the past.

When she finally returned to work, Rita was given a new detail. She was sent back to Transit. Terror alerts throughout the city were on high, and more officers were needed to patrol the rails and conduct random searches and bag checks as passengers filed in and out of terminals. When she learned the only shift available was the midnight-to-eight, on rotating subway lines, Rita decided to eagerly embrace it. She had no one to answer to anymore, and she was convinced that living life in an opposing plane to reality—sleeping days and working nights—would allow her to readjust to things on her own terms.

Her instincts proved valuable. Even with the extra work enforced by the potential of terror threats, the graveyard shift was a lot less stressful than a daytime tour. Fewer people in the subways meant less to contend with, and the schedule of the trains, in and out of each station at regular intervals, restored a much-needed sense of order and structure to Rita's life.

After hours, Rita spent her free time at dance class, and she tried to reconnect with friends she'd let slip away over the course of her relationship with Billy. She also maxed out her credit cards on purchases to decorate the new apartment, and she even began investing in a new wardrobe. She'd dropped to a size three—the skinniest she'd ever been in her life. It wasn't by choice. But rather, an underlying sense of vigilance had diminished her appetite.

She hadn't seen or heard from Billy for weeks, and though physically absent, he constantly invaded her thoughts as if he were still stalking her, watching her from afar, hiding in closets, under the bed or even behind the closed shower curtain. She still feared that at any moment, she could turn the corner and there he would be. He could spring up again, his rage waiting in the wings.

The terror of that near-fatal afternoon—the crazed look on Billy's face like he wanted to kill her—was impossible to shut off. Rita was convinced that some people, people like Billy, never really leave your life. They haunt you even more after they're gone. It left her to slip her revolver beneath the pillow and to keep the lights and the television on while she tried to sleep. All of these efforts became a very bad habit she couldn't break. And nothing could change what she felt. Not even Gary Hill.

He checked on her every day with a phone call both morning and night.

"How you doing there, Twinkle Toes? Having a good day? Hanging in?"

Being able to count on hearing his voice was a bulwark against Rita's loneliness. When they shared the same days off, Rita and Gary went to dinner and the movies. Together, they would laugh, debate and find contentment just being with each other. Even the silences proved companionable. Gary was more cerebral and tended to be more rigid, while Rita's style was more outgoing and carefree. Despite their differences, they shared an instinctual type of shorthand, where they often finished each other's sentences. Unlike Billy, Gary had no inhibitions when speaking about the job, the pressures, the dirt and the politics of the force. Sharing his company was a relief, as if his presence in Rita's life allowed her to come up for air and breathe again.

But it was through spending time with Gary and feeling the bond between them grow tighter that Rita began to question her past. She tried to understand what it was, exactly, that drew her to Billy. Why had he become so important to her? From her perspective now, and especially in the context of her relationship with Gary, it was clear that she and Billy really had nothing in common outside of the police force. Was Franko right? Did her attraction to Billy stem from her being enthralled and starry-eyed with an older man, a man in uniform, a decorated cop who was attentive to her? Had she made Billy into the person she needed him to be in order to fulfill some need within herself rather than seeing him for who and what he really was? She kept turning the horror of the situation over in her mind, trying to take away some positive lesson from the relationship that would make her future better and brighter. But would she ever get past the hurt and fear?

Caution. Restraint. It would take a conscious effort on Rita's part to do things differently this time. She would need to keep the channel open between her head and her heart. But once Rita became free of the past, old strings and attachments, she knew that her relationship with Gary would need to move to the next level. He never said so, but Gary sent signals that he wanted more. And it was more than Rita was ready or willing to give. How could she possibly allow herself to get closer to him when she was so afraid that she might lose him, too, just like Franko?

When she and Gary finally talked about their relationship and she shared her feelings, he said, "Life is risk, Rita. Nothing's permanent. And don't you see what you're doing? In trying to keep Billy and all he represents out of your life, you're making yourself a prisoner."

# FIFTY-SEVEN

*Every day is payday when you come back to being your own boss.*
That's what Billy Quinn thought as he headed toward his old
stomping ground in Harlem.

It felt good being a free man again. For more than a month,
he'd been successful at keeping a low profile. As required, he'd
gone for counseling with the department shrink, and he gave an
Academy Award-winning performance of repentance and atone-
ment to the powers that be regarding the incident with Rita. It
was concluded that Billy's mind was even and his emotions, in
check. He was cleared and given a rubberstamp to return to
work, and Captain Steuben and Internal Affairs finally backed
off. Luck was on Billy Quinn's side, and he appeared to have
landed on his feet, as sly as a cat with nine lives.

Things went back to being business as usual, except that
Billy Quinn was now working his beat alone. His last partner,
Rudy Palumbo, had hurt his back and had been assigned to an
administrative detail. This meant that Billy could look forward
to reaping even greater financial rewards from his solo efforts.

With a spry, optimistic bounce in his step, Billy strode down
the street, past the infamous shiny white Cadillac with the
initials M.T. on the license plate. It was parked illegally on the
sidewalk. But not since that very first confrontation had Billy
ever again asked to have it moved.

With his heavy gun belt fastened around his waist and static from his police radio squelching on and off, Billy eyed his watch. Right on time. It was four-thirty in the afternoon. If all went according to plan, he could be in and out of the bodega in five minutes, tops.

"I've got some business to do. Why don't you fellas beat it for a while," Billy told a bunch of street-smart-looking teenagers who were loitering by the front entrance of the shop.

Billy pulled open the door and stepped inside. The place was void of customers but well stocked with soda, beer, junk food and cigarettes. Past the racks of X-rated magazines and condoms, Billy found the well-dressed Mr. M.T. behind the sandwich counter.

"Hey? How's business?" Billy asked, not really expecting the man to answer. "Aren't you glad I'm back on the job?"

M.T. didn't say a word. It was clear he knew the drill, the routine, and he wasn't happy about it. This wasn't a social call. It never was.

When Billy squeezed his body sideways around the counter, M.T. squatted down. He lifted a large sheet of plywood that covered the back area of the floor behind the counter and revealed a stash of guns and drugs below. M.T. reached into the hollowed-out portion of the floor and pulled out a brick of money.

"Here." M.T. didn't seem happy handing Billy the cash.

"I hear business is booming, so maybe you ought to give me a few more of these today." Billy moved the stack of bills to his ear and thumbed through them. Then he held out the palm of his free hand, waiting for the rest of his hand out.

M.T. sneered, but did as he was expected.

With a stack of money in each hand, Billy gloated. He held up the wads of cash and slowly kissed each one. Then he stuffed the wrapped bundles of green inside his pants. He wound his way through the narrow aisles that led out of the bodega, straightening his hat and whistling like a happy addict who'd just gotten his fix.

Officer Billy Quinn was oblivious to the fact that he was under close surveillance. Based on the little bit of information they'd squeezed out of the Jinx and the confirmations they'd received from Rudy Palumbo, Internal Affairs technicians had installed a video camera inside a phony cable TV box across the street from the bodega. It was able to pick up images inside the store, and those images were beamed digitally to a media-equipped, unmarked police van just a few blocks away.

"Look at that cocky bastard. He's kissing that money like he's gonna make love to it," one of the I.A. detectives said, watching Billy's performance on the video monitor inside the van. "We've been putting the pressure on him for weeks now. You'd think he'd at least be a little discreet."

"Okay, cut. We've got him," another suit said to the techie who was running all the video equipment. "If you could make us a couple of copies of that before we go."

While the I.A. cops waited for their DVDs to be burned, the one detective said, "First Palumbo and now Quinn. They took the bait. I wonder how many more we'll snag before this is over."

"I'd imagine they're like cockroaches," the other detective said. "We might only see one or two for now, but once we start fumigating the place, a whole army of them will start crawling out of the woodwork."

"And now that we can show Quinn how well he photographs, that arrogant s.o.b. is finally gonna make our jobs a helluva lot easier."

# Fifty-Eight

It was getting more serious now. Sergeant Hill even switched his shift so he and Rita could both sign in for the twelve-to-eight A.M. rotation.

"I'm bored. All I do is twiddle my thumbs when I'm not with you," he explained. "I might as well be burning the midnight oil, too."

They worked different districts, but they made it a habit to meet every night at four o'clock in the morning at Rockefeller Center or thereabouts. It just took a few phone calls and a couple of inquiries of "Where are you?" and "What's taking you so long?" and they'd have their dinner breaks together. It didn't matter where they'd go or what they would eat. It only mattered that they were together.

It was easy for Rita to be with Gary, and yet it wasn't. Her uncertainty and the vacillation of her feelings created a constant niggling inside of Rita, a voice of warning: *Be careful. Don't lose yourself for the sake of love. It's not worth it.* And whenever Rita would subtly try to retreat from Gary, the pull and tug of loneliness only deepened her craving for him. No matter how hard she resisted, it was happening again. Rita was falling—counting the hours until she'd be in Gary's presence, checking her phone and texts every few minutes, getting that tingly feeling at the mere thought of him.

They rented a movie one night, but only watched the opening credits roll. With Gary's rock-solid arms holding her while the two of them cuddled on the couch, he brought his face to hers and kissed her slowly and tenderly. Her heart pumped wildly beneath his touch. And it all seemed so right, so inviting. It made her feel warm and wanting, until that voice cried out again from the recesses of her mind: *If you get too close, this could break your heart.* She tried to shut off her doubts, compelling herself to become totally swept up by Gary's caresses and his deepening desire. Yet no matter how much Rita longed to get lost in the moment, Billy was there in her mind, rankling her. She could see and hear him again, lashing out. His presence was like a film slide that had been slipped into a projector at the wrong time—the heft of his body straddling hers while pointing that gun in her face.

"I'm sorry," Rita said, easing out of Gary's embrace. "I can't."

Gary sighed. He smoothed his hair with his fingers. "What's going on?"

"Nothing."

"It's him again, isn't it?"

"He called me today."

"What?" There was a hardened edge to Gary's voice. He sat bolt upright on the couch. "You didn't talk to him, I hope."

"No. But he left messages on the machine to tell me about some new threats launched against Officer Quinn."

"I thought all that stopped after Franko died."

"Me, too. But according to Billy, threatening calls have started to come in at the apartment now. He thought I should know."

"And you believe him?"

"I'm just telling you what he said."

"He's lying." Gary stood up from the couch. He paced to the other side of the room. "Don't you get it, Ree? Don't you see what he's doing? Billy's lonely. He's playing head games. And he's succeeding in manipulating his loving wife all over again."

"I'm not his wife anymore."

"Well, you might as well be."

"In case you forgot, we're legally separated now."

"Yeah, on paper. But he's still got such a damn hold on you."

Tears burst out of Rita. "It's not by choice. You don't understand."

"No, I don't. What is it going to take for you to realize that I'm not Billy? I'm not going to hurt you," he said, sitting next to her on the couch. He reached out to gently touch her cheek, but when she pulled away, a cold, hurt look overtook his face.

She didn't want to be touched. She didn't want to talk. What she wanted was for him to just go away and leave her alone.

"I don't get you. You're one of the strongest, most independent women I've ever met. You weren't dependent on Billy while you were married, and yet you're somehow allowing him to control your life now. I understand that you've been through a really tough time, and I've tried to be patient and loving. But I give up."

The room went still. And the quiet that wedged between them seemed a dangerous sign. Was Gary expecting Rita to lash out, to plead and fight for him? But Rita didn't say a word. She couldn't. She hugged her bent legs to her chest, unable to look at him.

"Ree, I'm sorry, but I can't do this anymore. I can't compete with Billy. I won't. And there just isn't room for three people in this relationship."

Defeated, Gary rose from the couch. He tucked in his shirt, lifted his jacket, which was hung over the back of a kitchen chair, and left. She didn't try to stop him.

After he was gone, Rita crawled into bed and searched for sleep.

Days passed . . .

A week . . .

Two . . .

Gary's absence left her feeling empty, while it also created a growing love and longing for him. Somehow these feelings so engulfed her, they started to ease out and erase her painful memories of Billy. And what she discovered was that when she closed her eyes to sleep, she no longer saw Billy's face, but rather Gary's from their last night together: the turn of his lips, the astonishment of his sad, wounded eyes. Something in her soul lurched. It ached. What had she done? Hadn't being in love with him—his goodness and patience, his heart-wrenching tenderness—made sense when nothing else did? But oh, how she'd let him down and hurt him.

Her phone no longer rang, displaying Gary's number. There were no more texts signed *Sarge*. And whenever she was on duty and took the subway to their stomping ground at Rockefeller Center at four o'clock in the morning, there was no sign of Gary either. Rita's shadow was cast like a ghost as she searched for him, wandering through the dark, lamp-lit streets. But all she found were faces of passing strangers and emptiness staring back at her. Maybe she wasn't supposed to find him. Maybe she was supposed to find herself.

But life is lonely, very lonely, when you're trying to find yourself, and you're not sure just where to look.

# FIFTY-NINE

For almost eighteen hours, Internal Affairs agents kept hitting *stop* on the remote control of the DVD player and rewinding, going back over and over, again and again. Billy Quinn was forced to keep watching himself on the TV screen, his boldness from the money transfer inside that bodega in East Harlem. Add to that even more incriminating evidence gathered from his former partner, Rudy Palumbo, who'd squealed when he, too, was put in the hot seat.

*Palumbo. That little prick! That rat,* Billy thought.

"Whenever you want to start talking, we're listening," the I.A. investigators told Billy.

"I ain't tellin' you guys crap."

"Face it, Billy. We've got you backed into a corner. If you don't start talking, you've got nowhere else to go. Only upstate, and for a very long time."

What other choice did Billy Quinn have? Shouldn't a man try to save himself, if he can?

After twenty-two hours, the walls finally closed in tight enough, forcing Billy, who was worn down and worn out, to cave. He gave them the addresses of where the deals were going down. Then he started naming names of people on the street and the Mean Nineteen, including those of his two best buddies, Officers Tony Sanducci and Dirty Roy McSweeney. They might have been out of the circuit, but if Billy was going down, why shouldn't everyone go down with him?

But it didn't end there.

In exchange for a lesser sentence, Billy took the plea that was offered. He would wear a wire and stick close to the few "friends" he had left, while appearing to be an active member of their exclusive boys' club. The commission needed a few more weeks to coordinate the arrests, and Billy Quinn, now an official I.A. rat, was released on his own recognizance. His job was to bait the traps until there was enough evidence to prosecute the Mean Nineteen to the fullest extent of the law.

# Sixty

The Decree of Divorce arrived in the mail. It was a nondescript, business-sized envelope from the Supreme Court of the State of New York.

Rita slipped her finger beneath the seal and opened it. When she saw the date next to the official signature on the decree, the hair on the back of her neck rose.

The divorce became finalized exactly one year to the day that she and Billy were married.

*What the heck are the odds of this? And is it a good or a bad omen?*

Rita had left everything to the lawyers, who'd hired a mediator after they ran into a snag regarding the couple's grounds for divorce. When Rita initially filed the paperwork charging Billy with "physical abuse," he flatly denied granting her the divorce. Things came to a standstill while the legal fees mounted higher and higher.

There was banter back and forth between the two attorneys. After Rita finally consented to grounds of "sexual abandonment," the proceedings ran smoothly. In the end, things moved speedier than she'd anticipated. This was, no doubt, because Rita forfeited the apartment, all of her belongings, and a great deal of pride in exchange for self-preservation. What mattered most was that she knew the truth about Billy, and she was finally free of him. She wanted to banish that part of her life and go back to being Rita Marie Del Vecchio as soon as possible. And now, with the papers signed and officiated, that actually was possible, as even changing her name was included in the retainer she'd paid for the divorce, up front.

Rita stood at the door to her apartment and kept reading and re-reading that decree. She wanted to make sure there wasn't any fine print she was missing—that this was real. It was hard for her to believe that in little over four months, it was over.

Done.

Finished.

The end.

Rita had longed for this day, to hold the divorce papers that made it all official in her hands. But when she'd envisioned this moment, she imagined it would feel different, more significant like a big turning point. Close the book. Clear the slate. But it wasn't so clear-cut or black and white. The feelings were more muddled and gray.

She felt all alone in the world. It was as though she were suddenly unanchored, lost in an abyss, and truly scared. That fear of the unknown forced her tears to drip, one by one, onto the decree, slowly dampening it, until the emotional impact of everything hit her like a punch thrown in the gut. Here, she'd done her damnedest to keep herself together, body and soul, all the while she'd been married to Billy and all through their divorce. But now she let go. She let everything out, unleashing a deluge of bottled up pain and anguish. She cried, gulping, fractured sobs, until she thought she'd never stop.

But she did stop—eventually. And when her eyes were dry, she hung the decree beneath a magnet on the refrigerator. Then she opened the door and pulled out a bottle of champagne that had been chilling since Gary brought it over the night she'd moved into her place in New Rochelle. They'd gone out to celebrate instead, and she decided to save the bubbly for another special occasion. Tonight was that occasion. With Gary absent from her life for nearly a month, she figured that now was as good a time as any. She undid the foil wrap, twisted off the wire securing the top, popped the cork and with the sparkling wine foaming over the top, she took a swig right from the bottle.

"To freedom," she roared, lifting the ice cold bottle of champagne toward the decree tacked up on the refrigerator. "To being Rita Marie Del Vecchio. Again."

She filled a glass and sipped the delicate, golden-colored champagne. Against her palate, it tasted dry and sweet, but she felt empty as the fizz nudged against the lump mounting in her throat. Freedom, she learned, was more fun when you had someone to share it with.

At that moment, she wished that Gary was there. She wished that he would've clinked his glass against hers and savored this milestone with her. But they had been apart for weeks and it made her wish that, when everything started to come undone between them, he would've fought harder for her. And she, for him. Was it too late?

Maybe it was time to find out.

Rita reached for her cell phone. She contemplated the key pad. *Do I or don't I?*

It was only four o'clock in the afternoon and Rita, having made a daytime court appearance for an arraignment, had the next forty-eight hours off. Maybe Gary would join her.

She powered up her phone, hit the button and scrolled through the contacts. Gary's number was still the first one. Top of the list.

*Maybe I shouldn't call him. My contacting him again, after all this time, it might catch him completely off guard. I'd hate it if he sounded defensive. Maybe a text would be better?*

Rita took another sip of the bubbly, the gears in her mind turning. She was gaining confidence. But where, exactly, was her confidence coming from? Receiving the divorce decree?

Indulging in champagne on an empty stomach?
*What have you got to lose? Go for it! Take the leap.*
With fingers busy on the tiny key pad of her phone, she hammered out the text:

> *sarge—need to get over a wall. care to help?*
> *meet me @ TavernOnTheGreen-7pm-2nite? my treat.*
> *xo-the divorcee*

Rita shut her eyes. She blessed herself: forehead-to-chest, shoulder-to-shoulder. With the phone pressed between the steeple of her hands, she gazed heavenward. She said a little prayer. Then she hit the button on the cell marked "send."

# SIXTY-ONE

While Rita Del Vecchio was ripping clothes from the hangers in her closet, trying them on and peeling them off, Internal Affairs was dotting all the i's and crossing the t's. They had finally gathered all the evidence they needed to make their move on the remaining seventeen members of the Mean Nineteen. Some fifty officers simultaneously ambushed dozens of locations. Nine dirty cops were arrested right at their homes and paraded to police cars in their own neighborhoods. Two more cops were raided while on the golf course. And six were read their Miranda rights and taken into custody while on duty.

Billy Quinn was still a free man. He had a little more than forty-eight hours before he had to turn in his gun and badge—and himself—down at District Headquarters. He spent the time he had left drowning his sorrows from a barstool at Finnegan's Pub. Billy knew that from the minute he set foot in District Headquarters, he'd be referred to, then and always, as a rat: someone who *used to be* a cop.

He thought there would be nothing harder, until he was forced to go home later that night, and he carried up the mail.

There it was, a letter from the Supreme Court of the State of New York. A decree of divorce issued on what would have been Rita and Billy's one-year wedding anniversary.

*Nothing like kicking a man when he's already down.*

After all was said and done, only one thing would be certain in all of this. Billy Quinn would no longer have a life to go back to. And whatever life he did have left would surely not be worth living.

# SIXTY-TWO

Rita received three things before she left for Tavern on the Green that night. First there was a delivery from a florist in New Rochelle, a sunflower corsage with a note attached:

> *Your treat?*
> *I'm there.*
> *Sarge*

She was tickled head-to-toe—and relieved. After all, Rita hadn't worn a corsage since her senior prom in high school, and tonight would be an even greater thrill.

The second thing Rita received before she left for Tavern on the Green was a run in her stockings.

And the third was a phone call. Rita had been running late. Thinking it might be Gary on the other end of the line, she'd made the mistake of picking up the phone before the Caller ID and the answering machine kicked on.

"Congratulations, Rita. Looks like you finally got what you wanted."

Upon hearing Billy's voice on the other end of the phone, Rita's heart froze. All those old feelings of being off balance, on guard and nervous suddenly rekindled in her.

"Bet you almost forgot what I sounded like. Right, Ree?"

"What is it, Billy? I'm on my way out," she told him.

"Hot date?"

The line went silent. Rita considered the quiet and let it answer for her.

"Okay, I get it. You want me to mind my own business. Granted," he told her. "I'm really just calling to give you another heads up. I've been getting some more of those threatening calls for Officer Quinn."

Rita was relieved that she was no longer a Quinn, but she wasn't about to go there with Billy. Not now. Instead, she tried to call his bluff. "You know, I checked with the district office. I was surprised to learn that you haven't filed any new reports about this. Why?"

"Well, I did, a while back. But then the calls stopped. I hadn't gotten one in months, but just recently, they've started up again. They're coming in on the home line. And the weird part is, I just changed the number a few weeks ago. I don't know how they keep tracking us down."

*Us?* Rita thought.

"I don't know either," she told him. "But thanks for the heads up."

"I know that they've never suspected that the threats were aimed at you, but you never know. It couldn't hurt to keep watch and stay a little more vigilant."

"Okay, I'll keep my eyes peeled," she told him, trying to end the call.

"I guess you got the divorce papers today."

"Yes, I did."

"Did you notice the date? How the paperwork was processed on our first wedding anniversary?"

"Yeah, some coincidence. Isn't it?"

"Coincidence? Listen to you. The superstitious girl who seeks the advice of astrologers and psychics."

"Well, not anymore, Billy. I've changed."

"Oh, yeah? That's something because so have I."

"Good for you," she told him, now poking earrings into the pierced holes on her earlobes.

"You don't sound like you believe me—"

She cut him off. "Is there anything else, Billy? Because I've really gotta go."

Billy hedged for a moment then said, "You know, I'm sorry about the way things ended between us, Ree."

*Yeah, sure.*

"I-I know I didn't treat you right. I see that now," Billy stuttered, sounding meeker than ever. "And I-I don't want us to hate each other anymore."

"I don't hate *anyone*," Rita told him.

"Well, I'm glad. And now that I finally have you on the phone, I was wondering if maybe I could ask you something?"

*Oh, no. Now what?*

"I thought maybe we could make a deal."

Rita listened more intently. Suspicion seeped into her voice when she asked, "What kind of deal?"

"I was hoping that maybe you'd consider giving me back the wedding band. I mean, it was my great-great grandmother's, and my mother, well, she would really like to keep it in the family."

*A-ha, the ring. Of course!*

"And now that I've packed up all your things, your clothes and books and CDs and all of your pictures and stuff, I thought maybe we could make a swap. An even exchange."

Rita weighed his words. "How come you didn't ask for the ring back during the divorce negotiations?"

"To be honest, there had been a lot going on, and I just didn't think it was proper of me to ask for it back . . ."

*Proper? Since when was "proper" ever a consideration with you?*

". . . It's my mother. She's the one who wants the ring returned. She's been heartbroken about it. So if it makes you feel any better, you'd really be giving it back to her, not to me."

Rita had no qualms about Billy's mother. She never did anything to hurt Rita. And while Rita knew that she could live without her clothes, books and CDs, her pictures—photographs of her parents and her relatives, images from her childhood; photos and yearbooks and scrapbooks from her high school years—those were things she'd really like to have back. What was she giving up by returning that ring? She'd never liked it anyway. And it certainly had no meaning or place in her life anymore. But the sentimental value of those pictures and mementoes . . . they were priceless.

When Rita didn't answer for a while, Billy upped the ante. "I mean, if you don't want or need your stuff, I totally understand. I just figured I'd take a chance before I started throwing everything out."

Billy had pushed the right button. The thought of Rita's pictures sitting in a garbage dumpster or a recycling plant really irked her. "When were you thinking we could make this little exchange?"

"I was hoping very soon. Like tomorrow or even the next day," he told her. "I wouldn't be in such a rush, but the thing is that my girlfriend and I are going to re-do the apartment this weekend. Paint, wallpaper, the works, and I would sort of like to get this stuff out of here. It's not a lot. Just a couple of boxes. I packed them light so they'll be easy for you to carry."

It felt strange hearing Billy say that he had a girlfriend. *Poor thing!*

"Well, let me think about it. We might be able to work something out," Rita told him, eyeing her watch. It was already six-thirty. She'd told Gary seven o'clock. If she didn't hurry, she'd be late. And that wouldn't be a good thing if she was to regain footing in Gary's life. "Let me see if I can dig out the ring. If I find it, then maybe we can set up a time for me to stop over tomorrow. Maybe the afternoon sometime."

"That would be perfect. And I'm really glad we can be grown-up about this, Ree. We've both been through a lot, and I think it's important that we finally sever our ties on a peaceful, positive note. I really don't want there to be any more hard feelings between us."

"I'll call you," Rita said, hanging up.

Was Billy for real? Had he been reading self-help books or something? Had all that departmental counseling worked some kind of a miracle on him and his attitude? Or was his sudden change of heart all to do with that ring? Maybe his mother *was* really pressuring him? Rita couldn't understand Billy. But maybe she didn't have to. Giving the ring back and getting her stuff was a win-win situation, and maybe it would be a good thing for them both to be rid of any attachments to each other once and for all.

Rita might've told Billy that she'd have to dig out the ring, but finding it was much easier than she'd led him to believe. She knew exactly where it was. It was right in her jewelry box, in the ring holder, top tier. She pulled the band from the box and slipped it into the change purse in her pocketbook, vowing to put Billy and her decision on hold until tomorrow. Tonight she had other, more important plans. She slipped on her heels, spritzed herself with perfume and headed for the door.

While Rita was hurrying toward the taxicab parked outside her building, a message was being left on the phone inside her apartment:

"I know where you live, Officer Quinn, and I'm finally going to get you." *Click!*

If Rita hadn't been so late and in such a rush, she might've glanced at the newsstand on the corner. She might've seen the bold-faced words sprawled across the front page of *The Daily News,* the late edition:

### NYPD Busted!

As Rita hopped into the backseat of the cab, she heard someone whistle from behind her. If she wasn't so late, she would've turned and seen that the gesture had come from Billy. He was standing at a payphone near the corner, one of the very last of its kind since the advent of cell phones. With his sights glued to Rita, Billy disconnected the call with a touch of his finger. He had disguised his voice and left the message at what appeared to be the right time. As he replaced the receiver on the cradle, he ogled Rita's mini-skirt and her toned, thin legs rooted in her high heels as they stretched into the cab.

*Look at her. Like a whore!*

Billy had done checking. It appeared as though Rita and her little boyfriend both had the next forty-eight hours off, and they obviously had big plans. They'd have much more important things to do than read the papers or watch TV, where news of Billy Quinn, the lynchpin behind one of the largest corruption sweeps ever in the history of the NYPD, captured the headlines. *Perfect!* Things were right on schedule, and the threatening phone call would serve as Billy's necessary alibi.

When the cab with Rita pulled away, Billy picked the front door lock and made his way into her building. He strode up the stairs to her apartment and, finagling the lock, he broke in there, too. Once he was inside, he helped himself to the rest of the champagne in the bottle, grabbed himself a beer and devoured the leftover Chinese take-out he found in the refrigerator.

Then he waited. He watched TV and eyed the clock, flinging his gun around his finger. He had more than a little surprise waiting for his ex-wife when she got home.

# Sixty-Three

Rita turned more than a few heads when she waltzed into Tavern on the Green, and it confirmed for her that she looked as dazzling as she felt in her Chianti red cocktail dress. The outfit showed off her svelte shape, her dancer-toned legs and her black stiletto heels.

She settled herself at the bar and glanced at her watch—7:03 P.M. It looked as though Gary was going to be fashionably late.

"What can I get you?" the bartender asked.

Rita was tempted to say, "The man of my dreams. The one I almost foolishly lost forever." But the words, "I'll have a white wine spritzer with a cherry please," tumbled out instead.

For everything that had changed in Rita's life, some things just never would.

"Hey, how about I buy you that drink, lady?" said a voice next to her.

Rita swiveled her sights. They landed on Gary. He was beaming, wearing a dark suit and a striking red tie that matched perfectly with Rita's dress.

He circled his arms around her, and she buried her face against his chest, engulfed by the citrusy scent of his aftershave. It felt like only yesterday since last they'd been together. And when he kissed her, Rita remembered how good he always tasted.

Over dinner, they listened to the sounds of the string quartet as it played in the nearby gazebo. They stared into each other's eyes and reached across the table for each other's hands.

"So, you're back to being Rita Del Vecchio again, eh?"

She nodded. "Yes, I get my old self back. My name, at least."

Dinner was delicious. It wasn't the fare they were used to: fountain sodas, pizza, or greasy burgers and fries. But didn't everyone need to try roast duck and Dom Perignon at least once in a lifetime? And while they both agreed that the meal was superb, they felt the portions were a bit small and a little too sophisticated for their simpler tastes.

After a few objections, Gary let Rita pick up the hefty tab at the pricey, landmark restaurant.

*Thank God for MasterCard.* But Rita felt it was a worthwhile investment to get their relationship back on track.

Gary arranged for the second half of their night. After dinner, they took a carriage ride through Central Park. The dim white lights twinkling in the distance from Tavern on the Green made them feel as though a galaxy of stars had fallen down to earth. Gary smoothed his hand on her thigh, and his seduction, so far, was working. Their romance continued to build when they stopped in at the piano bar at the Plaza Hotel for a nightcap. Tucked close in the booth and lit by the warm, flickering glow of candlelight, Rita somehow felt grateful for the time they'd spent apart. It only made her appreciate and love Gary even more. In fact, she was convinced that she had never really been in love before this night.

Her feelings were so strong, that she burrowed deeper into the warm, loving safety of his arms.

"Please, don't ever let us be apart again," she begged, gazing up at him while he pressed his forehead against hers.

"I knew you'd come to your senses. Sooner or later." He grinned and Rita traced his lips with her index finger. "How about we take a room?"

"Here? At the Plaza? Are you crazy?"

"Why not?"

"It's too expensive. We're not Rockefellers. We're city employees."

"But, it's a special occasion. You paid for dinner. Let me spring for dessert."

Rita and Gary's passions uncoiled. They burned throughout the night in a luxury suite of the Plaza Hotel, but the intensity of their love couldn't match the fire that raged within Billy. His plan was not running on schedule. He paced and pounded his feet upon the floor of Rita's apartment until the carpeting wore thin.

By three in the morning, Billy knew that Rita wasn't coming home. *So much for her rule of not spending the night with a man until she's married!* He drove the empty, darkened streets, spanning the distance between New Rochelle and Long Island. When he found that Sergeant Hill's apartment was also vacant, Billy seethed in maddening agony, his imagination conjuring images his head could not contain.

The only way to quell his feelings was to open his wallet and roll up a fifty dollar bill. He cut a few lines of coke on the dashboard of his car and snorted, while seventeen miles away, Rita burst with ecstasy. Billy swore he could hear her pleasure-filled screams taunting him in the night. He could picture her in her lover's arms, and the images made him crazy. Wild. He knew there was only one way to erase her from his mind and from his memory. But to wait until tomorrow to execute Plan B seemed a lifetime away.

# SIXTY-FOUR

Rita and Gary slept well past check-out time. That made the room already paid for, so they decided to put the suite to continued good use. They spent the rest of the day dozing in and out of sleep in each other's arms. Beyond the opened drapes, they watched the changing light outside and how it started to slant through the windows, capturing glittering shafts of dust. For more than sixteen lazy hours, they had been happily sequestered from civilization, and they found that they really didn't miss the world, or its problems, a bit. But at six o'clock that evening, as they waited for the white-gloved butler service to wheel in their dinner, Rita suddenly remembered Billy.

"I thought we were through with him," Gary said, when she mentioned Billy's proposition.

"*We* are. I am. Believe me," Rita told him. "It's not a big deal. He just wants his stupid ring, and I'd really like to get my photographs and stuff. They mean a lot to me. This might be my last chance."

It had been a long time since Rita had dialed Billy and her old apartment. But she still remembered the number. Billy wasn't home, so she left a message that she'd call him at some point the next day to see if they could set up a mutually agreeable time.

But when she pressed the button to disconnect the call, she was puzzled. Hadn't Billy told her that he'd changed the phone number? Didn't he tell her how perplexed he was, wondering how the threatening calls kept finding him even with the new number? If that was the case, then how had she gotten through to the answering machine on the old line? Hadn't she heard the recorded sound of Billy's voice? Had she misunderstood?

When Gary came up behind Rita and snaked his arms around her luxurious hotel bathrobe, she jumped at his touch. That old fear. That uptight, jittery feeling. It was happening again.

"Everything all right?"

She turned to face him. She clapped her hands around his cheeks and kissed him. "Yeah, everything's fine. Nothing's going to spoil the magic of this time we've had together."

"But do you really think it's wise to do this? To see Billy again?"

"Yes, I think I have to. If I can do this, if I can pass this one last test, then I think I'll be strong enough to get on with the rest of my life."

"But is now the right time? You just learned that the divorce was finalized yesterday."

"Trust me, I can handle him now." Rita pulled apart the lapels of Gary's robe and ran her fingers through the coarse hair on his chest. Then she pressed her face into his pectorals and kissed them as if complimenting every muscle and ripple. "I can handle *any* man now."

Gary smoothed her hair. "Oh, you think so, do you?" He swept her off her feet and carried her in his arms back to bed.

Billy woke up back in the Bronx. He was hungover. He must've passed out on the couch. When he downed the last drop of scotch from the bottle on the coffee table, he saw the light flashing on his telephone answering machine. *Who called?* He reached across to the end table and pressed the play button. When he heard the sound of Rita's voice and the message she'd left, stalling him off, he picked up the empty bottle and hurled it straight at the TV. There was a loud *boom!* and a flash as sparks and plastic from the shattered screen flew out into the room, some even landing on Billy. But he just sat there in a trance, completely still and unmoving, staring at the smoldering TV set and the damage he'd done.

# SIXTY-FIVE

Between two and three o'clock in the afternoon—that was the time Rita finally worked out with Billy to pick up her things.

"After we check out, why don't we grab a bite to eat before we head for the Bronx?" Rita asked, calling out to Gary who was in the bathroom lathering up his face with shaving cream. "How does that sound?"

Gary's voice spilled back with, "I think it would sound a helluva lot better if we didn't have to go to the Bronx at all."

"I could probably just take a cab," she said, fixing her make-up at the vanity table. "It might even be easier than your driving all the way from Manhattan to the Bronx and then back up to New Rochelle. Billy said there aren't a lot of boxes anyway."

"You are *not* going alone. End of discussion."

On the drive from the Plaza Hotel to the Bronx, Gary and Rita talked about the best way for them to handle Billy and the meeting.

Gary said, "I'd feel better if you'd let me come in with you."

"No, that's a bad idea," she told him. "If you walk in there with me, it might set Billy off, and I don't want to provoke him."

"But it's foolish for you to go back into the lion's den alone."

"I'm not alone. You're going to be right in the car."

"In the car is not close enough to help you if you need it."

"I'll be fine. It's only for a couple of minutes. I told you,

266

you'll drop me off at the top of the street, just in case Billy's watching for me. Then I'll walk to the building. Give me enough time to get buzzed in and get up there. Then you can pull up in front and wait for me. It won't take long."

The way Gary was gripping the steering wheel, arms outstretched as though he were pushing it away from him, Rita could tell he was tense.

"I think we're making this into more than it needs to be." Rita ran her fingers gently along his arm.

"Have you forgotten what you looked like the last time you left that apartment?"

"I know, but that was then. Things are different now. This ring means the world to Billy and his family. I think they really do want it back. And I know Billy well enough to know that he won't do anything to jeopardize that. Plus the fact, he's anxious to get my things out of there because he and his new girlfriend are supposedly re-doing the place. Who knows? Maybe she'll even be there, and I can give her some pointers on self-defense moves."

Rita did some shadow boxing in the air, then flung out her hands in karate-type gestures.

Gary shook his head.

Rita gave him a poke in the arm. "Lighten up. I'm kidding," she told him.

"This isn't a joke, Ree."

"I know, but the way Billy presented this whole proposition was very rational. Very mature."

"Well, if he's so rational and mature, then why should he have any problem with my walking in there with you?"

Rita crooked her head and slowly swayed it from side to side. "Gar, I hear you, but I just think it's best if I do this on my own. At least if I take out the first round of boxes by myself."

"Do you have your gun?"

Rita laughed. "Gary, please. I'm not going to need my gun."

"Do you have it or not?"

"Yes, I have it. I always have my piece with me." She clasped a hand to the pocketbook sitting on her lap.

"And you're going to put it on the doorstop as you enter the building?"

"Yes," she said.

"And once you're in there, you're going to make sure the apartment door never closes behind you completely, right?"

"Check."

"I'm not kidding around, Rita."

"I know you're not. And neither am I."

"Well, once he buzzes you into the building, I'll give you three to four minutes to get up to the apartment. Assuming Billy answers the door right away, you should both be able to say what needs to be said and hand over the ring." Gary looked at his watch, pointing to the face. "That will probably bring the timetable up to five or six minutes before you start with the boxes. I don't see why you can't be back in the truck, buckled into your seatbelt, in a total of twelve minutes."

Rita sat dumbstruck, but in love, listening to him, how exacting he was and how the wheels of his mind were strategically mapping out the coordinates of her visit as though he were preparing for some sort of clandestine, tactical drill that would change the world.

"On the high side, let's say that if you're not out of the building with the first box by 3:13, I'm coming in."

"But I hate the number thirteen. It's unlucky."

"Luck? I don't believe in luck. But if it makes you feel better, we'll round things up to 3:15. But not a second later."

Once in the Bronx, Gary pulled his pickup truck around the corner from Rita's old street and slowed up. He double-parked alongside another car and kept the truck idling.

"I'll leave you off here. But fifteen minutes. 3:15. Got it?" he said, pointing to his watch. For a split second Rita thought she was staring into the stern-looking face of the Gary Hill she'd first met at the police academy.

"Aye-aye, Sarge," she said, offering him a mock salute. Then she softly ran her fingers along the smooth feel of his freshly shaved cheeks.

"Nice outfit." The hard edge of his voice evaporated as he fingered the spaghetti strap of her new sundress.

"Yeah, this hot, hunky guy bought it for me. It's from the gift shop at the Plaza. You like?"

"I love. Especially the lady wearing it," he said.

Emboldened, Rita planted a kiss on him then stepped from the car.

# Sixty-Six

It seemed strange, standing at the door to her old apartment as a visitor. But today that's exactly who Rita was.

Billy let her in. He was dressed in faded, ripped up jeans and a soiled, sleeveless undershirt, what some might call a "wife beater." *How apropos!* He was in need of a shave and shampoo as his hair was a matted mess. He looked and smelled like he hadn't slept or applied deodorant in days.

*Look at him. What was I thinking? What did I ever see in him?*

It was obvious that he hadn't gone to any great lengths to spruce up himself, or the apartment, in anticipation of Rita's arrival. The place was in complete disarray. Newspapers, empty beer cans, bags of junk food and pizza boxes were strewn over the couch, coffee and end tables. When she took her first step across the threshold, the heels of her shoes crunched upon the floor as if she were wearing cleats. She looked down. Was it broken glass? Plastic? She visually followed the scattered shards on the floor, and they led her to a gaping hole in the cracked television screen. Had Billy smashed the TV? Rita's scalp went all hot and prickly. She suddenly started to have second thoughts about this meeting, but she guided the apartment door closed behind her, making sure the lock mechanism didn't fully engage.

"I guess your cleaning lady is overdue?" Rita said, half in question and half in jest.

Billy laughed at Rita's remark. "I always loved your sense of humor," he told her, then explained, "I've been working a lot of overtime."

"Gee, then you must be tired," she told him. "Just point the way to those boxes, and I'll let you get some rest."

He gestured down the hall and motioned for her to help herself.

"This way?" she asked. She had hoped the boxes would be stacked up and ready, waiting for her, right there in the living room.

"Yes. That-a-way," he said, flinging his thumb in the direction of the bedroom.

Rita didn't like that Billy was forcing her to take the lead. But she started past him, down the hall. She could feel him trailing closely behind her. When she stepped across the threshold, she found the bed unmade, the ashtray full of cigarette butts and clothes scattered everywhere.

*There's no way there's a girlfriend in this equation,* she concluded as she scanned the room, looking for boxes. There weren't any. Panic rose in Rita.

"Where are my things?"

"Oh, it's all here. I thought I could get everything packed up before you came, but working so much, I just didn't have time," he told her.

*What happened to his telling me that he'd packed the boxes light?*

"Well, why don't I just grab my pictures and yearbooks?" she told him, her pulse quickening. "They should be right on the top shelf of the closet."

"Sure. Be my guest."

When Rita slid open the closet door, there was nothing inside. It was completely empty, except for some hangers dangling on the clothes bar. Rita's heart raced. A sick, terrible feeling washed over her.

"What going on here, Billy? I thought we were going to be

grown-ups about this and make a legitimate swap?

Billy stood, arms crossed, in the doorway. There was a weird, manic look in his eyes, and his lips curled into a crooked smile. He appeared pleased to see Rita beginning to squirm.

"Look, I don't know what this is," Rita told him, her quivering hands rummaging through her pocketbook and removing the ring from her change purse. She held it out and tried to reason with him. "But here. Take the ring, and we'll call it even."

Billy didn't budge. He stood, blocking the door. "What happened to you, Rita? When I married you, you were this sweet girl. Now look at you."

Rita took a deep breath. The bitter scent of burned tobacco and stale, dirty laundry filled her nostrils. She kept her sights glued to Billy and held up the ring like a priest might hold a communion host before a congregant. When he still didn't reach for it, she finally set it down on the dresser, then held up the palms of her hands in surrender. "There. There's your ring. I don't want or need my stuff. I'll just go."

"Are you sleeping with him?"

The room went still. Rita's heart tightened. She took a step and tried to ease her way around Billy, but he would not let her pass. When she tried to push her way around him, he blocked her with his body. He pushed her up against the wall and wedged her into the corner.

"Get away from me," she said, his body quickly becoming like a cage around hers.

"You ruined my life, Rita," he said, the scent of alcohol filling the space between them while he drew his gun from the back waist of his pants and pressed it against her face. "And now it's time for me to ruin yours."

Rita froze. Blood thundered in her ears.

Billy traced the barrel of the gun from her forehead down her nose and rammed it into her mouth. "Is Gary Hill the reason why you left?"

With the gun still in her mouth, Rita was terrified and rendered speechless.

A gust of his breath shouted, "Answer me dammit!" Billy's face went purple and the veins in his neck were popping out.

Rita flinched at his raw power. When Billy pulled the gun from her mouth, she flailed against him and screamed, "*You're the reason I left.*" Rita tried to topple him, but she wasn't nearly strong enough. Billy grabbed at her clumsily, pulling at her hair and her dress. Her purse went flying as he threw her onto the bed. With his legs and chest pinning her to the mattress, she screamed louder. He sealed a hand over her mouth, while with the other, he held the gun and ripped at her dress, digging for her panties.

Rita could feel her eyes bulging from their sockets. She thrashed in vain beneath his weight, but he was strangling her with his unbridled strength.

"Were you screwing him while you were screwing me? Just like you were doing with your little buddy, Franko? Flaunting him in my face!"

Rita kicked. With her nails, she clawed at him. But Billy's arms and legs had her trapped. "You're my wife until death do us part. And I'm having you one more time before you die."

With a sharp tug, he jerked down the zipper of his pants.

At the sound, adrenalin ripped through Rita until her pain and fear changed to a wild, animalistic fury. She twisted her head. She freed her mouth and sank her teeth down to the bones of Billy's fingers. Stunned, Billy allowed the gun to slip from his grasp. It landed on the other side of the mattress. With a warm, syrupy taste coating her tongue and her throat, Rita screamed as loudly as she could. She stretched out her arm, her quivering fingertips inching toward the weapon.

# SIXTY-SEVEN

Gary hated watching Rita amble away from the truck. But he let her go. With her pocketbook clasped to her arm, he watched her walk down the block toward her old apartment building. She needed to do what she had to do, and nobody, not even Gary, could stop her. He knew Rita well enough to know that by going back and giving Billy the ring, Rita was trying to conquer her past, face down the demons, in order to reclaim her future. And Gary hoped that future would include him.

When Rita completely vanished from his sight, Gary looked at the dashboard clock: 2:59. She would be right on time, right on schedule. He'd give Rita five minutes, or until 3:04, to get inside the building then it was on to phase two.

If Gary Hill had flipped on the radio instead of staring at the digital numbers and watching them change to 3:00, he would've heard the news at the top of the hour:

*"Eighteen New York City Police Officers have been arrested and arraigned. One officer, who plea bargained with officials in exchange for information leading to arrests in the biggest corruption scheme ever uncovered in the history of the NYPD, is expected to turn himself over to authorities this very hour."*

But Gary sat in silence in the idling truck. He turned his wrist and eyed his watch for the tenth time: 3:02. Only three minutes had passed? He hated waiting like this, feeling so powerless and at the mercy of time. There was nothing harder

274

than being in love with a strong, independent woman. You constantly ran the risk of losing her. And the fear always lingered that if you were out of her company for very long, you'd start to feel she no longer needed you, that being part of a pair might cramp her style, and she might change her mind and rather go it alone, without you.

*This time, I'm going to learn from past mistakes. I'm going to be less possessive, more laid-back and flexible.* In his mind Gary was talking to himself, making a million plans and promises. When the numbers glowed at 3:04, he engaged the transmission into drive. He hauled in a breath and slowly began to maneuver the pickup down the block, envisioning the sight of Rita sweeping out through the front door of the apartment building long before the 3:15 deadline.

He'd been stalking the apartment from across the street all afternoon, just waiting for the right moment. And now, here it was. That hottie in the low-cut dress had even left the door open for him. How easily he could slip into the building completely unnoticed. *What a cinch,* he thought, kicking the doorstop free and hearing the creak of the hinges and the click of the lock engage behind him. After today, his work would be done. All those weeks of waiting and watching. No need to place another threatening call to this address ever again.

A rush of excitement coursed through his veins as he disappeared though the foyer. He pulled his black ski cap down over his head and face and extracted a steel crowbar from inside the leg of his pants. Pummeling the cold bar in his hands, he hurried down the hall and up the stairs.

# SIXTY-EIGHT

Seconds seemed like hours. Rita's screams rattled her eardrums. The muscles in her arms grew tired as she struggled to reach across the bed for the gun, but Billy's grasp outstretched hers. It was his hand that finally found the weapon. He lifted it and pointed the cold, steel barrel between Rita's eyes.

She froze. The firearm blurred out of her vision, and she found herself staring at something dangling from a chain around Billy's neck. It hung outside his undershirt, and each time he breathed, the light from the window caught the ridges of polished gold and reflected back at Rita. There was a straight edge on one side and a rounded, curved corner on the other. She recognized the fractured shape immediately. It was the other half of Franko's New York Yankee heart charm.

Billy's madness spilled from his mouth as he rammed the barrel of the gun harder against her skull. "If you're not gonna love me, then you're not gonna love anyone."

As he attempted to force himself on her, Rita heard a sharp knock on the front door.

For a split second, the muscles in Billy's thighs clenched tighter around Rita. There was a moment's hesitation.

*Didn't I leave the front door unlocked?*

Rita watched Billy turn his crimson colored face in the direction of the sound. He waited. He listened.

Silence . . .

Stillness . . .

From the corner of her eye, Rita could see the green, digital numbers on the alarm clock, which read 3:13. *Thank God Gary doesn't believe in bad luck!*

Three hard knocks pounded again.

"Is that your little boyfriend?"

When Rita shifted beneath him, the tide of Billy's anger rose higher than a tidal wave. Enraged, his voice roared, "You're not going anywhere. I'm not through with you yet," as he blasted his weapon down on her head.

When she opened her eyes, Rita saw double: the closet, the dresser, the mirror. For a minute she didn't even know where she was. *Have I been dreaming?* But then it came to her. The bedroom she shared with Billy, the Bronx apartment. Rita tried to sit upright, but her head felt split apart. She gingerly put a hand to it. *What's happening? Where's Billy? And Gary? Where is he?*

Her vulnerability made her tremble cold. She heard yelling and wild thrashing coming from the other room. The living room. Moving as quickly as she could, Rita rolled out of the bed. When she lifted the blinds, a burst of daylight seared into his eyes. She squinted against it and found herself a prisoner behind the wrought iron security bars on the windows. There was no way out. She searched for her purse, but it wasn't there. Her revolver. She needed her gun. Where was it?

The banging and commotion from the other room grew louder.

Unable to find her purse, Rita gave up the search and angled open the bedroom door. Billy's handgun lay on the floor in the shadows filling the hall, and she went for it. The front door was wide open. As Rita edged toward the living room, she saw a figure wearing a baggy hooded sweatshirt, big pants and a knitted, black ski cap beating Billy with a crow bar. Whack after ruthless whack, blood was flying everywhere—the sofa, the end tables, the walls. Rita checked to make sure the magazine was loaded into the weapon while Billy scrambled to escape his attacker, darting for refuge behind the couch near the front picture window.

"You stupid, dirty cop," the figure in the black ski cap hollered. It was a deep, masculine voice. Billy was curled into the fetal position on the floor. His arms were bent, covering his head. Yet he was unable to escape the blows, the slaughter, that kept coming nonstop. "You stole my money. You took my drug stash. You broke my arm. Now you're gonna pay, you rat!"

The assailant threw down the crow bar and pulled out a gun, a semiautomatic. A shot rang out. Glass from the large front window shattered and dropped to the floor. Some of the shards and fragments slashed into Billy, piercing his raw flesh. He screamed.

"You probably don't remember me, dawg." The intruder trailed Billy at close range while he ripped off his ski mask. Rita could see the revealed face reflected in the mirrored side wall of the living room. The intruder was a teenaged kid with pearly white teeth and coffee-colored skin. "But I sure as hell remember you. Badge number 7-7 dash 5-7-7-2."

Weapon drawn, Rita moved toward the attacker. With her arms outstretched, she aimed the gun. She gripped it tightly with both of her hands and kept it pointed at the intruder's back.

"I told you I knew where you lived! Didn't you get my messages? Whatcha think I was playin' with you?"

Rita was close enough to see Billy, who was curled into a ball on the floor. Every square inch of him, his clothes and flesh, was saturated in blood. She firmed her moist fingers around the handle of the gun and stretched her index finger over the trigger, steadying her aim on the attacker.

A rumbling grew in the floor beneath her feet. The cracked panes of glass from the shattered window rattled louder and louder as the thundering roar of the elevated subway train was approaching. With the room seeming to vibrate all around, Rita firmly ordered, "Drop your weapon." But the earsplitting, eyeball rattling noise from the train drowned out the sound of her voice. She saw Billy shift his eyes around the attacker and when he did, the assailant turned. But he moved too quickly. Rita squeezed the trigger and fired.

The intruder fell. His weapon dropped with him to the floor. He lay motionless, passed out cold. The handle of the gun was hot in Rita's hand, but she tightened her grip and now took aim on Billy.

In a matter of seconds, the blazing sound of the train began to fade away until all that could be heard was a distant echo. Billy coughed up some blood and in a weak voice said, "Nice shot. Now finish the job. Put me out of my misery."

"You killed Franko, didn't you??"

Billy followed Rita's gaze to the chain around his neck. He fingered the bloodied charm resting atop his breastbone.

"Tell me you did it, Billy."

"Just shoot me."

"No, for once in your life, you're gonna look me in the eye and tell me the truth. You owe me that much. Say it!"

When Billy didn't answer, Rita's voice tore through her vocal chords with, "Say it, dammit! I want to hear it from your own mouth."

Billy's eyes and voice filled with tears. "I did it because I loved you—"

The shot that discharged from Rita's weapon silenced him.

"You don't know what love is," she said, heat oozing from the pistol. The bullet had landed in the wall alongside the front picture window, directly above where Billy lay slumped.

A piercing sadness sliced into Rita, then an ache. Her hand relaxed until the barrel of the gun tilted down toward the floor. Billy was fading fast, and the attacker stirred, groaning in pain at her feet. When she heard her own name being called from the doorway—"Rita?"—she half-turned.

It was Gary. He weaved into the room, arms outstretched, weapon drawn.

Rita felt herself breathe for what seemed like the first time in hours.

"What took you so long?" she said.

"Couldn't find a parking space," he told her.

# Epilogue

The punk in the black knit ski cap had a bullet removed from the back of his upper thigh and was released from the hospital in less than seventy-two hours. They charged him with assault and possession of an illegal firearm, but he copped a plea in exchange for information about Officer Billy Quinn.

For three weeks, Billy lay in the hospital with broken bones, a ruptured spleen and severe internal injuries. Physically he would be okay . . . but emotionally, he had reached the point of no return, and he would not be eligible for parole for at least thirty-five years. Billy testified against the Mean Nineteen, but the deal he'd cut wasn't enough to exonerate him from in-depth DNA tests that convicted him of the first-degree murder of Officer Francis O'Malley. He was also tried and convicted of assault against Rita. Billy Quinn finally made the papers, but as a dirty cop and a felon, not as a hero. His life sentence was more like a death sentence. And Rita believed that his past would rage like a smoldering flame trapped behind a brick wall, slowly destroying him from the inside out.

For Johnny the Jinx Delgado, the news of Officer Quinn's sentencing was an answer to prayer. From that moment on, the Jinx vowed—for real, this time—that he would turn his life around and finally belong to Jesus.

As for Nick the Spic? The shot from Billy's weapon went untraceable, as certain forensic reports from that particular homicide went missing from Central Records. Billy never

281

confessed to, nor was implicated in, that murder, so Nicky remained one of those casualties of the sinister cityscape that would never be accounted for.

In time, Rita's bruises once again healed, and so did her heart. She went back to working nights and meeting Gary Hill at four o'clock in the morning at Rockefeller Center. About a year after her divorce, after having shared all four seasons together, Gary, with ring in hand, finally proposed to Rita at Saint Patrick's Cathedral.

Rita soon learned that her mother was right. Gary Hill *was* Irish. His family name of *Cahill* had been changed to *Hill* when his ancestors were processed at Ellis Island.

"It's bad luck for an Italian girl to marry two Irishmen in a row," Rita's mother said when she learned the news of Gary and Rita's engagement.

"I'm marrying him, Mother," Rita announced defiantly. "I think it is high time I prove you wrong about the Irish, once and for all."

And prove her wrong, she did. The truth was that Rita's folks took an instant liking to Sarge. He was "good people," as they liked to say, and he fit with their daughter—and the family—as if he had always been a part of their lives. Who could ask for more?

Rita bade goodbye to her old existence and looked forward to a fresh start as Mrs. Gary Hill. For the first time in her life, she knew true love, and it had nothing to do with a uniform. But happily-ever-after was no longer a done deal. Time. Time would lend perspective, until Rita's past would become like a train having left the station. The sight and sound of it would diminish, gradually fading into the landscape and weaving itself into the present as a memory. A memory of the days that changed her life while she was in transit.

# ABOUT THE AUTHOR

**Kathleen Gerard**'s fiction has been awarded The Perillo Prize, The Eric Hoffer Prose Award and was nominated for Best New American Voices, all national prizes in literature. Her prose and poetry have been widely published in literary journals and anthologies, and broadcast on National Public Radio (NPR). She lives in New Jersey and is currently at work on another novel. To learn more visit www.kathleengerard.blogspot.com.